MARILYN TURK

Secrets of the Desert Rose

Marilyn Turk

Published by Winged Publications

ISBN:978-1-968792-75-6

"For everyone who asks receives; the one who seeks
finds; and to the one who knocks, the door will be opened."
Matthew 7:8.

This book is dedicated to all the brave women who gave
unselfishly so others could live better.

Prologue

North Africa, 1942

Was this the day she would die?

Audrey covered her helmet with her hands and burrowed facedown into the sand as another shell landed nearby, shaking the ground and showering her with one more layer of dust in her desert dugout. She spit out sand and turned her head to suck in a breath. The relentless ear-splitting booming and shelling from German Panzer tanks continued as if their supply of ammunition was infinite. Would any of her fellow soldiers survive this time? Concern for their safety, those who had become more like family, was more important to her now than her own life. Maybe this would be her last moments on earth, a fitting end to the life she had chosen. What else did she have to lose?

Her mind flashed back to her best friend Monique and how they first met. Where was she now? No doubt someplace safe living out her protected life, enjoying the comforts of modern conveniences—something Audrey hadn't experienced for quite some time. Not that she envied her friend. Monique's life had always been more genteel than her own, and Audrey had long accepted their differences and the choices they'd made. Monique would have never chosen the path of danger and adventure Audrey lived.

Even when they'd gotten into a little trouble at school together, Monique always came out looking innocent. No one would have believed Monique with her delicate angelic face and dark curls would do anything wrong. Instead, Audrey was the one always suspected, and with just cause. She looked guilty, like she was up to something. At least that's what the strict nuns at the convent school said to her father. Not that she could disappoint him any more than she already had by being a daughter and not a son. Funny how these memories surfaced now.

A shell exploded to her left, raining more sand down upon her. Audrey tried to catch her breath in the foul, smoke-filled air. No, Monique had chosen the safe route, the normal domestic lifestyle expected of a young lady. She would never have survived this kind of life. A lump formed in her throat, and she pushed it down. Audrey had tried domestic life. She'd thought that's what she wanted too. Didn't last though. She wasn't cut out for it after all. Her heart squeezed at the memory. Forcing it away, she accepted her situation. Those plans hadn't worked out, so when adventure called again, her stint at domestic life ended.

Maybe she hadn't always made the right decisions. Except for one, and only Monique knew about it. And Monique would never tell. They'd always kept each other's secrets, and this one was the biggest of all. But Monique would keep it because she'd crossed her heart. She wouldn't give away the secret of the Desert Rose. Knowing that gave

Audrey a peace otherwise nonexistent in this place as the whine of another projectile whizzed through the air.

Chapter 1

Nicole

North Carolina, 2019

You're kidding me! No way!" Nicole stared wide-eyed at the phone in her hand.

"What, Nicole?" Mom finished pouring the second cup of coffee and glanced at her daughter perched on the barstool at the kitchen island.

Nicole dropped her phone on the counter and cupped her hands over her mouth. "Oh, my goodness, Mom. I got in! Can you believe it?"

"Calm down honey." Mom handed one of the cups to Nicole. "What are you talking about?"

Her heart pounding and hands trembling, Nicole took a deep breath to steady herself, then lifted the coffee, holding it close to her face as she blew across the top. Taking a tentative sip, she raised her gaze to her mother. "Mom. The year-abroad graduate program I told you about!"

"The one in North Africa?" Mom sipped her coffee and sat down on the cushioned stool next to Nicole.

"Yes, in Algiers. My chances of getting accepted were

practically impossible?"

Mom nodded, holding her coffee with both hands. "And you've been accepted? Nicole, that's wonderful!"

"Yes! Oh, Mom, I've wanted to go there for so long. That area has so much cool archaeological stuff with more to be discovered. By me!"

"Keep your voice down so you won't upset Mimi." Mom nodded toward Nicole's great-grandmother. The petite woman whose hair retained its original jet-black color, now streaked with silver, sat in a wheelchair nearby, staring out the window. "I wonder what she would think about you going back to the place where she grew up?"

Nicole's gaze followed her mother's. Ever since Mimi's stroke, Mimi hadn't been able to talk. Mimi was one of the reasons she'd wanted to go to Algiers. Her eyes moistened. "I wish I knew. I want to tell her and see how she responds. If only she could still talk to me. I miss her stories about growing up in Algiers."

"You'll miss her 100th birthday this summer if you're out of the country."

"I know. I hate that. Can we have an early birthday party for her? Maybe that will perk her up."

Nicole climbed off her stool and knelt beside her great-grandmother's wheelchair. Peering into Mimi's face, Nicole placed her hands on Mimi's arm. "Hi Mimi. It's Nicole. Can you hear me?" Assuming Mimi was watching the activity at one of the bird feeders Mom had placed in the backyard, Nicole said, "See anything interesting out there?"

Mimi turned to face Nicole, a crooked smile crossing her face as her green eyes brightened. With effort, she lifted her opposite hand and placed it atop Nicole's, patting it.

"Can I get you anything? Coffee? Tea?"

A little nod, and Mimi pointed one finger up.

"Coffee? Okay."

"I'll get it," Mom said, rising from her seat.

"Mimi, did you hear my news?"

Mimi shook her head ever so slowly.

"I'm graduating from college in archaeology this year." Nicole spoke slowly to make sure Mimi understood.

Mimi fixed her gaze on Nicole, patting her hand.

"And I applied to do postgraduate studies in North Africa. I've been accepted! Isn't that great?"

Mimi's brow creased as though she had a question.

"I'll be going to Algeria! I'm sure it's changed a lot since you were there." What must it have felt like during World War II when Mimi lived there? "Much safer, I'm sure. I hope to see where you lived in Algiers. Of course, I'll go to other places in North Africa too."

Mimi's eyes widened, and she squirmed in her chair, attempting to lean toward Nicole. A look akin to alarm covered her face, and her hand gripped Nicole's. Her lips moved, but no words came out.

"What is it, Mimi?" Nicole gave a worried glance to her mother. "Mom? I think she's upset."

Mom rushed over. "Mimi, are you okay? Do you need anything?"

Mimi shook her head but stared at Nicole. Her lips moved again.

"What is she saying, Mom?"

"I don't know." Mom bent over to speak to her grandmother. "Mimi, try telling us what you need."

Mimi's mouth moved again while Nicole and her mom

tried to figure out what Mimi was trying to say.

"F… father?" Nicole said.

Mimi shook her head again. "F..i..?

"Fi? Find?"

Mimi's head bobbed up and down.

"Find what?"

"Mom, can she write it out?"

"Maybe, I'll grab some paper and a pen." Mom rushed to the counter, retrieved the items, and grabbed a book to set them on. She placed the items on Mimi's lap, putting the pen in Mimi's hand.

"Mimi, try to write it down for us," Nicole said.

As Nicole held the paper steady, Mimi scrawled the word "Find" with a shaky hand.

"Okay, we got that one right, but find what?"

Again, Mimi's trembling hand worked to form some letters.

"Is that a 'd'? Dirt? Dinner?"

Mimi shook her head and continued.

"D. E. S?"

"You want dessert?" Nicole glanced at Mom. "Mom, do you have anything for dessert?"

Mimi shook her head again but continued to force her shaking hand to cooperate.

"D. E. S. E. R. T. Desert?" Nicole hated to see Mimi in such distress. Surely, whatever she had to say was important to her.

Mimi pointed to the first word, then the second.

"Find desert?" How could she not? "Of course, I'll find the desert. You mean the Sahara? You know, ninety percent of it is in Algeria."

But Mimi's agitation continued, and she shook her head again. She sighed, her hand dropping to her lap as if she were tired of trying to communicate. Her gaze returned to the window, and her expression lightened. Lifting her arm, she pointed out the window where the morning sun was brightening the patio.

"What is she pointing to? Mimi, do you want to go outside?"

Mimi shook her head, then nodded.

"I guess that means yes. Okay, it's a nice day, so why wouldn't you? It's good for you to get out in the fresh air."

Mom unlocked the brake on the chair and pushed it toward the outside while Nicole held the door. The fragrance of gardenias greeted them as Mom found a warm spot on the patio with sunlight streaming through the tree limbs above.

"We forgot her coffee," Nicole said.

Mom frowned. "I wonder if she's cold. It's not cold out here, but she chills easily." Mom turned back toward the house. "I'll run, get the coffee, and grab her sweater just in case. You keep an eye on her."

Mimi lifted her shaky finger again, pointing, and Nicole followed her gaze to the colorful garden.

"Yes, the flowers are lovely. They're really pretty this time of year," Nicole said. "I used to love working in the garden with you." Nicole paused, biting back a gulp. Oh dear. Would reminding Mimi of something she couldn't do anymore make her sad? "You know, these flowers are pretty as they are because of you." Nicole strolled along the small stone wall that formed the boundary of the garden, her hand sweeping over the flowers. "I think I remember what they are. That white one's a daisy, and those yellow ones are marigolds, right?" Nicole glanced at her great-grandmother for affirmation.

Mimi nodded but continued to point.

"Let's see. Those purple flowers are vinca, but I prefer to call them periwinkle." She smiled. "When I was a kid, I thought that was a funny name."

Mimi smiled her crooked smile, this time lifting her arm and pointing to another area of the garden.

"All right, I'll go to those. Are these big fat flowers hydrangeas? I've always liked them." Nicole glanced at Mimi for a response. A little nod and still the pointing finger. What on earth was Mimi pointing at?

"Your roses are doing well." The roses, Mimi's favorite flower, dotted the garden in various colors. "I think the red ones are my favorite. But I love the yellow ones too. Well, I love all of them, actually. I can see why they're your favorite." Nicole leaned over to sniff the roses as Mom came out the door with Mimi's coffee.

Mimi's head bobbed, and her eyes lit up.

"She must really want that coffee," Nicole said.

But when Mom tried to give it to Mimi, she turned away.

"Maybe she doesn't," Mom said. "I just don't know what she wants, bless her heart."

"But she just got so excited." Nicole blew out a frustrated breath.

"What were you doing?"

"Just naming flowers." Nicole gestured toward the garden. "She did seem more excited when I mentioned the roses, though. But then, she's always liked them the most."

Mimi nodded again, and her mouth tried to form a

sound, "Rrr. O.."

"Rose! Are you saying 'rose'?"

Mimi nodded and smiled.

"Okay, so you wanted to show us the roses?"

Mimi shook her head again. Then she pointed to the paper in her lap.

"Could the rose have something to do with the words she wrote?" Nicole asked.

Mom picked up the paper. "Find… desert … rose?"

Mimi let her hand fall back into her lap, and her shoulders relaxed. She nodded, then tried to say the words. "F.f.f.in d.d.zz..r..o.."

"Mimi, are you saying that when I go to Algeria, you want me to find the desert rose?"

Mimi forced her uneven smile, nodding again.

"Alright, Mimi. I will." Nicole gave her great-grandmother a reassuring smile and a gentle hug. When she leaned over, the large oval gold ring with an etched red-orange carnelian stone suspended on a chain fell out of her blouse. Mimi pointed to it. "Yes, it's the ring you gave me, the one your father gave you in Algeria. I wear it on a chain to keep you close to my heart."

Mimi's eyes moistened with tears, and she squeezed Nicole's hand. Nicole kissed her on the cheek.

She loved Mimi so much. Nicole would do all she could to find what her great-grandmother wanted, even if it did seem to be a strange request. But if finding a desert rose was that important to Mimi, it was important to Nicole, too. It had been a very long time since Mimi had lived in Algiers; in fact, she moved away shortly after World War II when she was a young woman. But the Mimi she knew had always loved to share her stories of Algiers. Nicole didn't remember one about a desert rose, but it must've been part of a story.

If only Mimi could go with her and show her around. What a shame her great-grandmother was no longer in physical condition for travel. At least Mimi was still with them, though, having outlived so many people from her era, even her own daughter. But if all Mimi wanted now was a desert rose, Nicole would do her best to find one for her. She'd do anything to bring a little joy back into Mimi's life. And even if she couldn't bring one back, she could snap pictures with her phone, and Mom could show them to Mimi.

Chapter 2

Monique

Cannes, France, Summer, 1931

Monique, ma chérie, come over here please. I'd like you to meet someone," Jacques Clermont, Monique's father, sat in the shade of the beach cabana near where she played in the sand.

"Yes, Papá." Monique stood and brushed the sand off her body, then hurried to her father. Beside him sat a large, pale man she had never met. Her first impression was that he was English.

"Monique, this is Colonel Arthur Reynolds. He used to be the British Consul in Marseilles."

She had guessed right then. The man, though reclining in the beach chair, looked stiff, a characteristic she associated with the English. They didn't seem to relax like French people did, in her opinion anyway. His folded hands rested on a big stomach, reminding her of a woman expecting a baby.

Colonel Reynolds's smug expression made Monique think of her cat Minette after he'd caught a mouse.

Apparently, what Papá said about the man meant he was somewhat important, which was interesting since Papá wasn't usually too fond of Englishmen in general. She eyed the man in his tan linen suit and white straw hat, a pipe stuck in the corner of his mouth.

Monique curtsied as her lessons in etiquette had trained her. "Bon jour, Monsieur."

"Hello, dear child." Colonel Reynolds turned to Papá. "She's a pretty thing."

Papá's pride was genuine when he smiled, gazing at his daughter. "We think so."

Monique returned Papá's smile before Colonel Reynolds looked back at her.

"Mercí." Even though he hadn't spoken to her, she thought she should reply. Monique glanced down at her bare toes digging in the sand. Why did Papá like this man who eyed her like he was examining a horse, making her uncomfortable?

"She speaks English?" the stranger said to Monique's father, as if she weren't able to hear him.

"Ah yes, Monique is well-spoken in English."

"Then good! She and Audrey can communicate."

Audrey? Who was that?

"Monique, Colonel Reynolds would like you to meet his daughter Audrey. I hope you can show her hospitality."

"Audrey!" the man called out, glancing at a girl down near the water's edge. "Come here!"

The tall, slender girl with curly, reddish blonde hair, looked over, frowned, then ambled toward the cabana, shielding her eyes as she approached. When she stepped into the shade, she paused, scanning the group. Her gaze rested on Colonel Reynolds. "Yes, sir?"

"Audrey, I'd like you to meet Monique. She and her family live in Algiers, but they're here for holiday as we are. I think you two are the same age, twelve. Perhaps you girls can spend some time together."

Audrey eyed Monique with curiosity. Monique offered a smile, then reached out her hand, hoping to ease the apparent awkwardness of the situation. "Come, Audrey. Let's go have fun."

Audrey's face relaxed, and she grinned. Taking Monique's hand, she said, "Yes, let's."

Before Monique could say another word, Audrey took off running, her long legs covering distance much more quickly than Monique could, but she did her best to keep up and not fall down face-first in the sand. When they reached the water, Audrey kept going, splashing into the surf. Monique let go of her hand to keep her balance as a wave rocked her, knocking her off her feet. The wave broke over her head, and she sputtered out seawater. Nearby, Audrey laughed and dove under the water. This girl wasn't shy at all, and quite unlike any of the girls Monique had ever known.

Audrey's head popped out of the water. "Hey! Are you all right?"

"Yes, just a little drink of seawater." Monique swallowed, the salty taste acrid on her tongue.

"You should have seen the surprised look on your face when that wave went over you!" Audrey laughed again, and this time Monique joined her. Audrey started a splashing war and Monique joined in. After she'd had enough, Monique stopped and backed away.

"Let's go sit in the sun," Monique said.

"All right." Audrey said. "Mother says I'll freckle, but I don't care."

"But Coco Chanel said a woman's tan is attractive."

"Who's that?" Audrey said as they slogged out of the water and plopped down on the sand. She laid back with her hands under her head and closed her eyes.

Monique stretched her legs out in front of her, not interested in lying down and getting sand in her hair. She lifted her face to the sun and sucked in a breath of fresh sea air while her hair dripped down her back.

"Coco Chanel is the most famous fashion designer in Paris!" Monique thought everyone had heard of Coco Chanel.

"Oh, I never heard of her. I don't care much about fashion. But I've seen some unusual clothes on the women here."

"Such as?"

Audrey sat up. "Those over there." She pointed.

Monique looked quickly, surprised by Audrey's gesture. Maman would not approve of pointing. "You mean the beach pajamas? They're very popular now."

"Is that what they are? Those wide-leg pants would get in my way!"

No doubt, they would, as fast as Audrey moved.

Audrey shrugged and looked away. "Let's make sandcastles!"

"I love to do that," Monique said. But it would be so much more fun to build them with someone else.

For the rest of the afternoon, the girls worked hard on their masterpiece, molding castles with turrets and moats out of the sand, chatting and giggling the whole time. Their excitement built as their imaginations ran free, adding to their project until the castle had grown into quite a large fortress.

"We can be the princesses and have handsome knights come visit us!" Monique said.

"Yes, and we can pick which one to marry!" Audrey added.

"Mine will ride a huge white horse," Monique said.

"Then mine will ride a black horse with a white diamond on its head."

More giggling ensued. Monique's side hurt from laughing so hard.

All of a sudden, a boy ran through their creation, destroying a section of it.

"Oh no!" Monique exclaimed. "How mean!"

"He can't get away with that!" Sand flew in all directions as Audrey jumped up and chased after the boy, who was no match for her speed and stride. Monique gaped as her new friend jumped on the boy's back and began pummeling him with her fists.

"Hey, get her off me!" the boy yelled.

Two older boys ran up, and one pulled Audrey off while the other held the boy. One of the older boys was Monique's brother Rene. She hopped up and ran over to the fracas.

"Rene! What are you doing?"

Holding the castle destroyer, her brother replied. "Capturing a rascal."

"Let me go, Hugh!" Audrey tried to free her arms from the other older boy, who seemed to be about the same age as Rene.

"Not until you behave," the boy named Hugh said.

"Please let Audrey go," Monique said. "She was just trying to … to…"

"I know what she was trying to do. But Audrey needs to act like a lady and not a hooligan," Hugh said. while Audrey wriggled in his grasp. "Who might you be?"

"That's my sister Monique," Rene said. Speaking to the boy whose arms were held behind his back, he said, "You, young man, need to apologize to these ladies."

The boy looked down at the ground, then mumbled. "I'm sorry."

"What? I couldn't hear you," Rene said.

"I'm sorry!" the boy shouted, making Monique and Audrey grin.

"All right then. You may go, but don't go around destroying other people's property."

"It weren't their property, it was just beach sand!" the boy retorted.

Rene tightened his grip. "Excusez-moi?"

"Ouch! Okay, I'm sorry!"

Rene let the boy go. As he ran off, Rene turned to Monique. "Hopefully, he learned his lesson."

"Now will you let me go?" Audrey said to Hugh.

He blew out a breath, then released her. Once released, she ran over to stand beside Monique.

Monique whispered. "Who is that?"

Audrey grimaced. "My brother Hugh."

Glancing between the two older brothers, Monique said, "Do you two know each other?"

"We haven't been formally introduced." Rene offered his hand. "Rene Clermont. This is my sister Monique."

Hugh accepted the hand and shook. "I'm Hugh

Reynolds, and this is my sister Audrey. I'm afraid her manners are lacking."

Shooting daggers with her eyes in the direction the boy had gone, Audrey said, "He didn't have good manners either."

Hugh shook his head, then turned to Rene. "Let's find something more entertaining." He glanced toward a pavilion where some young ladies had assembled. "That looks promising."

Rene followed his gaze and smiled. "I agree." Turning to Monique, he touched her shoulder and said, "Sorry about your castle's demise. It looked quite formidable, from what I can tell. Perhaps you can rebuild it."

Monique's adoring gaze followed her brother as he and Hugh strode away.

"Your brother seems nice, not a hosebag like mine," Audrey said, scowling at her brother's back.

"A what?" It wasn't a word familiar to her, but Monique understood it was not a compliment.

"Oh, it's someone who's not nice. Hugh is never nice to me."

"Rene is always nice to me. He's almost ten years older than I am and has always been very protective of me when he's home. But that hasn't been very often since he's been away at boarding school most of my life, and now he's going into the military." She looked in the direction where Rene had gone. "I wish he were home more."

"That's odd. Hugh has been gone most of my life at a boarding school, too. He's joining the Royal Air Force after this holiday. But he's never had any interest in me. He's quite like our father, who thinks boys are more important than girls.”

"He does? That's not fair. Women are just as important, just in a different way," Monique said. "My father dotes on my mother."

"My father pretty much ignores my mum unless it's a social occasion. He'll probably act real attentive tonight at the restaurant. That's his way, so Mum and I are used to it. I think Father would have preferred it if he had had two sons instead of what he got."

"Well, then he's a hosebag too!" Monique said.

Audrey's face registered shock at the comment, then she burst out laughing and Monique joined her. Audrey put her finger in front of her lips. "Better not let the adults hear you. Let's just keep that word a secret between us."

"Okay. I can keep a secret if you can," Monique said.

"You bet I can!" Audrey said. She made a sign with her hand of drawing an X across her chest. "Cross my heart."

Monique copied the motion. "Cross my heart too."

Chapter 3

Audrey

Cannes, France, Summer, 1931

Audrey eyed the petite French girl, whose delicate olive complexion and shiny black hair were a sharp contrast to her own curly and untamed mass of strawberry blond hair. Monique was small, graceful, cute, and charming—everything tall, gangly, and awkward Audrey was not. Audrey wanted to dislike her, but she couldn't. Monique was too nice not to like, plus she was fun. Audrey had felt an instant connection with her, an understanding that they would become instant friends.

Audrey's father had looked at Monique as if seeing a perfect example of a little girl. The familiar pain had tensed Audrey's stomach, knowing he'd never looked at her that way. Audrey would never be ladylike and poised like Monique, but it didn't matter anymore. Audrey had given up on acquiring those qualities a long time ago. She'd never please her father anyway, since he had wanted two sons instead of a son and a daughter. Mum tried to coach her to act more genteel, but Audrey preferred competing in sports instead of having tea and biscuits. So she settled for the "Tomboy" moniker, much to her parents' chagrin. But in the process, she had become a good runner and strong enough to take on any boys who challenged her.

Monique didn't seem to care if Audrey acted with perfect manners, though. On the contrary, she laughed with Audrey as if she were fun to be with. Too bad their friendship would be short-lived, since they'd be going back to their respective countries, she to England and Monique to Algeria, after their family vacations. At least they could have fun while they were still in Cannes.

"Where's your mum?" Audrey asked Monique as they tried to rebuild their sandcastle.

Monique glanced up, shielding her eyes. "Up there by the wall."

Audrey followed her gaze and spotted a pretty woman who could've been Monique's twin, except she was older. The lady's hair was black, sleek, and shiny like her daughter's, also cut in the latest bob from what she could see poking out from under a fashionable cloche. The woman sat with two other women at a café table under an umbrella. The table was one of many beside the stone wall covered in climbing roses separating the sidewalk from the beach. As Monique looked up, she caught her mother's gaze and waved. The lady smiled and waved back, then turned to the other ladies and laughed.

"Is your maman here?" Monique scanned the area.

Audrey shook her head, wishing her hair would swing the way Monique's did. "She's here in Cannes, but not out here at the beach. She doesn't want to get sunburned and doesn't like sand. She's more than likely back in our room reading."

"Your skin is getting a bit red, you know." Monique pointed to Audrey's shoulder.

Audrey shrugged. "It'll just turn to freckles."

"My skin gets dark if I'm out too long. Papá says I start looking like the servants."

Servants? Audrey tried to imagine Monique's home in Algeria on the African continent. "Do you live in a manor house?"

Monique laughed. "A manor house? What is that? We live in a nice house overlooking the city and the sea. My Papá bought it because he has a high station in the military. Our servants are assigned to his family."

Audrey's family had a small staff as well. She'd been raised by a series of nurses and taught school at home by governesses. But the image of her grandmother's old manse back in England, in the seaside resort of Torquay, was what came to her mind when she tried to envision Monique's house. Grandmother's house not only boasted a household of servants but contained interesting collections from travels her grandparents had taken around the world. She loved going to her grandparents' house on holiday, where she roamed the dusty library, finding ancient books and exploring the vast garden by herself. Did Monique's house look like that?

"Perhaps you could come visit me there." Monique's words ignited a flame of hope in Audrey and offered a chance to embark on new adventures. "I know we'd have a grand time!"

Dressed in a plain black dress, a woman Audrey had not seen before walked over to them. "Miss Monique, it's time to come in and bathe. You need to get ready for dinner."

Monique stood and brushed the sand off herself. Audrey followed suit. She glanced up toward the area where their fathers had been. Now empty, she scanned the beach and realized it, too, was almost vacant. She and Monique had such a good time that they had not noticed the time passing.

"Miss Audrey, I'm to take you back to your room so you can prepare for dinner as well."

Audrey nodded, and the girls trudged up the hill behind the woman. Audrey gave Monique a quizzical glance.

"That's Marie. She works for our family."

"So I assumed. I hope we get to play again tomorrow. When is your family leaving?"

"I believe we're staying until the end of the week. You?"

"The same. Unless Mum wants to go home earlier. She's not happy here." Or anywhere else, for that matter. With a husband who paid her no attention, Mum had separated herself from everyone else. Even her daughter.

When Marie dropped off Audrey at her door, she turned to say goodbye to Monique, hoping it wasn't the last time. She almost cried at the thought, but pushed it away, pasting on a grin instead. "We had great fun, didn't we?"

"Oui! Tomorrow maybe we see each other again?"

Father's voice came from inside the room. "You'll see each other tonight if you get in here and get ready."

Audrey and Monique exchanged wide-eyed glances and broad smiles before Audrey entered and closed the door behind her.

At the restaurant that night, the girls were seated across from each other, so they were resigned to making faces instead of talking. Father's rule of children being seen and not heard would be enforced. Audrey envied their brothers, who were allowed the privilege of speaking out loud, as long as they conversed about the same subject as their fathers. As usual, talk of their future in the military along with stories of their fathers' military exploits monopolized the dialogue.

Monique looked perfect in a pink dress with a wide lacy collar and matching bow in her hair. Audrey glanced down at her own dress, blue dress with puff sleeves and a bow at the neck. The sleeves irritated the sunburn on her arms, and she squirmed to get comfortable.

"You look very pretty, Audrey," Monique's mother said.

Audrey's face grew hot. No one ever said she looked pretty. Across from her, Monique smiled and nodded. Feeling all eyes on her, she wanted to hide under the white tablecloth. Her father cleared his throat. "Audrey?"

What did he want? She glanced at him, and saw his stern gaze, eyes darting to Mrs. Clermont. Of course, she'd forgotten her manners. Why did she think he might agree with the compliment?

She turned toward Mrs. Clermont. "Thank you, madam."

Audrey's mother looked at Mrs. Clermont and said, "Your daughter looks lovely too. Very dainty."

Your daughter? Did Mum not even know her name? And instead of looking at Monique, she looked at her mother. Just like Mum to only return formalities. Somehow, her comment didn't sound as sincere as Mrs. Clermont's. And "dainty"? Audrey's stomach turned.

"Merci," Monique said, winking at Audrey.

Audrey felt a giggle coming on but tried hard to stifle it. Across from her, Monique looked like she was having the same problem, which only exacerbated the problem. Audrey, sure she was going to burst out laughing, picked up her glass of water and took a sip. But while she was doing so, she made the mistake of glancing at Monique again, which unfortunately caused her to choke when she tried to swallow. A coughing fit ensued as her parents looked on with horror. Monique, on the other hand, burst out in giggles.

Audrey's eyes watered as she held her napkin over her mouth until she could catch her breath.

"Are you all right, dear?" Mrs. Clermont said.

Audrey nodded behind the napkin.

Glowering, Audrey's father said, "Perhaps Audrey needs to excuse herself."

Audrey glanced his way and her coughing stilled. She swallowed, then exhaled. "I'm very sorry. I'm fine now."

He pursed his lips and looked down at his menu, as if he were completely done with her. Audrey ducked her hot face. Could everyone see what her father thought of her? Worse, did everyone agree?

Audrey's stomach grumbled as a waiter passed by carrying a tray of luscious food aloft. Glasses tinkled in the background of the spacious restaurant while waiters in black short coats and pants, starched white shirts and black bowties scurried between the tables. After a waiter took their orders, the conversation turned to school.

"Monique has been tutored, but next year, she'll be attending the convent school in our city. The sisters run an excellent school," Monique's father said.

"Audrey was taught by her governesses until she began school this past year. She rides the tram with the three brothers who live next door," Audrey's father said, his brows creased. The fact that her only friends were boys was a thorn in her father's side. Despite her parents' efforts to introduce her to other girls her age, she failed to share their interests in dolls and tea parties. She was always getting her dresses torn from climbing trees and playing chase with the boys. "Perhaps she would do well to attend a convent school such as your daughter attends."

Audrey's mum's mouth dropped open and shock covered her face. "It is a Catholic school, is it not?" she said, as if to challenge his comment.

Monique's father answered. "Yes, of course, and a very fine school too."

Audrey's father's face was an angry shade of red, evidence of a stunned reaction to his wife speaking out against him, something she absolutely never did, much less in public. But being members of the Church of England, Audrey was almost as surprised at her father's suggestion as she was her mother's reaction.

"Please forgive my wife's comment. Her uncle was a vicar for the Anglican Church."

Now it was her mother's turn to be embarrassed. She glanced at the others seated around the table. "I don't mean to imply anything untoward regarding the Catholic Church, you understand."

Monique's mother spoke up. "No offense taken. We are all free to choose whichever faith we believe."

Were they? Audrey had always thought that if one were British, you were a member of the Church of England, but there were other types of churches in the country as well. However, even if there were other churches, she never thought her father would allow anyone in his family to attend them. Being a member of the Church of England was a matter of national pride. Would he seriously consider sending her to a Catholic school? And in another country? The idea excited her, even though she had no idea what a school run by Catholic nuns was like. But it sounded like a great adventure!

One thing she knew for certain. She loved the beauty of this place—the colors and ocean were such an inviting contrast to her dark home in England. The world was brighter here, and she wanted to stay. Having been taught the French language since the age of five, she could easily fit in with other French people. If Algeria was anything like Cannes, she knew she would like it too. And her new friend Monique would be there, so she'd already have a friend. She certainly wouldn't miss the cold, detached attitudes of her parents.

Maybe Audrey could help convince her father to make the decision to send her to the convent school in Algiers. What would it take? She couldn't wait to talk to Monique privately and hatch a plan.

In an obvious attempt to change the subject, Monique's father spoke up, exhaling a puff from his cigarette at the same time. "Arthur, do you play tennis?"

Audrey's father's demeanor changed as his favorite topic besides military stories was introduced. He leaned back with a glass of wine in his hand. "I do indeed. And you?" Father had been a keen player in his youth, from what she heard. Of course, he was older and fatter now, unlike Monique's father who was more trim.

Colonel Clermont nodded. "I do. In fact, I had a tennis court built at our villa in Algiers."

"Is that so?" Father glanced at Audrey as she hoped he would. "You know, Audrey is quite adept at playing the sport. We've admired the French player Suzanne Lenglen for several years."

Audrey sat up straighter, thankful for her father's positive attention. Tennis was the one thing she did that pleased him, which amazed her since the sport couldn't be considered ladylike, especially when Suzanne Lenglen started playing in shorter skirts and bare arms.

"Ah, what an outstanding player she was!" Colonel Clermont sipped his wine. "I cannot believe she has retired from the sport. And so young."

"I agree, especially after what she's done to encourage women to play the sport."

"I heard she started teaching a tennis school in Paris for children," Colonel Clermont said.

"Have you thought of sending Monique there?" Audrey's father asked, glancing at Monique.

Monique's eyes widened and she whipped her head toward her father.

"No, Monique is pretty good, but she has no interest in playing competitively."

Monique allowed a small smile, visibly relaxing with

his answer.

"I wouldn't mind sending Audrey if they accept non-Parisian children." Audrey's heart raced. Attending Suzanne Lenglen's school would be an amazing opportunity. Could it be possible for an English girl? What would she prefer? Living with Monique's family in Algeria or attending the tennis school in Paris? Either would be much better than where she lived now.

"Tell you what," Colonel Clermont said. "When you come visit us in Algiers, we can all play tennis on our courts. If the boys are home, they can join us."

"I'll take you up on that invitation!" Audrey's father grinned. But a glance at her mother revealed the opposite reaction. Mum had no interest in playing tennis, and the only place she'd like to go was home to England, where she could return to her life as a recluse. How she wished her parents were more like Monique's. Mutual affection reflected in each other's eyes, and they always looked adoringly at their children. Wouldn't it be nice if she could live with Monique's parents in Algiers instead of with her own parents in England?

Chapter 4

Nicole

Algiers, 2019

Nicole walked through the cavernous terminal at the Houari Boumediene International Airport in Algiers—unusually empty compared to the Madrid airport where she'd had a layover—rolling her suitcase and wearing her backpack. Hopefully, she had enough clothes for her ninety-day stay, the length of her visa. She didn't expect to need any nice clothes. After all, she'd be on an archaeological dig doing dirty work. And if she needed more clothes, surely they had stores here.

She tried to read the signs and figured out which one led to Immigration. Hopefully, the process of entering the country wouldn't be difficult or slow. The Madrid Airport hadn't been too bad, even though she hated proving to strangers that she was not a threat.

As Nicole made her way through immigration, she scanned the crowd of faces waiting on the outside of the area, then glanced back down at her phone. Sami Kateb. He was going to be her guide and field manager. He told her he had black hair and a short beard, about six feet tall. Well, that should narrow it down to a couple hundred men. He didn't say he would be holding up a sign. How were they supposed to recognize each other? Of course, there weren't many single, obvious-looking American women there. She then remembered what she told him she'd wear.

She took her light blue cap with the letters UNC out of her backpack and stuck it on her head, pulling her ponytail through the back hole. Being 5'8" helped her to stand above a lot of other people, too. As she cleared the final checkpoint, she stepped outside the area and searched the crowd of male faces again. One of them, a very handsome one at that, was grinning at her. Making eye contact, he waved. Was that Sami? This trip took on a new level of interest.

He stepped toward her and extended his hand. "Nicole?"

"Yes!" She accepted his gesture, a little self-conscious of being overly enthusiastic. "You're Sami, I assume. I hoped you would recognize me. Good thing I put on the North Carolina cap."

He laughed, then gave her one of the nicest smiles she'd ever seen, lighting up his tanned face. Like he said, his hair was black and cut stylishly short, matching his trim beard and mustache. As her hand heated, she became aware that she had not let go of his and pulled away. "I do believe I would have known you, even without the cap," he said with a twinkle in his eyes. "There aren't many young American ladies with blonde hair here."

Nicole's face warmed.

Sami glanced around her. "Is that your only bag?"

"Yes, plus my backpack. I thought I should travel light,

since I didn't know how much we'd be moving around the country."

"Good choice." He grabbed the handle of her suitcase. "Let's get you to your hotel."

Glancing around, she found herself the center of attention, based on the somber stares of people around her. Were they looking at her because she was different or what? Unease crept up her back, so she nodded and eagerly followed Sami out to a small car in the parking lot.

"Your English is very good," she said. "I was afraid I might have to use my French, since that's the only other language I know."

"I studied at Cambridge in the U.K." He loaded her suitcase in the car, then opened her door for her, an unexpected gesture. "But if you prefer to use French, I speak that too."

Of course, he spoke several languages. Only Americans seemed to learn no more than one second language. "English is fine."

Nicole stared out the car windows, surprised to see modern buildings. After studying so much about the antiquities of the area, she'd expected to see them instead. But as they approached the city, modern towers blended with the stark white-washed stucco of all the other buildings.

"Now I see why Algiers is called Alger la Blanche."

Sami smiled from behind the steering wheel. "Algiers the White.' Most of the buildings you see downtown were built by the French in the French Colonial style when we were one of their colonies."

"What a pretty city. It gleams. I had no idea." Palm trees lined the boulevard they were on, adding a tropical flair to the city. "It sure doesn't look like desert here."

"Algiers is close enough to the Mediterranean to get moisture, that is, humidity, from the sea. We have plenty of desert in this country, the Sahara, which is about 1400 miles to the south." He glanced at her. "Are you hungry? Would you like to go get something to eat?"

"I ate some things on the plane, but I could go for a good cup of coffee. Is there a place around here where we can get some?"

Sami laughed. "Ha! Is there? I will take you to my favorite coffee shop. I hope you like strong coffee."

"Mimi, my great-grandmother, grew up here, and she taught me how to drink coffee strong."

"Do you know where she lived?"

"I remember how she described it many times, but I don't know exactly. I do hope to find it, though."

"Are there any relatives here?"

"I doubt it. She left here during the Second World War."

Sami pulled into a parking garage. "Do you feel like walking or are you tired from your trip?"

"My goodness, after being in a plane most of the day, I need some exercise!"

He parked the car, then looked down at her feet. "Your shoes look comfortable enough."

"I'm a good Girl Scout." When he gave her a puzzled look, she added, "They say a good scout is always prepared."

"Yes, of course. But I thought that only referred to Boy Scouts."

Nicole frowned at him. "You know, there are Girl Scouts too."

"Sorry, I didn't know. So I probably shouldn't ask such

a prepared person, but do you have a scarf you can wrap around your head if you need to? We may be modern, but some areas observe the Muslim tradition of a woman covering her hair."

She opened her backpack and pulled out a black scarf, waving it in front of him. "I did my homework."

"So you did." The impressed look he gave her added a warmth to his dark eyes and flipped her insides. "Well, good. Let's go."

As they started walking, the streets narrowed and wound upward.

"Will we be near the Casbah? I'd like to see it."

"You're in it," Sami said. He waved his arm out in front of them. "This is the old city, over one hundred acres. The rest of the city was built below and around it." There were no vehicles in the area, thank goodness, since there was barely enough room for two people to pass each other in some sections between the whitewashed buildings alongside the alleys. Many of the men and women wore long, loose-fitting robes that reached to their ankles.

"That clothing," Nicole said. "What is it called?"

"A djellaba. It is not required, but it is traditional," Sami said.

Nicole noticed many of them had long sleeves and hoods. "Gee, they must be hot."

"And some even wear them over their street clothes."

"Will I have to wear those?" Nicole certainly hoped not. As they climbed the unending steps, she could only imagine tripping over such a long garment.

"No, you're not expected to," Sami said.

She breathed a sigh of relief.

They took another turn and walked down steps. "Down here on the right is one of my favorite coffee shops."

Above the entrance, a sign was written in Arabic, while on the right side, a tile sign read "Café Casbah." The doorway was the shape of the Moroccan keyhole style, or as some referred to as a "horseshoe." Intricate screens carved in wood were on either side of the opening. Inside, the walls were covered in tile, and one wall had two windows that matched the doorway in design. The shop was long and narrow, with small tables on each side.

Nicole was mesmerized by the assorted knick-knacks—different-sized vases and mosaic-covered dishes scattered throughout the store. When they reached the back of the place, Sami addressed the man standing behind the counter.

"As*salamu alaykum."

"Wa alaykumu as-salam," the man responded.

"This is my friend Nicole from the States." Sami stepped aside so the man had a clear view of Nicole. "She's here to study our archaeology."

The man nodded in greeting. He had a very unique style of dress. He wore the traditional red fez on his head, but the rest of his clothing was more American with jeans, a vest and several necklaces, once with a peace symbol. Nicole would call it "Old School Algerian hippie." He leaned forward with his elbows on the counter, propping his chin up on his hands. "I am Hassan. What would you like, dear lady?" His grin reminded her of the Cheshire cat in Alice in Wonderland. Nicole was thankful he spoke English, as she could not understand Arabic.

"Can you make a flat white?"

"That I can do. But wouldn't you like to try some attay

instead? You can get your flat white coffee anywhere, but you can't get attay where you come from.

"What is attay?" she said, glancing at Sami.

"It's mint tea. Very good and popular in Algeria. You should try it."

"All right, I will."

Turning to Sami, Hassan said, "And you want your usual espresso?"

"You got it." Sami reached for his wallet, but the man put his hand up like a stop sign.

"No. This is a gift for the lovely American woman. Just bring her back another time."

Sami answered him in Algerian, and the man just nodded and began to make their drinks.

Leading her to one of the tables, Sami motioned for her to sit.

"What did you say to him when we first came in."

"It's a traditional Algerian greeting. As-salamu alaykum means 'peace be to you.' The typical response is Wa alaykumu as-salam. It means 'peace be upon you too.'"

"Oz salami … what?" Nicole tried to remember the greeting.

Sami laughed. "Almost. Repeat after me … as salamu alaykum."

"As salamu … alaykum."

"Perfect." There was that impressed look again and the responding swoop in her middle. "Just keep practicing. You'll need to know it, since that's the way we always greet each other."

Nicole nodded, then said the phrase over again. Scanning the room, she said, "Interesting décor."

"Yes, rather unique," Sami said, smiling.

Eclectic was more like it. The colorful décor boasted plants, pottery, colorfully painted furniture, and various signs she could not read. A striped tabby strolled through and stopped to rub against her leg, then he continued over to a cushion on the floor that had a sign over it which read The Cat Café.

Hassan brought their drinks over and set it before them. He pointed to hers. "Taste."

She obliged by picking up the cup and inhaling the aroma—green tea and spearmint. Then she took a tentative sip and found that it was very sweet. "This is very nice. I like it."

"I knew you would. I make the best coffee and attay in Algiers."

Nicole smiled as he walked away. Holding her cup with both hands, she sipped it. "This is actually very good," she said. "By the way, can you please tell me where we are? We've gone up and down steps, so I'm not sure."

"When we get back outside, I'll show you. You can see the Mediterranean if you look between the buildings."

"I didn't know there was a 'between.' It looks like all the buildings are connected."

"Most are. It helped for protection against invasions back when they built this hundreds of years ago." Sami's voice took on the tone of a professor teaching class, but a professor who would be pleasant to listen to and not boring. "When the Dey, the governor of Algiers, built his palace in the 1600's, the rest of the citizens built their homes around his, and the city was walled in. The area near the palace is called the 'High City,' and the area below it, the 'Low City.'

Before the French took over, there were over 166 religious-related buildings like mosques and mausoleums in the Casbah. There are only about fifty now."

"You know, my great-grandmother told me that when she lived here as a little girl, she used to run up and down the streets in the Casbah." Nicole imagined Mimi running the same path she and Sami walked. "She said she loved the excitement of the markets."

"When did you say that was?"

"She was born here in 1919. Her father was assigned here with the French military."

"I see. That explains it, then. She would have been safer in the Casbah back then."

"Safer? Than now? Why is that?"

"It's not advisable for anyone, especially women, to come here alone at night."

"Why?" Was there anywhere in this world it was safe for a woman to be alone at night?

"Mainly theft. However, during the day, you also have to look out for pickpockets. You need to keep your valuables close to you."

Nicole patted her midriff. "Got my money and papers in a pouch right here under my shirt."

"Good idea." Again, Sami gave her that approving look.

"You know, I doubt my grandmother came here by herself though. She told me she came with her father or one of the orderlies assigned to their household. Mimi said one of them shadowed her, to make sure she didn't get into trouble." Nicole laughed at Mimi's story. "She also told me she tried to slip away from him, but he always found her."

They finished their drinks, waved goodbye to Hassan,

and then walked some more until they found an opening between the buildings. Like Sami said, the deep blue water of the Mediterranean sparkled below while the brilliant blue of the sky made Nicole catch her breath. "It's gorgeous! I don't think I've seen a sky so blue."

"Come," Sami said, "There is more to see."

She followed him through a passageway into an arched entrance and found herself in a courtyard surrounded by white spiraled columns and Moorish arches. A second-story gallery with matching columns and arches wrapped around the courtyard above them.

"This is the Dar Aziza. It was the palace of Dey Mustapha and was built in 1797."

"The columns look like marble. Are they?" Nicole resisted the urge to run her hand along the surface of one nearby.

"Yes, that's correct. And the woodwork around the double doors is sculpted cedar."

"It's beautiful. And these tiles are lovely," Nicole said, looking up at the blue and white tiles that trimmed the tops of the arches and around the top of the first floor.

"Yes, thankfully, this property has been restored and still in use, although not for a residence, but for a government office. One of the rooms is now the place for the National Agency of Archaeology and Protection of Historic Sites and Monuments."

"Oh, so you work for them?"

"No, I work for the university's archaeology department. But I have to comply with them." Sami moved toward the entrance. "Come, let me introduce you."

Inside of the ornate doors, Sami brought her to the desk of a balding gentleman with bushy black eyebrows who looked up and smiled. They exchanged the traditional greeting.

"Sami, my friend," he said in a deep, coarse voice. "What brings you here today?"

Sami motioned to Nicole. "This is Nicole Bennett. She is doing graduate studies in archaeology here. I will be her guide. Nicole, this is Amad Hamid."

Nicole smiled, uncertain as to offer her hand or not. "Nice to meet you, sir."

"So Sami will keep you out of trouble?" His eyes sparkled with the jest.

Nicole glanced at Sami and nodded. "I'm sure he will."

"Fine. You must sign and date this form to promise you will respect our antiquities and not take any out of the country." He slid a sheet of paper over to her, his forehead wrinkling in a warning frown.

She arched a brow, but Sami nodded his approval. Of course, she would comply. Any archaeologist would know how to treat antiquities.

Mr. Hamid explained the reason behind the documents as if he had to defend the practice. "Unfortunately, some people do not respect our property and have stolen items or vandalized them. They were, of course, prosecuted for their crime. I'm sure you wouldn't consider such a thing."

Was he warning her? How were "they" prosecuted? Did they have their hands cut off as she'd heard in more barbaric countries? She shuddered at the thought.

Hoping her cheeks didn't flush, Nicole tried to vouch for her innocence, even though she was not and would not be guilty of such a thing. "Absolutely not. I am a strong supporter of preservation in every country."

He nodded. "As you may know, we have several UNESCO World Heritage sites here in Algeria, but we have many more sites that have not yet been added to the list."

"My great-grandmother was born here, so I have extra respect for your country."

When she leaned over to sign the document, the ring on the chain around her neck fell out of her blouse. Mr. Hamid's eyes widened when he saw the ring. "Your ring. You buy that here?"

Nicole's hand flew to the ring, and she covered it protectively. "No, this belonged to my great-grandmother, who grew up here." She quickly tucked the ring back inside her blouse.

He studied her, frowning. "Is that so? What was her name?"

"Clermont. Monique Clermont. Her father was Colonel Jacques Clermont in the French Army."

Amid's eyes darkened. "A French." He muttered something in Arabic, then turned to Sami. "Sami will fill you in on the details of your role here in *our* country." Nicole didn't miss the emphasis on the word "our."

A shiver like melting ice trickled down her spine.

Amid moved the paper to the side of his desk as if finished with it. "Have a nice visit to Algeria," he said without looking at her. Changing his attention to something else on his desk, he indicated the conversation was officially over.

"Thank you, Amid," Sami said, taking Nicole's arm and escorting her out of the office.

Once outside, she shot him a glare. "He made me feel guilty for something I didn't do, much less, even consider doing! I certainly understand the importance of protecting antiquities. What good archaeologist wouldn't?"

"Ah. You see, then. Not all archaeologists are good."

"Seriously?" Nicole couldn't fathom why any archaeologist wouldn't place the integrity of their find above all else.

"Yes. Don't be offended by Amid. He does not trust anyone, with just cause."

Nicole blew out a breath, trying to shake off the negative reception she had been given. "That's too bad."

"Yes, it is. But not all people are as honorable as you."

This time her cheeks heated for another reason, and it wasn't anger. Was she just naïve?

"He's not particularly fond of the French, you know. His grandfather fought for Algerian independence from France."

"Oh no. I didn't even consider that. After all, it was so long ago."

"Not that long, really. Only about sixty years, actually. Many still harbor ill feelings toward the French. When you see the Martyrs Memorial, you'll get a better understanding."

She stopped and faced him, searching his face for any hint of animosity. "Sami, do you feel the same way about the French?"

He shook his head. "No. It was before my time. And no, my parents don't harbor any ill feelings either. My mother is half French, you see."

"She is?" Hearing that gave Nicole comfort that Sami's mother had something in common with her family. "Did she have to deal with any problems?"

"No. Her parents had a little trouble because her father married a French woman. But that's in the past now." He extended his arms out wide and smiled. "So you see, you and I both have some French in our bloodlines."

Warmth coursed through her at the sense of connection she had with him. She liked this guy.

"Are you ready to explore some more, or are you tired?" Sami asked.

"I'm not tired yet, and yes, I'd love to see more."

They continued meandering through the narrow streets where ancient, crumbling buildings connected to others in better condition. Lines of hanging laundry were strung between some of the more narrow passages, and beautiful red and pink bougainvillea spilled over the tops of some of the walls in sharp contrast to the stark white of the buildings. Sometimes the passages split into narrow alleys, and Nicole wouldn't have known which way to go if Sami hadn't been with her.

"I can see how someone could get lost in here," she said.

"That is true. It takes some time to know your way around, so I suggest you don't wander through here by yourself."

"I keep seeing scenes of *Casablanca* in my mind and feel like I could be in the movie right now."

"There are similarities, of course, except that the movie was in Morocco and not in Algeria. But both places were founded by the Phoenicians, and later ruled by the Ottomans and the Romans. Our architecture and history have been influenced by all of them."

"So I've read. How amazing to think how far back in time this area, this place where we are walking, existed. The United States is so young by comparison."

"There really is no comparison," Sami said.

"I suppose you're right. Ancient doesn't really apply to my country. I guess that's why I'm so interested in the past civilizations," Nicole said.

Down steps, then up steps they went, occasionally passing by an open door to a small shop.

"You can tell these steps are old, since some are crumbling," she said.

"Yes, there is a plan to repair some of the property with the worst wear, according to the area's assignment as a UNESCO site, but the progress is very slow."

The steps ended in an open area where a myriad of textures, colors and aromas greeted them from merchants arranged throughout the area displaying their wares.

"How strange to see so many people in this space, since we only saw a few people as we walked," she said.

"This is a souk, a marketplace," Sami said.

Many of the vendors called out to passersby, trying to draw tourists. Sami nodded to several men, and they nodded in return.

"These are beautiful." Nicole paused at one of the booths to admire some tapestries while Sami addressed the vendor in Arabic.

"He is honest, if you'd like to buy from him."

She ran her hand across the fabric, then glanced up at the man.

"It is good," he said in a thick Arabic accent. "I make you good deal."

She glanced at Sami, who nodded. "It is the custom to bargain, if you're interested in purchasing."

"Oh, I hadn't really planned to buy anything today." She didn't want to carry souvenirs around with her today. "Perhaps we can come back another time before I go back to the States?"

"Yes, of course. I'll tell him."

She lifted the camera hanging around her neck. "May I take a picture of the two of you?"

Sami spoke to the man, who smiled. "Yes, it is fine."

The two posed together, and she snapped a couple of pictures. They left his booth and strolled past others, stopping at a huge display of dates. The fruit hung from the roof of the canopy in long clusters and was piled on the table in clusters as well.

"My goodness, I've never seen so many dates."

"You should get some. They are our candy," Sami said.

She picked up her camera and took a picture of the date-laden table. "All right, choose some for me."

Sami obliged, telling the woman at the table what Nicole would buy. While they were talking, Nicole took pictures of the market and its different booths. She glanced back at Sami as he was taking a package from the vendor. "How much do I owe?"

He shook his head. "Nothing. They're my treat. Here, try one."

Nicole obliged, chewing the soft dried fruit slowly. "It's very sweet. I don't believe I've ever tasted one before."

"You'll acquire a taste for them. They're good for a quick energy snack."

As they walked away from that booth, a man stepped up to them and shouted something in Arabic, pointing to Nicole's camera.

"What's wrong?" she said.

"You took a picture of him without asking his permission."

"Oh, I'm sorry." She spoke quickly to defend herself. "I was just taking pictures of the whole market. I wasn't really focused on him."

"It's customary to ask permission before you take a picture of an Algerian. It's considered rude if you do not. I should have told you."

Her face grew hot. "Please tell him I'm sorry."

"I will." Sami turned to the man and adopted an apologetic expression as he explained that Nicole had not intended to be rude. The man frowned, then stormed away.

"Oh my gosh. I sure didn't mean to offend anyone."

"Don't worry. He'll get over it. Next time, you'll remember," Sami said, smiling at her.

"I haven't even been here a whole day, and I've managed to offend at least one person, maybe two, if you count the man at the antiquities office."

"You're just getting used to our culture, so it's not a big deal. I had to get used to being in the UK too."

"Well, I hope nobody yelled at you," she said.

"Actually, they did, but only because they were trying to talk to me. Why is it that when people don't understand your language, they think by yelling, you'll understand?"

Nicole laughed. "I know what you mean. I've seen that happen many times."

"So we're even. And I'll try not to get you in any more trouble." He paused. "I think you've had enough exposure to our culture today, don't you? You must be tired."

"Actually, I am. I would love to have a shower and relax."

"Then I'll take you to the hotel. Unless you'd like to get something to eat before we go there."

Much as she wanted to accept his invitation, she really did want to clean up and put her feet up. She hoped to send an email to Mom if she could figure out what time it was back home.

"Thank you, but I think I'll pass for now. The hotel has a restaurant, right? Maybe I can get room service."

"Yes, you can. But if I were you, I'd order in person at the restaurant and take it with you to your room. That way, you don't have to deal with opening your door to a stranger or messing with tipping."

She eyed him, questioning. It was nice that he was so thoughtful, but he seemed to be protective, too. Did she really need protection? An uneasiness sent warnings through her. He must be more aware of the dangers she faced than she understood. Thank God, she could trust Sami because who else could she trust here?

A few blocks later, Sami pulled into a parking space beside the hotel. They got out, and he retrieved her luggage from the trunk. She reached for it, and he said, "I'll take it in for you."

"You don't need to do that." There were only a few steps up to the entrance of the building. "I can manage from here, but thanks anyway."

He looked disappointed but gave her the suitcase. "I pray you'll get a good night's rest. We'll have a busy day tomorrow. There is so much to see."

"I can't wait," Nicole turned to go up the steps, feeling his eyes on her all the way. It would be so easy to let him do everything for her in this strange country. But she wasn't helpless. She needed to establish herself as a professional archaeologist, even if she had to stumble a few times before she got it right. Sami wouldn't always be around to help her.

Chapter 5

Monique

Algiers, September, 1931

S he's going to live with us?" Monique stared at Maman, almost holding her breath as she heard the news a month after returning to Algiers. She'd never had a sister, much less lived with another girl. But the prospect sounded like fun.

"Yes, she'll be going to the same school as you, so she'll stay with us. Her parents think she'll do better here," Maman said as she sat on their back patio working on a piece of embroidery.

If Monique remembered correctly, Audrey's mother hadn't been in favor of her daughter attending a Catholic school. Had Audrey talked her parents into letting her attend school in Algeria, or was she doing so poorly at home that her parents decided to ship her off? No, had to be that Audrey talked him into it. Audrey was too sunny, too smart, and too much fun to be around for her parents to want her to be somewhere else.

"Where will she sleep?"

"That's up to you. Would you like to share your room with her?"

Would she? Audrey was fun, but Monique had always had a room to herself. "I don't know. Maybe."

"Okay, you think about it. We can always put her in the guest room."

The guest room? That's where Grand Mere and Grand Pere stayed when they visited from France, although they didn't visit very often. But the room was for old people, not a girl her age.

The idea of having someone like a sister excited her, though. But what if they didn't get along? Could she change her mind later? Still, Audrey's personality radiated excitement and promised new adventures. Grand Mere used to say she prayed about important decisions before she jumped into them. This might be the most important decision Monique had ever made, so she should take Grand Mere's advice.

After praying and trying to imagine what it would be like to have Audrey so close, Monique believed she was supposed to say yes. Audrey didn't have a sister either, so they'd both have to adjust. Monique told her parents it would be okay for Audrey to move into her room. Maman was pleased, and they began moving furniture and toys around in Monique's room to accommodate Audrey.

Audrey's arrival was met with mixed emotions. Her parents delivered her to Monique's house, then stayed for dinner. Audrey's mother was stiffer than her father, in Monique's opinion, and scanned the house as if she were inspecting it, especially when she was shown where her daughter would be sharing a room.

"Audrey has never had to share a room," she said. Mrs. Reynolds sniffed like the idea of sharing a room was beneath her family.

"Neither has Monique, but I'm sure they'll get along fine," Maman said. "Won't you, Monique?"

Monique nodded, but Audrey's eyes brightened, and she answered. "We'll have a grand time!" She grabbed Monique's hand. "Come, Monique, and show me around."

They trotted down the stairs and out the door. As Monique gave her a tour of the property, Audrey's excitement was contagious. She was overjoyed to meet all the animals.

"You're so lucky to have so many pets!" Audrey's eyes were wide as she took in Monique's yard. "My mother wouldn't allow me to have any at our house. But at my grandmother's house, there were two huge cats."

"My Papá loves animals, so he often brings a new one home. Some of them don't stay long though. We once had a baby giraffe, but he ate all the leaves off the trees, so he went to a zoo."

"A giraffe?" Audrey's mouth gaped.

"Yes, Papá travels all over the country in his job, and often the tribal chiefs give him unusual gifts. We once had a lion cub too, but he started jumping at people in the park next door and scaring them. He'd never hurt them, but he was growing bigger. So he went to live with one of Papá's friends out in the country, where he could roam around."

Audrey laughed and clapped her hands. "I wish I had been here then."

"That was when I was little. I do have a picture I can show you, though."

Monique's two dogs ran up to greet them. "This is Cossette and Louie." Louie dropped a ball at her feet, so she picked it up and threw it. The two dogs took off after it.

A loud cry rang out across the yard.

Audrey jumped, eyes wide. "What was that?"

Monique turned and pointed to a shed across the yard. "That's Henri. He's our peacock."

"A peacock?" Audrey walked toward the shed, peering up at the bird. "Does it bite?"

Monique laughed. "He'll peck at the dogs if they get too close."

"I love it here!" Audrey spun around. "What an amazing home you have."

Matazan, the tall, dark orderly assigned to Monique's father, walked over to them. "Miss Monique, this is your friend?"

"Yes, this is Audrey. Audrey, this is Matazan. He works for my father."

Audrey studied the man wearing a white uniform and red fez. "Hello."

"Miss Audrey." Matazan gave a short bow before turning to Monique again. "May I get some lemonade for you and your guest?"

"Yes, thank you. Audrey will be living with us for a while."

"Is that so? Then welcome." He gave her a bow of his head, then walked away.

"He is your servant?" Audrey said, watching Matazan's retreating figure.

"Not really. He is an orderly and is also in the military, assigned to my father's household. He lives on the army base, but since it's far away, he stays on our property most of the week in a cottage in back of the property."

"But he does what you say?"

"Only if I don't ask too much. I have gotten in trouble with Papá for that because it is not my place to give him orders. However, Matazan is from Senegal, and since he didn't know how to speak French when he came here, I taught him, so he and I are more like friends. He has a unique gift of mimicking animal sounds. Sometimes you can't tell if it's a real animal or him."

"My grandmother has servants. She lives on the coast of England in a grand house, where my mother used to live. I liked to go there for holidays when my father went on a business trip and left me and my mum at home. I much preferred Grandmother's home to our house in the city," Audrey said. a note of sadness in her voice.

A short man in a uniform like Matazan's strode across the yard away from them.

"That is Tunis." Monique nodded toward the man. "He is our other orderly. He mainly does whatever Papá or Maman ask him to do. He does not spend time with me, and I do not think he and Matazan like each other. But I'm glad Matazan will escort us to school and in the city."

Audrey sat next to Monique, along with twelve other girls clad in their blue uniform dresses at one of three long wooden tables that formed a U in the classroom. Sister Julia stood at the front of the room in her all-white habit, droning on about arithmetic. Audrey scanned the room, taking in the faces of the other girls focused on the nun. How could they be so interested? Her gaze rose above the dull white walls to the high ceiling, looking for something more interesting. The windows in the room were tall as well, but kept open to allow air in.

She nudged Monique to get her attention. Monique cut her eyes toward Audrey but kept her head forward. "Do you think we could climb out of those windows?" Audrey whispered.

Monique's head lifted toward the windows, then back down. Between closed lips, she muttered, "If we had to, I'm sure we could."

"Let's try it later," Audrey said.

Monique's eyebrows lifted, but she didn't answer.

"Miss Reynolds!" A shrill voice echoed throughout the room.

Audrey jumped. She turned her head to face Sister Julia in front of the room. Audrey lowered her eyes. "Yes, Sister."

"Can you tell me what we have been talking about?" The Sister crossed her arms.

Who was the "we" she referred to? Audrey glanced up at the blackboard. "Multiplication?" Beside her, Monique shifted in her chair while the other girls tittered.

"Silence! Miss Reynolds, you have not been paying attention. Perhaps you need some extra time in the classroom so you can learn what's being taught."

More time in the classroom? Audrey stifled a groan.

"I'm sorry, Sister. I'll do better, I just need to go to the loo."

More tittering. A scornful glance from the Sister

silenced the room.

"You may go, but I expect you to pay attention when you return."

Audrey pushed her wooden chair back from the table, scraping the floor with an awful screech magnified by the stone walls. Monique looked down, trying to hide her smile. Too bad she couldn't get out of class, too. It was a lovely day that begged to be outdoors. A sense of victory filled Audrey as she strode down the hallway. She had won her freedom, albeit briefly, because she'd have to return to the classroom. But one day, she'd have freedom to do whatever she wanted, chase whatever adventure presented itself.

Much as she wanted to run down the hall, she restrained herself, not wanting to make more noise and gain the attention of other Sisters in the school. She still couldn't believe Father had allowed her to come here.

Poor Mum had been stricken by Father's decision to allow their daughter to attend a Catholic school. But much as she disliked his decision, but there was little she could do about it. And the funny thing was that Father thought the school would make a lady out of her, while Mum thought the school would make her a Catholic instead of an Anglican. Audrey, on the other hand, expected the school to have neither effect on her. For her, it was a new adventure and an escape from the daily doldrums of home and the silence between her parents. She was in Africa! And staying with Monique's family had shown her the type of family life she wished she had. Every day in Algiers had been a new experience so far, and Monique was a wonderful friend. She had that innocent look, but she was almost as adventurous as Audrey, with a little encouragement.

Audrey went to the loo, but instead of going right back to class, she sneaked down the hall and out into the brilliant sunshine. Sucking in a breath of fresh air, she relished the clear, warm days in Algiers, such a contrast to the overcast, rainy days back home. She strolled around the garden, keeping an eye on the school in case she was seen. In the center of the garden stood a majestic marble fountain with a statue of some saint standing on it. Maybe he was Saint Cyprian, the patron saint of North Africa. The fountain reminded her of some she'd seen on a trip to Italy.

A low wall of stacked stones encircled the fountain, inviting Audrey to sit and enjoy the refreshing sound of the water. She obliged, glancing up at the saint and hoping he didn't mind company. A brief moment of sadness pinched her heart when a wish for her parents to join her crossed her mind. She didn't really miss them, though. Did they miss her? She sighed, then stood, pushing up from the wall. As she did, one of the lower stones moved, and Audrey reached down to adjust it. But when she grabbed it, it came out in her hand. She glanced sharply around, hoping no one would accuse her of destroying the fountain.

Not seeing anyone, she bent down and looked at the place where the stone had been. There was a large space, large enough to hide something. But what could they hide there? Treasures? Trinkets? No, they weren't little children. They had bigger secrets. Secrets! Their secrets, in a place where only Monique and Audrey would know about it. Audrey stood and brushed off her hands. She couldn't wait to tell Monique about it.

She studied the school building and noticed the windows toward the rear weren't as high as the ones in front, thanks to the elevation of the land. Surely they could climb out one of those windows. Wouldn't that be fun? Hadn't she seen Matazan with some rope yesterday? Now where had he put it?

A bell rang inside, reminding everyone class time was over.

Time to get back inside to the boredom of class and sitting still, memorizing facts. Audrey cast a glance back to the fountain. Once she told Monique about the hiding place, school would become much more interesting.

After school, the girls were playing outside with the dogs when Colonel Clermont came home early, bringing another officer with him. He and the other man walked out to the tennis court that was in the backyard. Taking off their jackets and rolling up their sleeves, they began hitting the ball back and forth across the net. But when the colonel spotted Matazan, he called the orderly over. Monique had told Audrey that her father had taught the orderly how to play tennis so he'd have someone to play with because her brother wasn't home, away at school.

The men's voices carried through the still, hot air, and Audrey couldn't help eavesdropping.

"Now we have three, but we need four to play a game of doubles," Monique's father said.

"I can play!" Audrey jumped up and ran over to the court.

"Hmm. I remember your father said you played well. But can you play with gentlemen?" the colonel asked, his eyebrows lifted.

"I sure can. I practiced with my instructor, a man." Audrey straightened her spine and tried to appear taller, stronger.

He looked at the other man who shrugged. "Why not? Let's see how proficient you are."

Although eager to prove her skills, she was surprised that the colonel agreed. Her father would never invite her to play with his friends. But the colonel was a very nice man, not at all like her father.

Soon Audrey was playing tennis with the men, surprising them all by her finesse. Monique stood by and watched, applauding when Audrey made a good shot. Too bad she couldn't play with them, but perhaps she couldn't play well enough to join them. After the game, the men congratulated Audrey. Even Matazan seemed impressed.

"Perhaps you can help Monique with her game," the colonel said.

Audrey glanced at Monique, who smiled back. "Thank you for letting me play," she said, then ran over to Monique.

"You played very well," Monique said. "I've never seen Papá play with a girl."

"That's too bad because he should play with you, too."

"Oh, I'm not that good," Monique said.

"Well, you'll never get better by just watching. I can help you improve your game, then we'll take the men on!"

Audrey's boldness amazed Monique. Audrey didn't act like there were any barriers to what she could do, while Monique was used to following the rules of society. She wanted to be more like Audrey, but was afraid to take chances.

When Audrey told Monique about the loose stone in the fountain, Monique asked her father for a leather journal so she could keep a diary. She told him the truth, except that it would be a diary of sorts for both she and Audrey. They planned to leave messages for each other, then hide the journal behind the stone. It became quite the game, making sure no one saw them hide the journal and read their secrets.

Usually, the secret was about something or someone at school that they had heard. Sometimes the message was funny, other times revealing. Monique eagerly looked forward to retrieving the journal and discovering a new message from Audrey. The journal had the added benefit of giving them a way to "talk" without getting into trouble in class. They vowed to never share their secrets or their hidden journal with anyone else for the rest of their lives, crossing their hearts in pledge.

Matazan always walked them down to the school, which was several streets below their house on the hill. The path involved going down tiers of stairs that went behind and between other houses. After school each day, Matazan was there to escort them back home. Monique had always been glad he was there to look out for her, but Audrey wasn't used to having that sort of protection and wasn't convinced she needed it. Papá had to explain why it was important for the children of the French officers to have extra protection, because not everyone appreciated the French government in the country of Algeria. Monique wasn't sure what that meant, but believed Papá and knew it was important.

Their home at the top of the hill gave them a panorama that looked down on the white buildings of the city and out to the blue water of the Mediterranean. It was a white two-story stucco house with a central marble staircase and a very large, fenced-in yard with plenty of room to run around and play. Monique liked playing with her dolls, but Audrey didn't care much for dolls, so she suggested they dress the cats up in doll clothes instead and push them in the doll carriage. The cats tired of playing dress-up, though, so they sprang out of the carriage and ran off wearing the doll clothes. Audrey and Monique laughed so hard they cried, watching the cats run off in frilly dresses and lacy bonnets.

One side of the yard bordered a huge park, separated by a fence. There were so many trees and flowers, it was hard to see their house from the park. There was also a trail along the cliff that led to the next property on the other side of Monique's house, so Monique took Audrey to see the agricultural research facility that was at the end of the path. The facility had a citrus grove with orange, lemon, and grapefruit trees. Audrey eyed the fruit hungrily.

"Can we have any?"

"Yes, they told me to help myself," Monique said.

"Then what are we waiting for?"

Audrey shimmied up an orange tree and plucked a couple of oranges off, tossing one to Monique. After they ate the oranges, Monique climbed a lemon tree and grabbed two lemons. The girls made faces as they tasted the sour fruit. The grapefruit was as tart, but when they each finished one, they both climbed the orange tree and ate another orange each. Pretty soon, they were full, and their mouths burned. They hurried home in time for supper but couldn't eat because they were so full of fruit.

"That was the best fruit I've ever eaten," Audrey said.

"It doesn't grow where I live. You're very lucky to have it so close."

Monique considered Audrey's remark. She'd never thought herself lucky, in fact, never thought other people didn't have what she did. However, Audrey frequently pointed out differences between her life and Monique's, making Monique more grateful for her own life and sorry for Audrey's. Based on what Audrey said, Monique would never want to change places with her.

Chapter 6

Nicole

Algiers, 2019

When Nicole saw Sami in the lobby of her hotel the next morning, he was looking away from her, but she had a chance to observe him. Wearing a white shirt tucked in with rolled up sleeves and open at the neck, his trim, yet muscular build fit into the jeans he wore quite well. He turned around as she approached. Her face warmed at being caught checking him out.

"Good morning," he said with a warm smile. "Looks like you're dressed for the occasion."

Nicole glanced down at herself, clad in lightweight khakis and a white T-shirt with the necessary red and white scarf tied loosely around her neck. "Am I? I wasn't sure. Didn't want to offend anyone with my American clothes."

"You don't need to dress in our traditional wear." He spread his arms open. "I'm not."

No, he wasn't, not even close to the baggy pants and long vests she'd seen men wearing in the Casbah the day before. But enough focus on him. After all, she wasn't a college coed anymore.

"So where are we going today? Will we visit any digs?" She couldn't wait to join in one.

He motioned her to one of the couches in the lobby. Sitting beside her, he pulled a map out of his pocket. After opening it and spreading it out between them, he pointed. "Not yet. I want you to see some of our older architectural sites. So first we'll go past the post office. We won't go in, but it's one of the famous sites. Then we will go to the Casbah again, driving close to the Ketchaoua Mosque on the southern side, so we won't be walking through to get to it. After that, we'll go to the Basilica of Notre Dame, then maybe see the Martyr's Monument if we have time. However, we're going to spend most of our time visiting a couple of archaeological sites out of the city. It will be a full day."

"I'm ready!" Did she sound too eager? A few men turned to look at her.

"Did you eat breakfast? I brought some dates if you're hungry."

Her mouth watered, remembering the dates she'd sampled yesterday. "I did eat, so I'm good, but maybe later."

"I brought some bottled water too. It's best that you don't drink tap water. It may be good in some places, but just to be sure, drink the bottled type."

"I have my own water bottle in my backpack. I filled it up with the bottles in the hotel room."

"Okay, good. You'll need it."

Sami drove down a busy boulevard to a commercial area where a huge white building occupied a triangular city block. "This is the Grande Poste d'Alger, the post office built in 1910 when we were a French colony."

Nicole listened to his tone, trying to detect any animosity toward the French. She was well aware of the long war for independence that the Algerians had fought against them after World War II. Thank God, Mimi had moved to the States by then.

Next, they drove to the Ketchaoua Mosque, parking and going inside while Sami acted as a docent, sharing its 1612 Ottoman history, its 1962 French conversion to the Cathedral of St. Philipe, and its post-revolution return to a mosque.

Then Sami took her to the Church of Notre Dame of Africa.

"What a gorgeous setting!" Nicole said, as they parked near the domed cathedral at the top of a cliff overlooking the crescent-shaped Bay of Algiers. A brisk breeze blew from the water. "It also seems to have a combination of Moorish architecture and French."

"You're right. The French built it in the 1800's." He nodded up where a statue of Mary stood at the apex of the entrance with small minarets on either side of her at the corners of the building."

"That blue tile is so pretty," Nicole said, admiring the border of light and dark blue tile that ran along the top of the stone building just below the roof.

"It is also called the Basilica of Our Lady of Africa and the French name Notre Dame d'Afrique."

"Mimi mentioned this place." Nicole couldn't wait to visit the place Mimi had been. "She came here for some special events, although I don't think they attended here regularly. I think they attended the Anglican Church more often."

"That's probably true. It was hugely popular during the French rule."

"May we go in?" Maybe knowing Mimi had been there explained the feeling of being drawn to the place.

"Of course. They still have daily mass in several languages."

Nicole covered her head with her scarf and walked as quietly as she could when they entered. She scanned the walls and ceilings, an unexpected tear trickling down her cheek. Mimi had been there as a child and a young woman. Had she looked at the same things Nicole was looking at?

Sami whispered, nodding toward the front of the sanctuary. "The organ was donated by a wealthy English woman in 1930."

Nicole's memory triggered. "Mimi told me about that! Her father knew the lady."

Nicole's eyes were drawn to the stained-glass windows depicting scenes from the Bible. "So many beautiful windows."

"There are 46, but they were blown out in World War II and have been restored since."

Nicole faced Sami. "That's when my Mimi left Algiers. Her husband said it was too dangerous for her to stay."

"I can see why." People started coming into the church and sitting in the pews. Sami took her elbow and steered her toward the front door. "We're not staying for mass. I hope you don't mind."

She shook her head. As they exited, she said, "I'm not Catholic, but I can appreciate the beauty of their cathedrals."

Especially this cathedral with its connection to Mimi. She would definitely come back another time.

Back in the car, Sami turned to her. "Are you all right?"

She nodded, wiping her eyes with the back of her hand. "Yes, I'm fine. I had such a strong sense of feeling Mimi here. I could almost see her. Her father wasn't Catholic, but he was friends with people of all faiths, and since he was a French official, he was invited to quite a few events at the cathedral, so I know she accompanied him often."

"So are you ready to see more of the country?"

She jerked herself back to the present. "Drive on! Where are we going next?"

"Tipaza. You've heard of it?"

"Yes, of course! It's well known for being one of the crossroads of civilization from the sixth century B.C. to the sixth century AD. I can't wait to see it."

Sami smiled and soon they were on a highway that bordered the sea.

"It's about an hour from here, so enjoy the scenery."

Nicole breathed in the fresh air, mesmerized by the sun sparkling on the blue water of the Mediterranean. She sat back in the car seat, closing her eyes against the glare and enjoyed the breeze through the open window. She must've dozed off, because the next thing she heard was, "We're here."

Startled, Nicole blinked and came to attention. Before her lay ruins along the waterfront as far as she could see. "Wow! This is amazing."

She climbed out of the car and stretched as Sami came around. "It's difficult to capture in photos."

Roman ruins spread as far as she could see along the

banks of the water. Tourists clustered around a guide talking about the city that once stood here. Nicole and Sami walked around the group, overhearing some of the information the guide was giving. "The earliest identified ruins are from the Phoenicians, who had a large trading port here."

When Sami and Nicole were away from the group, Sami provided Nicole with further commentary as they explored the grounds. Sami explained that the Phoenicians were the first known civilization here. "This was a very popular seaport for trading on the Mediterranean. Artifacts from Greece, Iberia, and Italy have been found here."

"And then the Romans took over, right?" Nicole pulled from her history of the area.

"Yes, the Romans ruled it for many years before the Vandals ruined it. But it also had significance and examples of Christian and Byzantine influence. And actually, the Berbers lived here before anyone else. With each invasion, they were pushed farther into the interior of the country."

They stopped in one of the areas where remains of a wall stood. "This is where the Basilica Alexander was. There were three churches, or basilicas, here in Tipaza, and cemeteries surrounded each of them. The churches were built when Christianity was very popular here in the third and fourth centuries." Sami waved his arm following the expanse of ruins along the coastline. "This settlement covered three hills."

"I'm impressed with how well this place has been excavated," Nicole said.

Nodding, Sami said, "Yes, this is a good example of the change that has been made since it became a UNESCO site in 2002. Since then, extensive archeological work has been done, with more left to be discovered."

Excitement ran through Nicole as she envisioned working on the site and discovering more ruins. "Will I be assigned here?"

"Not at first."

Nicole bit back, disappointed as she followed Sami among the ruins up and down the hills, finding archways, an amphitheater, the site of thermal baths, and the other churches, including many more tombstones, some with inscriptions carved on top. There was a mosaic visible in what was thought to be the nave of the Basilica of St. Salsa, supposedly built to commemorate a young Christian girl who was martyred for her faith. The largest church, the Great Basilica, had seven aisles. "Under the foundation of the church, they found more tombs."

She glanced away toward the water, then shielded her eyes to focus on an object on one of the promontories along the coast. "Oh, there's a lighthouse!"

"That one is relatively new," Sami said, still in tour-guide mode, "built in 1860-something."

"New?"

"It's not the first lighthouse built in the harbor," Sami said with a slight smile.

Nicole crossed her arms. "So the Romans built one, right?"

"Yes, when Rome controlled, this area was called Mauretania. It was ruled by Queen Cleopatra Selene and her husband Juba II from around 35 or 25 BC. She wanted to copy the great lighthouse of Alexandria in Egypt, the place of her birth."

"Wait. She was Cleopatra's daughter, wasn't she?"

"She was. In fact, the only heir of Cleopatra that lived until adulthood, as far as we know."

"I remember reading about her. What a fascinating story," Nicole said.

"Yes, there are lots of legends surrounding her and her reign, but when her son, who ruled with Juba after her death, was killed by Caligula, their history sort of disappeared."

"That's sad, especially since all the Romans in authority were related in some way too."

"You're right about that." Sami turned toward her. "Speaking of Cleopatra, I have something else to show you, but first, let's get lunch. There's a place in the modern town nearby that has decent food."

"You promise?" Nicole grinned. "I can always break out my trusty granola bars."

"Save your granola bars. This will be better, I assure you." Sami took her hand and placed it on his chest, a serious look on his face. "This heart doesn't lie," he said. The gesture almost knocked her off her feet, but she desperately tried to keep her cool. Hopefully, he didn't notice her shock.

They drove to a small modern restaurant similar to a deli. There appeared to be only one dish on the menu. "Have you even had shawarma?" Sami nodded to the area behind the counter, where two employees prepared something that looked like a sandwich wrap.

"I don't believe I have," Nicole eyed the food as her stomach rumbled. "But I'm hungry enough to try it."

"It's similar to a gyro with meat and vegetables wrapped in pita bread."

"Sounds good."

Sami ordered two of the sandwiches, which were served

with fries and a cola. Picking up a tray, he carried the food to a small table. Bowing his head, he blessed the food, praying naturally like he was used to talking with God. This man was not what she'd expected here in Algeria, but he was evidently Christian. She took a bite of her sandwich and savored the taste.

"What do you think?" Sami asked.

She nodded, unable to answer with her mouth full.

She swallowed and took a sip of cola. "I like it. I could eat this again."

Sami chuckled and wiped his mouth with a napkin. "I'm sure you will. It's as popular here as hamburgers are in the US."

"I wonder if my Mimi ever ate shawarma."

"Hmm. I don't know that it was popular back in the 1940's."

The thought of Mimi triggered her memory. "Sami, maybe you could help me find something."

He leaned forward. "I'll try."

Before I left home, Mimi asked me to find the desert rose. Do you know what that is?"

"A desert rose? Like a flower?"

Nicole shrugged. "I think so. She loves flowers. I'm not sure how I can bring her one, but maybe if I find one, I can take a picture with my phone and send it to her. Hopefully, that will satisfy her."

"Sure. I know where there is a big variety of flowers. I'm sure we can find it there."

"Great. Thanks." Nicole relaxed. If she could do this one thing for Mimi, maybe she can make her a little happier.

Chapter 7

Audrey

Algiers, 1932

ademoiselle Audrey, you have a letter." Matazan gave a slight bow as he handed her the white envelope.

Audrey glanced at Monique and rolled her eyes. "Thank you, Matazan." Why did he act like a servant if he wasn't really? She had to admit he made her feel important, though. She studied the envelope in her mother's handwriting and fought conflicting feelings. Would she be going back to England this summer or to Cannes?

"Well, aren't you going to open it?" Monique said.

"Of course. Wonder if I'll see her this summer?"

She opened the envelope and unfolded it, her heart beating a little faster in anticipation. But as she read the contents, her heart slowed to a stop, dropping in her chest. Fighting back tears, she swallowed, then hurriedly placed the letter back in the envelope, shoving it into her pocket.

"Audrey, what is it? Did they say where you'll spend the summer?" Monique studied her with concern.

She just couldn't let Monique see her cry. It was no big

deal anyway. Just because Mum and Father were separating was no reason to be worked up. After all, they barely coexisted anyway. So now they wouldn't even spend the summer together. But neither of them were going to see her either. Mum's letter said she was going away to "work things out." Going where? Work what out? Why couldn't Audrey go with her? Did Mum not want to see her, after all these months apart? She wouldn't expect Father to come see her, but Mum?

Audrey shook her head, sucking in a breath to steady herself. "I'm afraid you're stuck with me. Mum and Father are going their separate ways this summer, and I'm not invited."

Monique's eyes grew round. "They're not going to come get you?" Audrey glanced away, trying to hide the building moisture in her eyes. Monique took her hand and spoke gently. "I'm so sorry, Audrey."

Audrey sniffed. A rogue tear ran down her face despite her best efforts to stop it. "I hope your parents won't mind me hanging around longer. Are they going back to Cannes?" She hoped her father wasn't there. Wouldn't it be strange to run into him?

"They haven't said so. But Audrey, we don't mind you being here. In fact, you make things more fun."

She certainly didn't feel like fun at the time. "Fun? Are you sure you don't mean 'mischief'?"

Monique laughed. "Well, that too. But that's part of the fun!"

Audrey looked up at the sky, following the path of a bird flying high above. Wouldn't it be nice to have such freedom? Her gaze fell on the biggest tree on the property. Maybe she could climb it, jump down, and pretend she was flying. But the branches were too high to reach. She jerked as an idea hit her.

"Monique! Where did Matazan put the rope?"

"You mean the one that got us into trouble at school?"

Audrey rolled her eyes. "Well, yes, that one. I have an idea he can help us with."

Monique crossed her arms and lifted her eyebrows. "We don't want to get him in any more trouble."

"No, we won't. I bet your father wouldn't mind. Let's ask him if we can have a swing." She pointed to the large tree that stood at the edge of the patio behind the house. "From that tree."

"That one? It's pretty tall."

"Of course it is. And it's strong enough." She headed to the house. "Come on, let's ask!"

After some discussion between Monique's mother and father, they summoned Matazan and asked him to see if he could throw a rope over the lowest limb and create a swing for them.

"This is going to be so much fun," Audrey said, clapping her hands together as they watched Matazan toss the rope into the air until it cleared the limb and fell back over.,

Colonel Clermont stood watching with his arms crossed. "Looks like we need two ropes."

Matazan hurried to get another and repeated the process. Audrey was eager to test out the swing, but Colonel Clermont stopped Matazan before he could finish. "No. This isn't going to work."

Audrey's heart dropped to her toes, and she felt

traitorous tears threatening yet again. "But Colonel…"

The Colonel held up his hand, but his expression didn't look condemning. Rather, he appeared thoughtful. "Do you trust me, girls?"

Audrey and Monique exchanged glances. What did that mean?

"Of course," they answered.

"Okay, then. Tomorrow, you'll have your swing."

Curiosity about the Colonel's plans eased the dejection Audrey felt. She and Monique shrugged at each other and headed for the house to find something else to distract Audrey from her parents' news.

When Matazan picked them up from school the next day, he had an unusual smile.

"There be a surprise for you at your house," he said.

"What? Tell us, please!" Audrey and Monique begged and pleaded, but he wouldn't tell them.

When they returned home, the two girls ran to the swing. But instead of ropes waiting for them, there was a round piece of wood attached at the bottom.

"What is this?" Monique said, running her hand over the smooth surface.

"It looks like a table," Audrey said, turning the disc to look underneath at the hole where the rope went through, a large knot tied to hold the wood in place.

Matazan walked over. "Your Papá, he found that old table and we made it for you to sit on while you swing."

The table was wide enough for them both to sit on, but Audrey climbed on first, straddling the rope. "Would you please push me?"

Matazan nodded and obliged, pushing her away. She swung way out close to the edge of the cliff. Each shove pushed the swing farther up until it was as if she were flying over the city and out to the Mediterranean beyond. Wouldn't it be wonderful to fly off the cliff, free as a bird? But much as she wanted to stay on the swing forever, she wanted Monique to know how it felt as well. She glanced back at her friend waiting patiently behind her, a smile on her face as if she were on the swing too.

"Monique, it's your turn!" Audrey let the swing stop and climbed off, then held it steady while Monique climbed on. Monique gripped the ropes with both hands, and Audrey pushed her.

"Whee! This is magnifique!" Monique shouted. Colonel Clermont came outside to watch, smiling at the girls. "Papá. Thank you!"

"Oh yes, it is wonderful," Audrey said, gazing at Colonel Clermont with appreciation. Not only had he allowed them the swing, but he'd also given Audrey a taste of adventure she never wanted to end. Even though her parents had abandoned her, the pain shrank when she was on the swing, as if her cares blew away through the air around her.

They took turns pushing each other. After a few times sitting on the swing, Audrey decided it would be more fun to stand.

"Audrey! Be careful!" Monique said. "You might fall."

"It's fantastic!" Audrey grinned, holding on with one

hand to wave. "You must try it too."

Monique crossed her arms and shook her head. "No, I can't. That scares me."

Audrey let the swing slow down seeing the fear on Monique's face. "Monique, it is fun."

Still, her friend shook her head. "I am not as brave as you, Audrey."

"Someday, you'll have to be brave too, Monique.

At the dinner table that night, Colonel Clermont made an announcement. "As you know, I have to make trips south into the country for my position in the Topographic Service." Monique had mentioned how he was sometimes gone for long periods of time. His job was to inspect the territories he was responsible for all the way to the Niger River with side trips to Morocco and Tunisia. Why was he telling them this? Was he leaving again? "I may be gone for a month next time."

Monique and Audrey glanced at each other.

"However," he continued, "since you girls will be out of school for the summer, you can go with me. Would you like that?"

"Truly, Papá? We can go too?" Monique asked the question while Audrey gaped.

"Yes, we will camp out in the desert and the mountains, but Matazan and Tunis will go with us, as well as some of the men who work for me, so you will be safe. Maman and I have discussed it and believe the experience will be a great adventure for the two of you."

Monique and Audrey's grins couldn't be any bigger. Audrey's heart almost thumped out of her chest with excitement. An adventure! A real adventure!

Monique turned to her mother. "Maman, you are not going too? You'll be alone?"

Mother shook her head. "No, I've accompanied your father on many trips before, but this time, you girls get to enjoy the experience. However, I'm not going to stay here. I'm going to visit Grand Pere in France at his summer house in Brest. I'm looking forward to seeing my aunts and uncles."

Colonel Clermont looked at Audrey. "What do you think, Audrey? If your parents agree, does this sound like something you'd like to do?"

Audrey grinned. "When do we leave?" she said.

Chapter 8

Monique

North Africa, Summer, 1932

The brilliant blue of the Mediterranean sparkled on the right side of the army vehicle as they left Algiers behind. It had been two weeks since Papá had announced the trip, and Monique's excitement had built with each day. But Audrey's anticipation was even greater, having never gone on one of these expeditions before. She had asked Monique a thousand questions. Would it be fun? Would it be scary? Would they see wild animals, be attacked by angry Bedouin tribes? Many of her questions were things Monique had never considered, because Monique had always felt safe with her father.

Audrey pointed out plants along the way, and Monique giggled at her friend's comments. The sea breeze blew Audrey's strawberry blonde curls into a tangled mass.

"I'm going to cut all my hair off, if it keeps getting in my way!" Audrey said, trying to tuck some of her curls behind her ears.

"Oh, please don't," Monique said. "I like your pretty

curls. I just have this straight hair."

"Girls, you might want to look on the other side of the car. There's something interesting up ahead," Papá said.

Their car was in front of a convoy of six Renault army trucks. Monique guessed there were fifteen men riding in them, bringing equipment they needed to survey the land, according to Papá. He told Julian, the driver, to turn to the left, and all the other vehicles followed, stopping in front of a strange, round building with a peaked top. It reminded Monique of a circus tent built out of stone.

"What is this place, Papá?" Monique asked.

Papá, sitting in the front seat, turned his head to look at her in the back seat. "This is called the Royal Mausoleum of Mauretania."

"That old thing?" Audrey scrunched up her face. "It looks like a huge mound of rocks."

"True. It doesn't look like much now. People have been trying to tear it down for hundreds of years."

Monique frowned, trying to understand what she was looking at. "But why? And why is it royal?"

"Supposedly, it was the burial place, the mausoleum of King Juba II and his wife Cleopatra Selene, not the Cleopatra you know about but her daughter. They ruled this area a couple thousand years ago when it was called Numidia."

"But why is it such a mess if it was built for famous people like that?"

Papá shook his head. "I don't really understand. Why, even the French Navy has tried to use it as a target and shoot it from the sea."

"They have?" Audrey said, looking out at the sea. "But aren't there tombs inside?"

"Well, the odd thing is, no graves have ever been found. There are a lot of stories about that. Some say they were stolen, and some say they were never there in the first place."

"But wouldn't it have treasures like King Tut's tomb?" Monique said, remembering hearing about the discovery at school.

"If it ever did, I'm afraid they were stolen a long time ago."

"Maybe we can look around and find something," Audrey said.

Papá laughed. "I'm afraid it's too late for that. Anything that was valuable has already been taken. However, I've never heard of anything important being found or placed in a museum."

"Well, I wish we'd been here first. Then we would have found the treasure!" Audrey gave her head a firm nod of affirmation.

"I'm sure you would have." Papá turned toward Julian and told him to leave, then looked back over his shoulder at Monique and Audrey. "We need to head to the mountains now. Maybe someday we can look at the Roman ruins at Tipaza and Cherchell. They're pretty amazing too, but our expedition is not about archaeology."

The caravan turned away from the sea.

"Are we going to the desert?" Audrey asked Papá.

"Not for a while yet. We'll spend some time in the mountains first. There's much more to see before we get there, though."

Entering a dense forest, the air cooled as light was overshadowed by the trees. The roar of the vehicles sounded strangely out of place, as if they were disturbing the peace.

No other vehicles were in sight on the narrow road.

"I feel like we're being watched." Audrey looked from side to side.

Monique had the same feeling but didn't dare tell Audrey there could be unfriendly tribes of people around. She had overheard talk of such things when she wasn't supposed to be listening. Sudden movement in the trees distracted them, and they looked up through the open roof of the car as monkeys swung from tree to tree, even across the road overhead.

"Look at them!" Audrey pointed.

"And look over there!" Monique exclaimed, turning her head to follow one of the monkeys as he made his way alongside the caravan.

"That one has a little baby!" Audrey said.

The caravan came to a sudden halt when they reached a place where a tree had fallen across the road. Papá got out and motioned to the other vehicles. Several of the men got out of the trucks and walked over to the tree to move it. While Monique and Audrey waited, a monkey landed with a thump on the front part of their car. He climbed up the windshield and peered over.

Audrey gasped, her eyes wide as she followed the monkey's movements. "Do you think he'll come inside the car?"

Before Monique could answer, the monkey hung down and snatched some dates out of Julian's hand, stuffing them in his own mouth.

"Hey!" Julian yelled and reached for the monkey. But the animal was too quick, and with its long arms, grabbed the driver's hat. "Give that back!" Julian tried to take the hat away from the monkey, but the animal pulled himself out the car, jumped down and ran for a nearby tree, scampering up the trunk where it perched on a limb high above the road. From there, he examined the hat, sniffing and turning it in his paws.

Audrey and Monique laughed so hard, their sides ached. "Mon Dieu!" Julian said, then mumbled other words under his breath. Papá came back to the car, eyebrows raised.

"What is going on here?"

The girls couldn't catch their breath as they pointed to the red-faced driver, then up to the trees. Papá looked from one to the other, then said with a wry smile.

"Julian, where is your hat?"

The driver lashed out in a flurry of French that even Monique had trouble understanding.

"I see. I suppose I will not write you up for not wearing your entire uniform."

Julian's stricken look made Monique feel sorry for him.

Then Papá laughed and patted the man on the shoulder. "It is all right, Julian. Sometimes we have no control over such things, especially monkeys."

"I can shoot it down," said another soldier standing nearby. He withdrew his pistol, aiming it at the monkey in the tree. "No!" the girls screamed, their eyes wide.

Papá put his hand up to signal "stop." "You will not. The hat can be replaced. Put your gun away." Papá signaled to the others. "Let's go."

Monique and Audrey exchanged glances as both released sighs of relief. Thank God, Papá' had a heart for animals.

The caravan continued as the road climbed higher and

higher. The vehicle's engine noise grew louder as they maneuvered through steeper terrain. Occasionally, a space between the trees revealed valleys beyond.

"We're getting really high!" Audrey said, viewing one such scene.

"We are in the Atlas Mountains," Papá said. "They run east and west, all the way from Morocco to Tunisia."

"But I thought we were going to the desert," Audrey said with a hint of disappointment.

"We will get there eventually. The desert is on the other side of the mountains, which we must pass through first. We still have a way to go before we see the desert."

Finally emerging from the forest into a more open area, the sand-colored stone walls of a small village drew their attention. Fields spread out on either side of the village, where people could be seen working among the plants. As they headed toward the town, they passed two men leading donkeys draped with colorful striped blankets and baskets hanging on either side.

Papá turned in his seat. "We're making a brief stop here so I can give my regards to the local magistrate."

"Why do some of the buildings have cracks from the roof to the ground? It looks like they might split open," Audrey said.

"Yes, this area had a very bad earthquake many years ago, and you can still see the damage." Papá traced his finger through the air in a jagged line like he was tracing the fracture marring the nearest building's wall. "Many of the homes were destroyed, and sadly, many people did not survive."

Monique and Audrey exchanged worried glances.

"An earthquake? People died?" Monique asked. "Will there be an earthquake while we are here, Papá?"

"Oh no, don't you worry about that. There hasn't been one for a long time."

The caravan of trucks rolled into the center of the small town, where they parked near a fountain. "Girls, stay here with Matazan. I'll be back soon. "

Julian got out to wait beside the car. Monique and Audrey climbed out, too, happy to stretch their legs. Matazan, who had been riding in the car behind them, walked up to stand by them. A souk, or marketplace, had been set up along the walls of the town where there was some shade.

"People are staring at us," Audrey said in a low voice.

"We are the only Europeans here, haven't you noticed? We don't look, act or dress like they do." Monique was so accustomed to the native clothing styles that it never occurred to her to question them. Indeed, the people in town all wore the garments that covered them from head to toe.

"I'm so hot now, I would die of heat if I had to wear that much clothes," Audrey said. "How can they stand it?"

"It is their custom, but Papá said it also protects them from the sun and dust. They think we're the strange ones."

"Us? Well, we are different, I guess." Against the wall in the shade of one of the buildings was an older woman garbed in a long striped brown dress, sitting beside a table laden with oranges. She wore a turban on her head and large loop earrings. Audrey eyed the fruit hungrily. "Those oranges sure look tasty," she said.

The woman motioned for her to come over. Without asking, Audrey hurried toward her.

"Mademoiselle Audrey. You must wait," Matazan said, following the girl while Monique followed him. Try as he might to keep her safe, Matazan had a hard time keeping up with Audrey, much less keep her out of trouble.

At the table, the woman smiled a gap-toothed grin. She held an orange out to Audrey, nodding. Without hesitation, Audrey took the fruit. "Thank you!" The woman then pointed behind Audrey toward Monique, holding another orange.

"Monique, you can have one too!" Audrey said, peeling off the skin and taking a bite of the fruit.

Matazan stopped at the table and spoke to the woman in some kind of language. He pulled a coin from his pocket to hand her, but the woman shook her head. Instead, she offered him an orange too. He looked at the fruit, then at Audrey with juice running down her face, and seemed confused about whether to accept or not.

Monique accepted an orange from the lady and began to peel it. Poor Matazan. He wanted so badly to do what was right, according to her father. She looked up at him. "I think Papá would not mind if you had an orange too, Matazan." After more hesitation, he finally accepted the fruit, putting it in his jacket pocket.

"We must return to the car," he said, ushering the girls toward the vehicle. As they crossed the square, Audrey darted over to the fountain, rinsing her hands and splashing water on her face. Monique joined her at the fountain, cupping her hands for a drink.

"Ah, this water is great," Audrey said.

Seeing Papá walk toward the car, Matazan urged them back.

"That lady over there gave us oranges," Audrey said, as soon as they neared Papá.

He quirked an eyebrow. "She did?" He glanced at Matazan, whose gaze had lowered.

"They were very good, Papá," Monique said. "Would you like us to get you one?"

Matazan reached into his pocket and withdrew the orange he had, offering it to Papá.

Papá grinned, putting his hand up. "No, you keep it, Matazan. It is all right. These people grow oranges in groves outside the city. They are some of the best in the country."

Obvious relief relaxed Matazan's features, and he put the orange back in his pocket. Thank God, Papá didn't reprimand him. But Monique worried that Audrey's daring behavior might get him into trouble another time. She'd certainly gotten Monique into a few situations.

They climbed back into the car and drove out of the town. Ahead of them rose a wall of mountains, reaching as far as they could see from east to west. "Are we going to those mountains, Papá?"

"Yes, we are. In fact, we will be spending a week or two there. But since, it'll take us the rest of the day to reach our destination, you girls might want to take a nap."

Monique and Audrey played finger games until they got bored, then gazed out the open windows looking for wild animals. But there was nothing to see. The mountains didn't seem to be getting any closer either.

"Have you been to this place before, Monique?" Audrey asked.

"No, I don't think so. It's been a long time since I traveled with Papá, though."

Audrey lowered her voice, which was unnecessary since the car made enough noise, and Monique's father talked to Julian up front. "Do you think we'll be attacked by someone?"

Monique faced Audrey with a frown. "Why would you say that?"

Audrey glanced around, pointing ahead and behind them. "These soldiers are carrying guns."

"They always do. It's part of their uniform," Monique said. "And Papá has to have protection whenever he takes trips." She paused. "I don't think he's in danger, but it's just the way the military does things. Besides, he wouldn't bring us along if it were dangerous."

"Has your father ever shot anyone?"

Monique jerked her head. "Papá? I never asked. But he was in the big war before I was born, and he got a special medal for something. When I asked him about it, he said he just did a

good job. He's never talked about the war. But there's no war now, so we don't have to worry about it."

"I think I'd like to shoot a gun," Audrey said. "Not at any people, of course. I just want to know what it feels like."

Monique shook her head. "Well, I don't. Women don't shoot guns anyway."

"Nonsense. I knew a lady in England that was a great trapshooter. It's an Olympic sport, you know. In fact, even the queen shoots because she likes to hunt."

"I don't want to shoot any animals," Monique crossed her arms, abhorring the thought.

"No, I don't either, but what if a lion attacks us out here?

Would you shoot it?"

"I wouldn't have to because the men have guns."

Audrey huffed and looked out the window again. Knowing how spontaneous Audrey was, Monique cringed at the thought of her friend with a gun.

Chapter 9

Nicole

Algiers, 2019

Sami pulled into the parking lot in front of an ancient, round stone building several stories high. The top of the building had a mound on it, which might have been a type of pyramid at one time.

"This is a mausoleum, isn't it? "Nicole said, peering at the structure.

"It is. It's the Royal Mausoleum of Mauretania. This is supposedly the family tomb of Cleopatra Selena and King Juba II."

"I've read about it!" Nicole opened her car door, eager to investigate.

Sami joined her in front of the car and they walked toward the mausoleum. "According to ancient records, it was built to be a tomb for the couple, however, no human remains have ever been found here, perhaps due to tomb raiding. But the general consensus is that they were buried here initially."

"And no one knows where the bodies are now?"

"No, I'm afraid not. But there's also a belief by some that their followers took the bodies to protect them from invaders. You see, Juba II was of Berber descent, and some think the Berbers took the bodies with them when they left the area. So whoever stole the bodies didn't tell anyone where they took them."

"How interesting." Nicole studied the building as she strolled around it.

"Another very interesting fact, at least to me, is the nickname, if you will, for this place.

Nicole stopped and faced him. "Nickname?"

Sami nodded. "Yes. In French, it's called the Tombeau de la Christiene."

"The tomb of the Christian woman?" Nicole said, with her knowledge of French.

"That's correct. We think it was because there is a large Christian cross that is formed by the pattern of lines on the false door."

"So Cleopatra Selene was Christian?" Nicole scrunched her forehead in thought. "Wait. When did she die?"

"5 B.C."

"B.C.? So how could she be a Christian before Christ lived?"

"That is indeed a good question. History records her as a very influential person with a say in Mauretania's government, trade, and construction projects. During her reign, the country became very wealthy by exporting a number of products throughout the Mediterranean, especially with Spain and Italy. The couple had coins minted with their likenesses on either side."

"Have any of those been found?"

"Yes, they're in several museums, including the museum in Algiers."

"Back to the Christian reference. How could that be possible?" Nicole and Sami continued walking alongside the monument.

"Cleopatra Selene had a reputation for being very intelligent and interested in learning. She hosted many advisers, scholars and artists from the royal court in Egypt, the place of her birth. It's quite possible she heard the prophecy regarding the Messiah."

"Hmm. That's very strange." She stopped to pull her water bottle out of her backpack and take a swig. It sure was dusty here.

"There's even more strange history about this place," Sami said. He too stopped and drank some water.

Closing her water bottle, Nicole glanced up at Sami. Beads of sweat glistened along his forehead. "What else?"

"In 1555, when the Ottomans controlled the area, the Pasha of Algiers gave orders to pull down the mausoleum. But when they tried, hordes of large black wasps swarmed out and stung the workers. Many of the workers died as a result, so they abandoned their effort."

"Seriously?"

Sami nodded. "True. Then, late in the 18th century, Baba Mahommed, the Dey in Algiers at the time, tried to destroy the monument with artillery. But that failed too."

"No kidding."

"And on top of that, when the French occupied the country, they used the monument for target practice by the French Navy!" Sami chuckled and shook his head. "This place isn't meant to be destroyed."

"Did you say the French used it for target practice by their navy?" Nicole glanced toward the water on the opposite side of the road.

"That's what they say. Since it was built on a hill, it's not too difficult to see from the water. Plus, based on the size of the foundation, it was probably 130 feet high when it was built. Perhaps that accounts for the crater up there on one part of the roof."

"How terrible that they were so destructive."

"You know, people didn't care much about preservation in the past." They stopped in front of a door with a cross design dividing it into four quadrants. Below the symbol were some other markings. "This is the false door that gives the place its Christian name."

"Do you think that's enough to call the place the tomb of a Christian woman?" Nicole pursed her lips.

"It does seem like a stretch, doesn't it?"

"There must be more to that name."

"Maybe so, but no one knows what. At least not anymore."

"I saw a sign coming in. This is a UNESCO site, too?"

"Yes, it is, but it hasn't been protected well. Unfortunately, the place is still subject to vandalism, not to mention normal deterioration."

Nicole observed the pillars that separated the stacked stones of the mausoleum. "Are these ionic columns? I see a little bit of something at the top, but I can't tell for sure what kind of capitals they had.

"You're right. There are sixty columns, and they were ionic like similar mausoleums in the world. But most of the identifying capitals have been stolen, too."

"That makes me so angry!" Too bad no one cared about preservation. "Wonder where they ended up?"

"Someone's palace or house?" Sami ventured a guess.

Nicole glared at the damaged ancient building. "Have you ever been inside?"

"Yes. But we're not allowed now. I wish I could show you, but I can't without special permission. There's a passage about 400 feet long that leads to the center of the building, where there are two vaulted chambers separated by a short passage with stone doors that can be moved up and down by levers. One of the chambers is about 140 feet long by eleven feet wide and eleven feet high. The other chamber is smaller. And of course, they're completely empty. If you really want to go in another time, I'll request permission."

Nicole really did want to go inside, but she wouldn't insist. "Maybe another time." She stared up at the dome of the building. "Did Cleopatra Selene have any descendants?"

"Yes, after she died, her son Ptolemy ruled with her husband Juba II until he died. Ptolemy took over the kingdom then. He had a family, including a daughter named Drusilla. Even though her father was killed, she survived, having been married off to an important Roman official."

"Why was her father killed?"

"You know how crazy the Romans were. Apparently, Ptolemy had a very wealthy kingdom, and when he went to Rome for a visit, even though he was recognized as a friend and ally of the empire, the emperor Caligula had him killed. No one knows exactly why, but it may have been as simple as jealousy. The interesting thing to me is that after he was killed, the Berbers, who considered him their king and fellow Berber, caused a huge revolt against the Romans. Strangely enough, there are still statues of Ptolemy in Algeria and Morocco today."

"Well, that answers the question of why the family isn't buried in the family tomb."

Sami laughed.

"I wonder what kind of treasure Cleopatra Selene was buried with? There must have been some kind of valuables in her tomb, so she could have them in the afterlife, as they believed."

"We could probably figure it out, based on the type of wealth that existed here at the time. "I'm sure there was lots of jewelry, and maybe some furniture too. One of the things this area had was citrus trees, so they made furniture out of citrus wood, but none of that has been recovered either."

She glanced around the area. "I don't see any roses around here. Guess I won't find Mimi's rose here."

"Probably not. If there had been any, they're gone now." The circuit around the building completed, they headed toward the car. "Are you ready to go to our next stop?"

"Yes, this has been very interesting. I hope I get to see some of the museums. I'd like to familiarize myself more with the various civilizations that have been here. Will we have time for that?"

"Yes, of course we will."

As they climbed into the car, Nicole noticed a man dressed in a black tunic similar to the white ones she'd seen in the Casbah. He stood in the shade of a tree by the parking lot and wore a turban that partially covered his face. Some cords crossed in front and over his shoulders. Was that a large knife attached to the cords? An uneasiness crept over her with the distinct impression he was watching her. Was she imagining that? After all, many of the men dressed in a similar style, and frankly, made them all look alike. But realization jabbed her. Had she seen the same man at the Tipaza ruins?

She looked away, self-conscious for staring at the man.

Sami glanced at her, a frown creasing his brow. "Are you all right?"

"Yes, I'm fine. I was just curious about that man over there. He's dressed differently than anyone else I've seen."

He looked past her in the direction of the man.

"I don't see anyone."

She jerked her head toward the tree where she'd seen the man. Where had he gone?

"But he was just there." She pointed to the spot where she'd seen him. "And I think I saw him at the Tipaza ruins too."

"What did he look like?"

Nicole described the stranger. "He kind of looked like he stepped out of the pages of a history book on Algeria."

Sami nodded. "Sounds like a Tuareg. They're a Berber tribe. But they normally live in the Sahara, not around here."

Nicole scanned the area looking for him, but he had disappeared.

"Why would he be here?"

Sami shrugged. "Sightseeing?" He gave her a broad smile, and Nicole felt like an idiot. Why did she assume the stranger was dangerous? Just because he looked different? Sami must think she was too suspicious.

She faked a laugh. "Of course. I guess I expected to see

a camel with him."

"That wouldn't be unusual. They're still pretty common among the Berbers, especially those who live away from cities."

"Will we be going to the desert?"

"Yes, there are some digs out there we will visit. But the Sahara is on the other side of the Atlas Mountains, so it'll be a longer trip. We'll have to pack for overnight when we go there."

"Sounds intriguing." Nicole imagined camping out under the stars in the desert with Sami. How romantic that would be. Heat rushed to her face at the scene her mind conjured up. She'd die if Sami could read her mind. Her hand grabbed the ring around her neck, as was her habit as if it were a security blanket. Feeling the etching on the stone, she had a strange feeling she'd seen that same etching somewhere else.

Sami continued. "It's quite nice being out there at night, actually, but it can also get very cold. You wouldn't believe how clear the sky is in the desert at night. The stars are so brilliant, it feels like you can reach up and touch them."

Another vision of Sami with his arm around her, watching the stars at night, appeared in her head. She pulled off her cap and fanned herself with it, glancing away from Sami's twinkling eyes.

"Are you hot?" He reached behind him in the car seat and retrieved a canvas cooler. Opening it, he removed a green bottle with a yellow label reading Hamoud. "Here, try this." He handed her the bottle.

She took it, turning it over as she tried to read the label. "What is it?"

"It's like a fizzy lemonade, kind of like some of the American drinks. It's pretty good."

Nicole twisted the top off and took a swig. The beverage was tart and sweet, reminiscent of some drinks back home. "It's not bad. Thanks."

"You're welcome." He took a bottle for himself and gulped down about half of it before replacing the cap and putting it back in the cooler. "Feel better now?"

"Yes, thank you. Where to next?"

"Chercell. It used to be the capital of Numida and Mauretania under King Juba and Cleopatra Selene, so there's another site of Roman ruins there. Unfortunately, the ruins are right in the middle of the town, so the setting isn't quite as nice as the ones at Tipaza." Sami started the car and backed out of the parking space. "However, there's also an archaeological museum we will visit."

"Is it far from here?"

"Only about 25 minutes." He turned the car back onto the highway that traveled beside the Mediterranean.

"I can see why the Romans would want to settle here. It's such a beautiful location."

"Not only that, but a strategic port for shipping and a great vantage point for defensive purposes."

Nicole glanced back over her shoulder at the Royal Mausoleum as they drove away. The man she had seen before was there again, standing near the road. Watching her. Holding the reins of his camel.

Chapter 10

Audrey

North Africa, 1932

As the sun lowered over the mountains, sunlight began to fade. Suddenly, the car slowed down. Colonel Clermont held his hand up high to stop the vehicles behind them. Audrey focused ahead and saw the low flat roofs of buildings that blended into the dirt and stacked against the side of a mountain. On the road about a hundred feet ahead, two men stood with their arms crossed in front of their chests.

The men wore shorter caftan-looking black robes, belted and crossed with colorful straps, and black scarves wrapped around their heads like turbans that covered all but their eyes. When their truck came to a stop, Colonel Clermont removed his gun and laid it down on the car seat before opening the door and climbing out.

"Who are those men?" Audrey asked, her eyes focused on the strange-looking men.

Matazan looked over his shoulder at the girls. "Berbers. Those are Toureg guards."

"They look very fierce."

"Where is Papá going?" Monique asked as they watched her father walk down the rocky road toward the men.

"He must tell them who we are, and that we are coming to visit the chief. Otherwise, they might not let us in," Matazan said.

"What if they kill him before he can talk?" The fierce-looking men unsettled Audrey.

Monique's head jerked toward her, eyes wide with fear. "They wouldn't do that, would they Matazan?"

He shook his head. "I do not think so. They should see that he is not wearing a weapon. The chief is a friend of the colonel, so he should be welcomed."

Matazan's answer wasn't reassuring.

Monique grabbed Audrey's hand. "Pray for Papá, that they don't shoot him!" She squeezed her eyes shut.

Pray? Out here? She thought prayers were only done in church. How did one do that? What should she say?

Audrey watched her friend's lips move with no words coming out. Was she praying? Since Monique was taking charge of the praying, Audrey decided she should watch and see what happened.

Colonel Clermont lifted both his hands above his head. They could not hear what he said, but one of the guards said something to the other guard, then nodded. Colonel Clermont turned around and signaled the trucks forward, and the guards stepped to the side of the road.

As the trucks rolled past the guards, Audrey got a closer look at the men. Thick black beards covered half of their faces, not covered by their turbans. A shiny silver curved knife or sword hung from a strap around their shoulders. She shuddered at the sight, from fear or excitement, she wasn't sure. The men's dark eyes stared straight ahead, but Audrey got the feeling they could see in all directions without turning their heads, like the people in one of those creepy old portraits. In fact, she was certain the man on her side of the car looked her in the eye when they passed. She smiled, not because she meant it, but to see his reaction. But she didn't get one.

"They aren't very friendly, are they?" she asked Monique.

"They're not supposed to be," Monique said. "I think they're supposed to look scary."

Audrey turned her attention to the houses. They appeared to be made of red clay bricks and stacks of stone, blending in with the land around them. All the roofs were flat, and some had dogs lying on top of them.

"Monique, they have dogs on top of their houses!"

"They do!" Monique said as one of the dogs stood to observe them. "Matazan, why are the dogs on the roofs?"

"Slooghee. Amazigh dogs. They protect the village from wild animals and strangers."

"Strangers like us?" Audrey said, as one by one, every dog on every house stood, watching them as if ready to pounce, their long legs reminding her of greyhounds. The dogs were skinny, as if they hadn't been fed, but obviously prepared to attack.

"Sighthounds. The dogs, they have eyes that can see a long way off. If they see lion coming, they all take off together to chase it away. They are very fast."

"There are lions out here?" Audrey's head swiveled, her

heart racing.

Matazan nodded. "Yes, they will attack the village's sheep and goats, but the dogs keep them away."

"How could such skinny dogs kill a lion?"

"They all get together to attack the lion, or just chase it away."

Monique tapped Audrey on the arm. "Audrey, look at that man Papá is talking to."

A very tall man, wrapped in a long, striped robe, spoke to the colonel at the entrance to one of the houses. The colonel turned toward their vehicle and pointed. The man nodded and motioned for them to come, so the colonel nodded and beckoned Matazan.

"Come. We go to the house of the chief of the tribe." Matazan opened the doors for the girls to get out, then ushered them toward the two men. Audrey glanced around to see if the guards were nearby, but they had not moved from their positions, yet keeping a watchful eye on all of them.

"Audrey, Monique, this is Chief Badis Amastan. He is the leader of this settlement."

Monique dipped a curtsy, so Audrey followed suit. The man was fascinating to look at, as he was one of the tallest men Audrey had ever seen. His face was dark as leather and wrinkled as if he had spent many years in the sun. His ankle-length cloak had colorful stripes, and he wore a long cloth of a different color wrapped around his head to create a turban.

His broad smile revealed a couple of missing teeth as he said, "Welcome. Please come inside and meet my family."

The girls glanced at the colonel, who nodded, then motioned for them to go in.

"No." The chief held up his hand to stop them, then pointed to their feet.

"We must take off our shoes before entering the house," the colonel said. They complied, then stepped inside the dark room with the colonel and the chief followed. Inside, an older woman, a girl that appeared to be a teen, and a younger girl greeted them with warm smiles.

The chief pointed to each woman. "My wife, Gellida, my daughters, Nanna and the youngest, Mira."

The colonel returned the introduction. "My daughter Monique and her friend, Audrey."

Audrey gaped as she stared at the jewelry the women wore. Rows of necklaces hung around their necks, and cuff bracelets covered their arms. Colorful jewels decorated the jewelry in shades of red, orange, and amber. They also wore headdresses that had rows of coins or fringe with jewels crowning their hair, and the two older women wore rings with large stones.

"What fascinating jewelry," Audrey said to Monique. The women didn't seem to know French or English, but they smiled and noted the attention their attire was getting.

"Very pretty," Monique said, pointing to a bracelet the chief's wife wore.

The woman nodded shyly. Behind them, the colonel said, "They make all the jewelry themselves. They are quite skilled in silver and gold work. The men do not wear much jewelry, only rings, which are often etched with family symbols and passed down through generations."

The chief entered and said something in a language Audrey didn't understand, but found out later it was Tamizigh, then he pointed to the cushions on the colorful rug. "Sit, please. We will eat."

A room filled with brightly colored woven pillows invited the girls and the colonel to settle down and get comfortable. The colonel looked at Audrey and Monique, nodding toward the chief. "The chief is a friend of mine and wants to show us hospitality. Let us show him our appreciation."

Audrey leaned toward Monique. "I wonder what kind of food they will serve us."

Monique glanced at her father. "I don't know, but we're expected to try it. If we don't that's considered rude and bad manners. Papá would not want us to offend the chief."

The two women and the girl had disappeared from the room, but when they returned, one carried a bowl with water and went from person to person.

Audrey's brow furrowed. What was she supposed to do?

She watched as the chief rinsed his hands, then wiped them on a cloth the woman carried. So they were washing their hands. How reassuring to know they cared about cleanliness. She followed suit, and after they had all washed, the woman left. Next, the other woman came in carrying a large bowl of something that looked like a soup and placed it in the center of the floor within reach of all of them. The young girl set down a bowl of flat bread beside the first bowl, and the woman with the water returned with a tray of small cups containing a liquid. She bent over to offer a cup to each person.

Audrey took one tentatively, glancing at Monique, who did the same. The cup had no handle like the teacups she used back in England, so she held it in both hands. She leaned over to sniff the beverage within. The aroma was not unpleasant, so she brought it to her lips and took a tiny sip. A wonderful taste of mint awakened her taste buds, providing a welcome treat to her parched mouth. She lifted her gaze over the rim of the cup and noticed the women watching her.

She smiled at them. "Good. This is very good. Thank you."

The women understood her compliment, based on their pleased expressions.

"Eat," the chief said, pointing to the bowls in front.

"Where is the silverware?" Audrey whispered to Monique, who looked to her father for an answer.

"They do not use utensils," the colonel said. "They use the bread to scoop out food from the bowl. Watch me." The colonel took a piece of bread, tore off a piece, then dipped it in the bowl and put the soaked bread in his mouth. Nodding, he said, "This is called 'tagine.' It is a traditional Amazigh dish and is very good. You will like it."

Thankful, they had all washed their hands, Audrey did the same. The broth was reddish and had carrots, potatoes, and some chunks of meat in it. She tasted it and was pleased by the spicy, tomato flavor. It was odd to have people watching her, but they apparently wanted to know her reaction. So she smiled and nodded and hoped that sufficed as a compliment. Her mother would be appalled to see her daughter eating with her hands.

Soon, everyone was sitting around, dipping bread in the mixture. To pick up the vegetables, one had to put their fingers in the bowl to place them on the bread. Audrey developed the hang of that, but when it came to the meat chunks, she gave up. That task was a little too messy in her opinion, as one had to tear the chunks by hand.

"What kind of meat is that?" Audrey whispered to Monique.

"I think it is lamb."

Audrey had eaten lamb before, but she hoped their hosts wouldn't be offended if she didn't partake of it this time.

When the bowls were empty, the women removed them, then returned with another bowl of water to rinse their hands. Next, more cups were brought with the aroma of steaming tea.

Audrey took a cup as did Monique. Taking a sip from it, she discovered it was very sweet, more so than what she'd had before, like the mint tea back in Algiers. She glanced at Monique. "I don't like this. Do we have to drink it?"

Monique sipped hers and made a face. "I don't care for it either. Maybe if we just hold the cup, it'll be acceptable." She looked at her father, who smiled back.

"You don't have to drink it. Don't worry, they will not be offended if you do not want it."

The chief noticed and understood, then motioned to the women and said something. The women nodded and took the girls' cups away.

The colonel and the chief stood. "You girls stay here and visit with the other ladies. The chief and I have to talk, so we're going to take a walk. Perhaps they'll show you how they make the jewelry," Colonel Clermont said.

When they stepped out of the house, Audrey and Monique glanced at each other, then at the women. Audrey found them to be very beautiful, their long black hair and dark eyes possessing an aura of the exotic. Their teeth seemed especially white against their dark olive skin. Audrey glanced down at her own pale, freckled skin. She was practically colorless compared to these women. She pointed to the jewelry.

"Beautiful," she said, hoping they understood what she meant.

The older women nodded to the girl named Mira and spoke in their language.

The girl removed one of her bracelets and put it on Audrey's arm. Audrey gasped at the gesture and blinked her astonishment at the girl. Running her fingers over the smooth orange stones, she admired the detail of the silver designs in the band. The width of the band was half the size of the older woman's bracelets, as wide as the length of her little finger, but was surprisingly lighter than it looked. She held her arm out for Monique to see, and Monique touched the stones as well.

"This is beautiful!" Audrey looked at the girl in appreciation. She began to remove the bracelet, but the girl put her hand out and held the bracelet in place. "Do you mean for me to keep this?" Did Audrey understand what the girl was trying to convey? She glanced at Monique, then back at the girl who nodded.

Audrey's eyes filled with tears. "No one's ever given me something as beautiful."

The girl pointed to one of the amber stones, then to Audrey's hair, smiling and saying something in her native Tamazigh language.

"Audrey, I think she's saying your hair is the same color as the stone!" Monique laughed. "It truly is!"

Audrey held the cuff bracelet up by her hair, and the girl

nodded and smiled.

"But what about you, Monique?" Audrey pointed to the bracelet and then to Monique.

"Oh no, Audrey. That's rude to ask," Monique protested.

But the girl nodded, removed another of her bracelets, and handed it to Monique. "Thank you, but…" She shook her head, and the girl looked confused.

"Monique, you have to accept it or she'll be offended."

Glancing from Audrey to the girl, Monique smiled and put on the bracelet. "Thank you, it is lovely." This cuff bracelet was the same size as the one Audrey was given, but the color on top of the silver in shades of green and blue with a small red stone in the center of a diamond shape.

One of the women who Audrey assumed was the girl's mother nodded her approval. "You keep." She looked from Audrey to Monique. "Amazigh gift." She stood and motioned to them.

"Come. We dance."

Audrey exchanged glances with Monique. "Dance?"

The woman and the girls grabbed shawls and threw them over their dresses, fastening the shawls together with ornate silver triangular clasps connected with silver chains. The mother picked up two shawls and handed them to Audrey and Monique before going out the door, turning back to motion to Audrey and Monique to follow. Outside, night had settled in the mountains, and the temperature had dropped. Audrey rubbed her arms and pulled the shawl tightly around her as she hurried to keep up with the women who walked around to the back of the buildings. Stars sparkled in the clear sky, the only light visible, but bright enough to seek their footing. The village was shrouded in pitch darkness, and the only thing she could make out was the silhouette of the mountains. Dogs barked from the rooftops as they walked up the sharp incline behind the houses.

What was that strange sound? Was it singing? Instruments? The path wound around until the light of a campfire was visible. People could be seen under a tent supported by poles. As the girls approached, Audrey saw some other women with children sitting cross-legged on the ground under the tent. The chief's wife and daughters went under the tent and sat with the others, beckoning Audrey and Monique to follow, which they did. Some men banged on circular drums while others danced in a loose circle with no particular uniformity of style, singing an unrecognizable song.

All of the women wore jewelry similar to their hostesses' jewelry, with rows of beads and decorated silver. The headdresses were ornately decorated as well in a variety of styles that had jewels hanging from them. The French soldiers who had come with the colonel stood beyond the edge of the tent, watching the activity, while the local men urged them to sing along and dance too. Matazan stood by himself outside the tent.

Audrey grabbed Monique's hand. "Come on. Let's dance too!"

Monique pulled her hand back. "No!"

"But there are other children dancing," Audrey insisted. "Didn't they say we were going to dance?"

"I'm not sure they meant for us to dance. I only see boys and men dancing."

Monique glanced over at Matazan, who shook his head.

Audrey crossed her arms. "Pooh! You're no fun!"

Monique lowered her gaze.

Audrey regretted her words. "Hey, I'm sorry. I'm just tired of sitting around so much."

They sat and watched for what seemed like a ridiculous amount of time. Monique yawned.

Audrey glanced around. "Where's your father?" she said to Monique.

Monique peered at the people in the tent and the men outside. "I don't see him."

Audrey continued to scan the area, a little nervous about where they were. How deep was the valley below them? From her point of view, the edge of the area next to the tent dropped down into darkness. The sound of the singing and the drum beat under the stars in the dark night was mesmerizing and so foreign, it felt like a dream.

"There!" Monique pointed. "I can see the light of his cigarette. He is with the chief."

Audrey stared out into the darkness in the direction Monique pointed and saw the outline of the two men as they talked, Chief Badis towering over the colonel. They were some distance from everyone else, so they must've wanted their conversation to be private. Audrey was reassured to know he was still in the vicinity, not that he would leave them. She and Monique glanced back and forth between the activity at the tent and the colonel and the chief.

Monique yawned again. "I'm tired. I wonder when we'll go to bed."

"I wonder where we'll go to bed." Audrey answered.

The two girls looked back at the colonel, wishing they could convey their questions to him, but the men appeared to be in deep conversation and obviously did not want to be interrupted. The chief glanced around, then slipped his hand inside his cloak, and Audrey startled, a brief image of the man withdrawing a sword. But when he withdrew his hand, he extended his it to the colonel, who extended his in return. The chief placed an object in the colonel's palm, and the colonel closed his fist over it. The chief patted the colonel's closed fist, nodding, then both men glanced around them while the colonel put the item in his shirt pocket. Whatever it was, the item was too small to see from a distance and in the dark. Why did she think they didn't want anyone to see the exchange? Who would care? She, too, glanced around and noticed two other people watching. One of them was Matazan, the other another Amazigh man. Neither of them were singing and dancing with the others. The Amazigh man looked angry.

Audrey glanced at Monique. "Wonder what he gave him?"

Monique shrugged. "Probably a gift. People are always giving Papá gifts. He says it is a gesture of goodwill. He is very thankful to receive these gifts from the local tribes because he wants very badly to have peace between them and the French. He says some tribes are still not happy about the French being here in North Africa, but he hopes to create better relationships between them."

But were they in danger from the tribes who didn't like the French?

Chapter 11

Monique

North Africa, 1932

Monique woke the next morning to the aroma of food being cooked. She glanced around and sat up. She and Audrey had slept on the floor of the chief's house on top of rugs and covered with colorful striped blankets. No one else was in the room with them. Monique had been so tired, she fell asleep right away, not caring whether she was on a proper bed or not. She shook Audrey, who was soundly sleeping, sprawled out next to her.

"Audrey! Wake up!"

Audrey roused, then sat up, looking around. Rubbing her eyes, she yawned. "Where…Oh, that's right. In the Berber chief's house."

"I smell food. I think we'd better get up."

Audrey's stomach growled, and the girls giggled. "Look. I still have my bracelet on."

Monique looked at Audrey's, then at her own. "Me too."

They stood and crept to an open doorway, following the

sound of voices. In an outside kitchen area under a tented canopy beside the house, the women prepared a meal cooked over an open fire. The house was apparently built around the courtyard.

"Tifawin!" The chief's wife said to them with a smile. The other lady and the girls said the same.

Monique and Audrey exchanged glances. "What do you think they said?" Audrey said.

"I don't know, but I think it would be polite to repeat it back to them," Monique said.

Monique and Audrey made an attempt to repeat the word, getting laughter from the other women for their effort.

"We eat soon," the chief's wife said.

Audrey tugged Monique's arm. "Where is their bathroom?"

As if reading her mind, the chief's wife said something to Mira, who stopped what she was doing and came over to them, motioning for their feet.

"Our shoes! We need to put them on to go outside."

Mira put up her hand as in a gesture that indicated "wait," then she removed her shoes, which were similar to slippers, hurried through the house, and returned with Audrey and Monique's shoes. They all put their shoes on, then followed Mira away from the house to an area behind an animal stall where a donkey was tied. She pointed to the area.

"Is that where we're supposed to relieve ourselves?" Monique asked.

The girl nodded and squatted. "Apparently so," Audrey said, glancing around. "Glad we put our shoes back on."

Monique nodded her agreement.

Afterwards, they went back inside, Monique thankful her home had an inside bathroom.

When they returned, Mira's mother told her daughter something, pointing inside. Once again, they removed their shoes, leaving them just beyond the open door, and followed Mira into the main room where they had eaten the night before, motioning them to sit. Her father and the chief entered from the front entry.

"Bonjour, mademoiselles." Papá said, ever so jovial. No wonder people liked him so much, as he was friendly to everyone.

"Tifawin!" Audrey said, drawing laughter from the chief. Audrey grinned with self-pride.

"You learn Tamazigh language!" the chief said.

"We know that one word," Monique said. "That's what the ladies said to us this morning."

Papá smiled his approval. "Well done. The people are honored when you try to learn their native tongue."

The men sat down, and Mira passed the pitcher of water and bowl to wash their hands as before. Next came cups of mint tea, which the chief poured from a silver pitcher. The women brought bowls of dates, olives, nuts, and bread. Mira set down a bowl of some kind of paste beside Audrey and Monique.

"Papá, what is this?" Monique said.

"It's almond butter and is very good. Tear off a piece of bread and drag it through the butter."

Monique did as he suggested and so did Audrey.

"This is good," Audrey said. "But it makes me thirsty."

A pitcher of milk appeared before them. "Milk, Audrey!" Monique said.

"Wonderful," Audrey said. "But I didn't see any cows."

"It's goat's milk," Papá said. "It's good too." He grabbed a handful of almonds. "Today, girls, you'll get to see some of the desert. We will be hiking the mountains to survey them, and you'll be able to experience the Atlas Mountains."

Audrey's eyes lit up. "An adventure! Monique, this is so exciting!"

Monique was just as excited, but why didn't she seem as exuberant as Audrey? Audrey was always ready to try new things, like the dancing last night, but Monique was much more cautious. If only she had a more adventurous spirit like her friend.

After the breakfast was cleared away, they all put on their shoes, then Monique and Audrey went out the front of the house. Now in the bright daylight, they could see the wide valley before them. Sheep and goats were scattered throughout the valley and several women were out there with them. The sound of sheep bleating arrived around the corner of the house as the chief's wife, Nanna and Mira, appeared leading a flock of sheep.

Mira waved shyly as they passed.

"Would you prefer to stay with them instead of going with us?" Papá asked.

"I don't know. Audrey, what would you like to do?" Monique asked as she watched the women head down the road and into the green fields, reminding her of the verse in the Bible about leading sheep to green pastures. What a peaceful scene it was.

"I want to see what the men are doing," Audrey said. She leaned over to whisper in Monique's ear. "It's bound to be more fun than watching sheep."

Although she wanted to disagree with Audrey, she didn't want to get into a quarrel with her. Audrey was much more headstrong than she was, and Monique never seemed to win any arguments with her. She was probably right this time, too. Whatever the men did would be more exciting, so they loaded up in the trucks with the men. This time, Papá rode in a truck with the chief instead of with them. Matazan followed dutifully as the vehicle bumped along the rocky mountain road.

They climbed higher and higher until her ears popped, and the valley lay far below. Every so often, the trucks would stop, and the men would get out with their equipment. Monique and Audrey climbed out too, to watch the men. Monique knew only a little of what they were doing. Since her father was in charge of the topographical team for the government, he needed to take measurements of different places. The men set up tripods and looked through a type of viewer at the top, then called out numbers that another man wrote down. The process, indeed, was boring, but the view was amazing. The mountains seemed to go forever, creating different levels and colors as she looked from one range to the next. While the men worked, Audrey and Monique spent their time looking for wildflowers. Audrey wanted to help the men, but Papá told them to stay out of the way and not be a distraction.

As dusk approached, Monique wondered if they would spend the night at the chief's house again. The day had been long, and she was getting a little bored.

"Monique, look!" Audrey pointed to a place above them.

Monique followed the direction Audrey indicated and saw an animal on a ledge high above them on the side of the mountain overseeing them below. The deer-like animal had grayish-brown upper parts with a blackish band that ran from the hind legs to the front legs. Barely over two feet tall, its underside was completely white, and its face had a dark strip from the eye to the mouth. Two horns on its head slanted backwards. Two more of the same animals stood even higher on the side of the mountain.

"What are they? Deer?" Monique said.

Papá stood within earshot and looked up to see where Monique was pointing. "Those are Cuvier's gazelles. You'll only see them in the Atlas Mountains. The one closest to us, the biggest, is the male, and the two others appear to be a female and a younger one, probably their baby."

"They're so pretty!" Audrey said. "Do you think we can touch them?" She walked toward the mountain, clearly looking for a way to climb up.

"Don't bother. They won't let you get near them. Normally, they stay hidden among the trees until nighttime when they come out to graze."

As usual, Audrey had already reached a spot below the gazelles and had a hand on the rock face as if to climb it. A rock broke loose, spooking the animal so that it scampered farther up and into a copse of trees.

"Audrey! Now look what you've done. You scared them away!" Monique's hands rested on her hips. Why couldn't Audrey just leave well enough alone instead of chasing after the animals? Why couldn't she be content with admiring them?

Audrey turned around and came back looking

frustrated. Monique bit her tongue to rein in her anger.

"I'm sorry, Monique. I just thought…"

There was no need for her to finish because the truth was, she didn't really think. She just reacted. Bravery was one thing, impetuous another. Audrey resorted to her tactics to make Monique forget her anger by being funny. She made some comments about some of the men in their party that Monique couldn't help but laugh at. Oh, her dear friend. How could Monique stay angry with her?

Papá approached. "Well, that's it for today. Time to pack up and leave."

"Are we going back to the chief's house?" Monique asked.

"No, we're too far from it now. We are close to the desert. We'll camp out on the other side of the mountain. You two get in the car." He strode away toward his men.

"Camping out? That sounds like fun." Audrey said, always ready for a new adventure.

"I hope so," Monique said. She didn't know what to expect and was more leery about the idea.

"And the desert. Monique, we're going to the desert!"

The caravan wound around the mountain for at least an hour before it reached the other side. The sun had slipped below the horizon, so it was dusk when they stopped. The temperatures had dropped considerably, too, and Monique wished she had one of the blankets from the chief's house. The men began unloading their supplies and putting up tents.

Peering away from their campsite, Audrey said, "Is that the desert out there?"

Monique peered into the gloaming. The ground appeared to go on forever with not a tree in sight. "It must be."

A camel appeared out of the darkness, ridden by a man dressed in black clothing and a turban wrapped around his head, a knife with a curved blade hanging from his belt.

"Oh!" Monique jumped back, her heart racing.

"Where did he come from?" Audrey stared wide-eyed at the sight. "Out of nowhere?"

"Out of the desert," Monique said.

The mysterious man rode up toward Papá, who greeted him in Amazigh. The man responded in kind, then tapped on the camel's necks and the camel bent down so the man could climb off. Moniqe looked around for Matazan and found him standing near the unloaded supplies. She hurried over to him, and Audrey followed.

"Matazan, who is that?" Monique said, keeping her gaze fixed on the stranger.

"He looks dangerous!" Audrey added.

"He's a Touareg, another tribe of the Amazigh. They are desert people. He will be our guide in the desert." Matazan looked down at Monique and Audrey. "Do not worry about him. He will not hurt you. He is a relative of Chief Badis." While they were talking, two more men who looked like the first one rode up on camels behind the other camel.

Monique decided to stay close to Matazan. "Where will Audrey and I sleep?"

"You two will be in a tent next to me and your father's tent. No worries, Mademoiselle." Matazan gave her the warm smile he used only with her.

Audrey stared at the strangers. "Will there be more men coming like that?"

"I do not think so."

When the tents were ready, the men built a campfire and sat around it on three-legged stools. The Touareg people sat on the ground cross-legged. Food skewered on sticks was cooked over the hot coals, its aroma tantalizing after the long day.

"Where did the food come from?" Audrey asked.

"The Touareg provided. They are guardians of the desert, and so are our hosts as well as guides."

Flat bread, such as they had at the chief's house, was passed around, and everyone partook of the bread and the meat when it was cooked. Dates were passed around for dessert, accompanied by water from canteens the colonel's men had brought. The Touareg men sat beside Papá and spoke low. Monique tried to see the men's eyes, but they were dark and shaded by the black turban.

When they retired to their tents, Audrey and Monique lay down on camp cots with army blankets, coarse but warm in the cooler desert air. Tired as she was, Monique had trouble going to sleep, listening to sounds outside the tent.

"Are you awake, Audrey?" Monique whispered.

"Yes. I hear noises outside and wonder what they are."

"Me too. Listen. What does it sound like?"

"Wind? Yes, the wind is whistling, even singing at times." The tent shook when an occasional gust blew against it. The sound of tiny things hitting the tent was next.

"What was that?" Monique sat up.

"Sounds like someone is throwing something against the tent." Another whoosh and another pelting of the tent. "Should we get out and see what it is?"

"No! Matazan would come for us if there is a problem."

We will stay put and pray God will protect us." Monique proceeded to do just that, knowing Audrey would expect her to take the lead, since Audrey often said she wasn't good at God things.

The next thing Monique knew, the sun was shining on the tent, penetrating it with warmth. She sat and looked around, then turned and put her feet on the floor. She stretched, then heard people talking outside. The tent flap opened, and Matazan's head poked in. "Time to get up and have breakfast. We will start our work early before it gets too hot."

Audrey stirred, then sat up too. She yawned wide, making as much noise as she could.

Monique stood. "We'd better go. Papá would not like to have to wait for us."

Audrey stood as well, and they climbed out through the tent opening, then looked around. One side of the tent was partially covered in tan desert sand. "Look at all this sand! That must be what we heard hitting the tent last night," Audrey said.

"Yes, it must have been." When Matazan walked over, Monique asked him. "Was that a sandstorm last night?"

Matazan chuckled and shook his head. "No, that was just normal desert wind. If it was a real sandstorm, your tent might be completely covered."

What if their tent had been covered in the sand? Monique shuddered at the image that appeared in her mind and prayed they would leave before a major sandstorm.

Once again, they gathered around the fire and ate before all the men stood to go. Monique got a better look at their hosts and realized they were younger men than she originally thought.

The surveying men climbed into their trucks, and the Touaregs got on their camels. The girls got back into Papá's truck with him and Matazan, who was driving. The men on camels got in front of the trucks.

"I'd really like to ride a camel," Audrey said. "Wouldn't you?"

"I'm not so sure. I hear they spit at you."

"They do? Is it because they don't like someone?"

Papá spoke over his shoulder. "They do it when they feel threatened or bothered. You can usually tell if they're getting ready to spit because the cheeks fill up and bulge. If you see that, get far away as quickly as you can. They can spit pretty far."

"Papá knows about camels," Monique said, boasting. "He has ridden one across the Sahara."

"He has? You have, colonel?"

He pointed to a symbol of a tarantula on his shirt. "They decorated me for it, too."

Audrey slid forward to poke her head over the front seat to see it.

For the rest of the day, Audrey and Monique kept their distance from the camels as they traveled through the desert. They were in an ocean of sand with no other people or animals in sight. How far were they from another village? Around noon, they spotted trees. Amazingly, a small pond surrounded by palm trees appeared in a dip of the rolling hills of beige sand.

All the vehicles stopped, and the men got out to enjoy some shade and refill their canteens from the cold water. Monique and Audrey strolled around the oasis, remarking on the surprise of seeing it in such a barren land. A snake the same color as the light brown sand suddenly slid out of the undergrowth beside the water and slithered across the sand near them. Monique squealed, and Audrey grabbed her arm. Was it one of the poisonous snakes Papá had warned about?

"Don't move!" A male voice commanded. Monique glanced up to see one of the Touareg men raising his gun to fire at the snake. But before he could, a huge tan lizard with brown stripes circling its body scooted over the sand, its long tongue reaching out and wrapping around the snake. In an instant, he sucked down the snake like a piece of spaghetti.

Monique covered her mouth with her hands, too terrified to speak.

Audrey had no problem though as the lizard walked away, sauntering as if he was proud of his accomplishment before disappearing into the undergrowth. "Is that a dragon? That's the biggest lizard I've ever seen. It must be over one meter long."

Papá and Matazan ran over to them.

"You are all right?" Papá said, putting his hands on the girls' backs. Monique leaned against him for comfort.

The girls nodded their heads, although Monique still shook from the experience.

"Do those lizards hurt people?" Audrey said.

"Those are monitor lizards, and no. They only eat animals."

"He saved us from the snake!" Audrey said.

Monique looked at her friend in disbelief. She'd been too afraid to think about that.

Papá laughed. "And so he did. But you must be very careful not to wander too far off. There are other animals in the desert and other snakes."

Monique had no thoughts of doing otherwise. She'd explored enough today and would rather sit in the hot truck if it was safer. "Was that a poisonous snake?"

"I do not think so," Papá said. "I didn't have a chance to see it well."

Monique decided any snake was a bad snake, and she didn't care to come across any more.

The Touareg who had been about to shoot the snake strode over to them with purposeful steps. He stopped and addressed Audrey. "You want to ride a camel?"

Audrey glanced from Monique to Papá. "Can I?"

Papá nodded. "Yes, you can. You will sit on the camel with him."

"But what if the camel spits on you?" Monique said. After all, they'd tried to stay away from the camels ever since they learned of the spitting possibility.

"I do not let him spit," the Touareg said with a tone that let them know he expected his orders to be obeyed, even by camels. No wonder he wore the same tarantula decoration as her father.

Audrey's blue eyes shone even brighter against the sea of freckles on her face, and she grinned. "Yes, please." She looked at Monique. "Don't you want to ride too?"

Monique shook her head. This was Audrey's adventure, not hers. "No. You go ahead, and I'll watch."

Audrey tilted her head in question, but then turned and followed the man to his kneeling camel. He climbed onto the blanket, which rested on the animal's back, then reached for Audrey and pulled her onto the camel to sit in front of him. With a click of his tongue and a Touareg word, the camel rose, rear end, then front end, until Audrey was seated far above Monique, at least three meters high. The camel began walking, two legs on one side moving together, then two legs on the other side, resulting in a swaying motion for the riders on top.

Audrey's grin stretched across her face as she enjoyed every moment of the activity. Would she ever be as brave as Audrey? Even though Monique wanted to act as adventurous as her friend, she held back for some reason. Was it fear? Audrey waved from the back of the camel and Monique waved back.

"It is not comfortable to ride a camel," Matazan said, standing beside her. Did he know what she was thinking?

If it was uncomfortable, you'd never know it from Audrey's face. She couldn't be enjoying herself more. Monique wondered if she would regret not taking the opportunity. Maybe next time, she would do it. Next time she would be more brave.

The camel and its riders made a large, slow, circular route before returning to its starting point. When Audrey disembarked the animal, she ran over to Monique.

"Monique! It was great! I can't even find the words to explain it. The ride was not exactly bumpy, but I felt like I was rocking from side to side, like in a boat tossing in the waves. I'm so sorry you didn't go too."

"Maybe I will another time," Monique said. "I just didn't feel up to it today."

That night when they bedded down in their tent, Monique prepared herself for the wind and sand, praying it would be minimal. She had fallen asleep when she was awakened by a strange noise, like people laughing, not too far away. But it wasn't exactly like a person's laugh. She sat up with her knees bent and pulled the blanket to her chin.

Audrey sat up quickly. "What is that noise?"

Monique shook her head, unable to speak.

The unnerving sound continued. Was it getting closer?

The two girls sat wide-eyed, listening to the noise.

Then gunshots were fired, and the noise stopped.

"Did somebody get shot?" Audrey said. "But who?"

Chapter 12

Nicole

Algiers, 2019

Nicole and Sami stepped outside the museum, so the waiting attendant could lock the doors behind them.

"Would you like to get some coffee?" Sami asked. "There's a little place just down the street."

"Sounds great," Nicole said. There were so many things going through her mind after all the antiquities she had seen that day. So many things to talk about with Sami.

Entering the small café, the aroma of coffee awakened her senses. Sami motioned to a small table against the wall. "You go ahead and sit down. I'll get our order." He glanced at the counter, then back at her. "Tea or coffee?"

"Coffee, please. And can you see if they have cream?" Nicole sat down and studied the place. The customers wore modern western clothes instead of the traditional garb she'd seen in the Casbah. The café had plain white walls with styleless modern tables and chairs. After seeing so many historical items and places, modern culture was lacking in design and color. Was that really progress? Maybe she really belonged in the past. Perhaps that's why she'd always preferred studying ancient civilizations.

Sami returned to the table with his charming smile and their coffee. He handed Nicole hers and a small pitcher of cream before sitting down across from her, his chair facing the window. "So what do you think? Learn something new?"

"Oh my gosh, yes. I'm fascinated by all the cultures that lived in this area. I knew the Roman civilization was widespread, but I never thought about them being here in Africa."

Sami sipped his coffee. "They ruled the entire known world for about a thousand years. What's amazing to me is that Roman ruins are throughout Europe, even as far as England."

Nicole nodded, pouring some of the cream into her cup and stirring it. "Hard to believe. But I'm just as interested, if not more, in the different civilizations that have flourished in this country. The Berbers and King Juba the Second and his connection to Cleopatra—they had such an impressive kingdom here. And I guess the fact that the Berbers didn't disappear but still exist intrigues me." She took a sip of her coffee, adjusting her taste to its strength.

"It is rather interesting that the Amazigh have maintained their culture, only taking advantage of the modern world as needed. In fact, some of the villages have only acquired electricity in the last decade. And some still don't have running water. But they are not backwards. They are simply proud of who they are."

Nicole clapped her hand over her mouth. "Oh, I'm sorry. I shouldn't call them 'Berbers' anymore. I'll try to remember Amazigh." She glanced over at two men at a table sipping from small espresso cups. "I'd love to see the women in their jewelry these days, not to mention how it's made."

"Tell you what. I'll be sure to schedule a trip to one of the villages while you're here." He studied his cup, turning it around in his hands. "We have a whole country to cover, plus putting you to work on a dig."

"Is it possible to do both - sightsee and work on a dig?" She studied Sami, hoping he didn't think she was asking too much. "When was the last time someone discovered something on one of the sites? Anything recently?"

He shrugged. "A little, here and there. But you know that civilizations build on top of each other, so we have to keep digging down."

"Yes, I know. That's why I hope I can still discover something."

"And it takes time too. Perhaps more time than you'll be here. But who knows? You might be lucky." His gaze met hers. "I know one thing you'll have to find."

"What's that?"

"The rose your Mimi asked you to find."

"That's right! I haven't thought about that today."

"Tomorrow, I'll take you to some gardens around the city, and perhaps you can find it."

"Thank you. That would be great, I mean, I hope it won't take too much from the schedule."

"No, it's in the city where we're going to be anyway."

Should she ask him for another favor? "Um, do you think we would have time to look for my Mimi's old house? I know some of the homes have been changed or maybe they're not there anymore. But I brought a couple of black and white pictures she had that maybe you can recognize."

"Of course. I assumed you'd want to see where she lived. When were the pictures taken?"

"In the 1930's."

"Before World War Two, then?"

"Yes, she lived here before it and even after it started. She moved to the States sometime before the war was over."

"So she lived here during the Vichy government when the Nazis were in control."

"Yes, and then for a while after the Allied Forces invaded."

"An exciting, not to mention dangerous time to be here."

"Yes, but she hasn't talked a lot about the dangers."

"Has she mentioned anything about where her home was?"

"Yes, it was on a hill that overlooked the city. She said you could see the whole city and the Mediterranean from where she lived. She also said her home was next to a park."

Sami was quiet for a few minutes, his brow furrowing as he studied his coffee. When he lifted his gaze, his eyes twinkled with excitement. "I think I know where the house was. I'm not sure what it looks like now, but we can compare your pictures to the area. We'll go tomorrow."

Excitement bubbled inside her. "That would be great!"

A shadow crossed Sami's face as he focused on something outside. Nicole's spine tingled with the sensation she was being watched. "What is it? What are you looking at?" Should she look?

Sami's frown vanished as he looked back at her. "It's nothing. I was just thinking about the area where your Mimi lived and the changes it has undergone. No worries, though. I'm sure we can find it."

Nicole didn't believe that's what made his expression change. He was definitely looking at something outside the window. And it was something that bothered him. But what? Or who? She slowly turned to look over her shoulder, but didn't see anything suspicious. When she turned back to face Sami, he offered a smile, revealing dimples she hadn't noticed before. Maybe she was just being paranoid.

They talked for almost an hour about the different artifacts in the museum and where many had been found in the area.

Sami pushed his chair back. "Ready to head back?"

"Sure."

They left the table and went outside. From where they stood, Nicole could see the harbor and a lighthouse at the entrance. "There's another lighthouse! It looks fairly modern."

Sami's gaze followed hers, and his eyebrows lifted. "If you consider 1881 part of the modern era."

"It's that old? Could've fooled me. It looks spotless."

Sami laughed. "That's the Fort Joinville Lighthouse or in French, the Phare de Cherchell. I believe it may have an Arab name now." Facing her, he said, "Are you ready to head back?"

"I am. My head is swimming with all the historic places and things I've seen." As they walked back to the car, Nicole glanced around. Would the mysterious man show up again? She looked over at Sami who gave her a warm smile. For some reason, she wanted to hold his hand as they strolled through the town, but that would be very unprofessional. He was just so comfortable to be with, it was as if they'd been friends for a long time. But when he jerked his head around, she got the impression he was looking for someone or something. And whoever it was, Sami did not welcome them.

When Sami picked her up the next day, Nicole was eager to get started. Not only was she excited about the prospect of seeing Mimi's home, but she also looked forward to seeing Sami almost as much. He was always cheerful and accommodating with all her questions, not to mention nice to look at. Hopefully, he didn't think she was a typical student, naïve and unprofessional. She'd wanted to be an archaeologist all her life, even writing an essay about it in the fifth grade. Of course, seeing her mother's favorite film *Raiders of the Lost Ark* and its sequels could've fed that desire.

"First, I thought you'd like to see the Martyrs Memorial."

The towering structure could be seen several blocks before they reached it. Sami parked at the base of the hill on which the monument stood, the massive concrete structure rising almost three stories. Nicole and Sami walked up toward the obelisk that contained an eternal flame at its base. The monument featured three sections that were supposed to resemble palm leaves and joined in the middle, midway towards the top. A bronze statue of a soldier stood at the base of each of the "leaves."

"This is known as the symbol of the city these days," Sami said. "It was built to commemorate those who died in the Algerian War of Independence."

Nicole nodded, knowing the war was against the French rule over the country. "It was a long war, wasn't it?"

"Over twenty years." Sami gave her an apologetic glance.

An uneasiness crept through Nicole's shoulders. Her Mimi was French. Mimi's father belonged to the French Army. Was she not welcome here? Was she supposed to apologize for being part French?

"Do the Algerians still harbor resentment toward the French?"

"Some do, but that was last century, and the Algerians have changed almost everything to Muslim culture now. When did your relatives leave here?"

"Either 1942 or 43."

"So she didn't live here during the revolution."

"No, and she never spoke of it either. She went to the U. S. with her American husband, and her mother went back to her relatives in France. I don't know of anyone in the family who stayed here after World War II. From what she said, there was a good relationship between her family and the locals."

"That's probably accurate. The conflict escalated after the war was over. The local Algerians thought that if they fought with the French against the Germans, they'd earn their freedom after the war. But it didn't happen that way. It wasn't until 1962 that Algeria became independent of the French rule."

"And that explains why the names of places are being

changed from French names," Nicole said, remembering the airport's new name.

"Exactly. There's still a lot of French colonialism evident in the architecture, but other civilizations' influence is also seen."

"Which makes it harder to find things that no longer have the French names."

"Correct. But there are many who still speak the French language, so it's a matter of finding people who remember the former names."

"I hope there's no animosity toward people like me of French descent. But some people look at me suspiciously."

Sami touched her arm and looked into her eyes. "Don't worry. Only bitter people like to remember those things." He smiled. "If anyone is looking at you, it's probably because they want to know what a pretty American girl is doing with me!"

Nicole's face heated. But thank goodness, Sami is easy to be around. "I didn't exactly feel welcome by Mr. Amid at the Antiquities Office."

"Yes, unfortunately, Amid still carries a grudge. But remember, I'm half French too, so I'm probably more French than you are. Of course, there are some that resent any outside influence." Sami steered her away from the monument. "Let's go look at the Hamas Botanical Gardens next door. Maybe we can find your rose there."

Nicole blew out a breath, then focused on the lush vegetation ahead, her mood becoming more peaceful as she drank in the beautiful flowers and landscape of the gardens.

"How nice to find these gardens so close to the city."

"They weren't always. When these gardens were built

in 1832, the business district was farther away."

"So this could be the park Mimi mentioned!" The garden took on new meaning as Nicole tried to see it through Mimi's eyes. Was she standing in the same place her great-grandmother had stood?

"Yes, it probably is. It's very large, over thirty acres, and borders an older neighborhood higher up on the hill. At one time, that was where the wealthier people and French lived."

Nicole glanced up the slope as far as she could. Was Mimi's neighborhood there?

They strolled along a paved pathway alongside a pond as Nicole inhaled the scent of vibrant flowers all around them. "Were there ever monkeys here? Mimi talked about mischievous monkeys in the garden."

Sami thought for a minute. "Yes, I believe there were before the city encroached on the area. There's a little zoo near here, though, so that's where monkeys are now. But you can also find monkeys in the mountainous areas. The Barbary Macaque are native to the forested area of Algeria."

They stepped into a gazebo near a fountain in the pond. "Barbary again, huh?" Nicole said, enjoying the cool breeze.

"You notice a pattern?" Sami grinned. "I think we can blame the Romans for tacking the Berber adjective to so many things in this country."

Nicole pointed to some flower beds. "Look, I think those are roses." She just had to find the rose Mimi asked for.

Leaving the shade of the gazebo, they strolled to the vast assortment of roses arranged as if a master painter had splattered a giant canvas with color. "Oh my. These are gorgeous! But which one is *the* desert rose?”

"Let’s ask him and see if he knows.” Sami nodded toward a gardener working nearby. They approached the man, and Sami asked him in Arabic. The man shook his head and replied, his arm stretched out toward the flower beds.

"What did he say?” Nicole offered the man a smile.

"He said there is no rose by that name.”

"No? But I’m sure that’s what Mimi was saying.” Nicole couldn’t bear to disappoint Mimi.

"Wait.” The gardener hurried over to them, speaking rapidly.

"He says there is a plant named Adenium that has been mistakenly called the desert rose because it grows in the desert. But he says it is a dangerous plant and is poisonous to people and animals.”

"Poisonous? Why would Mimi want something poisonous?”

The man continued to speak. He pointed toward a small greenhouse.

"He said they have one in there, but not to touch it.” Sami thanked the man, then faced Nicole. “Would you like to go see it?”

"Yes, please.” But why would Mimi ask for that kind of plant?

The gardener motioned for them to follow him. When they reached the greenhouse, he pointed to a plant growing in a concrete urn beside the building. He pointed to the sign in front of it that was marked with an X.

"He says not to touch. That’s what the sign says, too.”

Nicole pulled her phone out and took a few pictures of the plant. “I’ll send these to Mom and get her to show them to Mimi. But if this is what Mimi meant, did she expect me to bring some back with me? I don't believe Customs would allow that, even if I could figure out a way to be protected by its poison." Nicole's heart ached with the prospect of failing Mimi.

Sami shot her a genuine look of concern. "I'm sorry, Nicole."

She shook her head and wiped her damp eyes. "It's not just the plant. It's just so sad that Mimi can't tell us what she means. The stroke has robbed her of her speech, and I'm afraid I misunderstood what she wanted."

"Maybe your mother can get some clarity when she shows the pictures. Let's wait and see what happens."

It was so sweet of him to care. This side trip had nothing to do with archaeology and was probably taking valuable time from his schedule.

"Sami, I'm sorry to waste your time. This was just a sentimental quest." She was touched by his warm gaze.

"It is not a waste of time. I understand that this is important to you." He glanced around. "Why don't we go see if we can find where your relatives lived?"

Nicole's enthusiasm returned. "I'd love that. Do you know where to look?"

Sami nodded. "I'm pretty sure I do. The house overlooked the city, so I think it was in the neighborhood above where we are now."

"Mimi told me that when she went to school, she went down the hill on a path behind other houses."

"Yes, I think I know the area."

Maybe this time, she'd succeed in finding something she was looking for. Her pulse increased, renewed with excitement as well as Sami's encouragement. As they strode back to the car parked near the monument, her skin began to prickle as if she were being watched. She glanced over her shoulder, half expecting to see the man with the camel. But there were no camels here in the city.

Sami paused. "Is something wrong?"

"I don't know why, but I feel like someone's watching me."

He looked around. "I don't doubt you are. You're a beautiful woman, and you stand out among the other women here."

Nicole's cheeks burned, and she averted her gaze. She noticed other women in the area, many wearing the hijab, the traditional long dresses, their heads wrapped in long scarves.

"I'm not the only tourist here." She nodded toward a group wearing American-style clothing and listening to a guide.

"Perhaps not, but you're the only one with blonde hair."

Nicole's hands went to her ponytail that was sticking out of her hat and tucked it underneath. "Now there's nothing to look at."

Sami's smile widened as he studied her. "I disagree."

Again, her face heated, and she looked away, embarrassed by the intensity of his gaze. Did he really think she was beautiful? Or just different than the other women? "Where is the car?" She had to say something to change the subject.

"Right over there." Sami pointed. Nicole increased her pace, reaching the car before he did. But as she waited for him to catch up and unlock the car, the same uneasiness she'd felt before returned. She glanced quickly toward the monument. Did someone just slip behind one of the statues by the monument when she looked? Or was it just a shadow? *Nicole, get a grip. You can't keep acting this way.*

Chapter 13

Audrey

North Africa, 1932

Matazan came to their tent in the morning, speaking through the opening. "Wake up, mademoiselles. We leave soon."

Audrey sat up quickly and hopped off the cot. Hurrying to the tent opening, she said, "Wait! Matazan, what was that noise last night? We heard gunshots."

Monique was awake now. She sat up as Matazan poked his head back in. "Did somebody get shot?"

He grinned, shaking his head. "No, the men fire the guns to scare away the hyenas."

Audrey and Monique exchanged glances. "Hyenas? So that was the sound we heard. It sounded like strange laughter," Audrey said.

"They are noisy. Make it hard to sleep, so we shoot guns to make them go away. Now, I must go help load equipment to leave and we need to take your tent down."

The girls hurriedly got ready, folding their blankets and tucking them under their arms as they left the tent. They handed the blankets to Matazan as they hurried to get some food. The meal was quick–dates and flat bread. Soon they were riding in the truck again.

They spent three days and nights in the desert as the men surveyed and measured the land. Once finished, everyone loaded up, and they headed back over the mountains to return home, passing herds of goats on the steep hillsides, their goatherders keeping a watchful eye on them.

This time, they did not stop at the chief's village, but went to another village with a marketplace that Matazan called a souk. Audrey and Monique roamed among the tented booths with Matazan staying close behind. Some of the booths displayed colorful rugs, while others presented a variety of jewelry similar to what the women at the chief's house wore. One of the ladies pointed to the bracelets Audrey and Monique wore, nodding and saying something.

"I think she likes our bracelets," Audrey said. "But I don't know what she said."

"Well, she's smiling, so I think it was something nice."

"Ooh, what are those?" Audrey pointed to another table laden with unusual small sculptures.

Monique followed, her attention captured by the display. She looked over her shoulder at Matazan. "What are these?"

"They are called desert roses or sometimes sand roses, as they are made from crystals in the sand." He pointed to one. "You see, it looks like a rose."

The sand sculpture had petals, just like a rose. "It really does," Audrey said. "Do people make them?"

"Oh no. God makes them. You can find them in the desert," Matazan said.

"You can?" Audrey glanced at Monique. "Wonder why we didn't find any?"

"We did not go to the area where they are most commonly found," Matazan said.

Some of the "roses" were multilayered, and others were more like bunches. Also, the colors varied from light tan to reddish tan. "Do you think we can buy one?" Audrey asked.

"Which one do you like?" Matazan said.

Monique pointed to a small, light-colored configuration that looked like a perfect rose. "That one."

"I will get it for you," he said, then began to speak with the woman behind the table in the Amazigh language. After giving the woman some money, he carefully lifted the rose and handed it to Monique. Audrey touched the object.

"It's heavier than I thought," Monique said.

"Will it stay together?" Audrey asked.

"Yes, those kinds are very solid." Matazan then took the rose and gave it to the merchant so she could wrap it in some cloth before handing it back to them.

At one of the booths, hundreds of dates were spread across the table and hung from the canopy. Matazan bought some for himself and the girls. Monique's father approached and pointed to another tent. "We must get some olive oil here. Mrs. Clermont says they have the best." Matazan nodded, then hurried over to the tent, picking up an earthenware jar and speaking to the merchant.

The captain looked at the girls, clasping his hands behind his back. "Have you girls found anything you like?"

"No, sir," Monique said. "We like the jewelry, but we already have some." She held up her wrist, showing the bracelet.

"So you do, and it is far more valuable because it was a gift." He looked over his shoulder. "Why don't you girls help me choose a new rug for our home? Monique, I think you know what your mother would like."

They followed him to one of the tents displaying rugs. "There are so many!" Audrey said.

"And they're all quite beautiful."

"I think Maman would like this dark red one with the blue diamonds in it," Monique said. "Do you like it, Audrey?"

"Yes, it's perfect!" If only she could buy a rug for her own mother. But Audrey didn't think her mother would like anything she chose. Even though their house had rugs and her grandmother's mansion had grand rugs, they'd always been there. And even if she could buy her mother a rug, when would she give it to her? Audrey didn't know when she'd see her mother again. She sighed, her heart heavy the way it got every time she thought of her mother. Audrey hadn't received even a postcard from her mother in all the months they'd been separated. Did she even remember she had a daughter?

Audrey swiped her arm across her eyes. Tears wouldn't accomplish anything, she'd learned that by now. The only people who cared about her were right here. Monique's family. Besides, she was able to go on so many adventures with them, and nobody expected her to act like a proper lady or perform a certain way. They never appeared to be disappointed with her. Surprised sometimes, but not disappointed.

The rug bought, the vendor rolled it up for them, and Matazan carried it back to the truck. On the way home,

Audrey and Monique chatted and laughed about all they had seen and done on the monthlong trip.

"I've never had so much fun!" Audrey said. "I am so happy your father allowed me to go."

Monique reacted with a quizzical expression. "Why wouldn't he? You live with us now. Besides, I wanted you to go. It's a lot more fun with you around."

Audrey grinned, her heart full. Maybe being abandoned by her parents wasn't such a bad thing after all. The bumpy ride eventually lulled them to sleep like an uneven cradle. The next thing Audrey heard was Matazan's voice.

"We are home now."

Home? Forcing her eyes open, Audrey yawned and sat up and realized the truck was parked in front of Monique's house. Glancing at the entrance to the house, she watched Colonel Clermont greet his wife with a big hug and kiss. When Audrey got married, she wanted to be in love just like the Clermonts were.

Monique woke up too, and seeing where they were, opened the door and climbed out. She ran over to her mother and embraced her. "I missed you, Maman! I wish you could have gone with us!"

Audrey got out of the vehicle and walked over to the family, feeling slightly out of place in the family reunion. Even though the Clermonts were not her real family, she wanted them to be. Mrs. Clermont extended her arm and drew Audrey into a hug. "How did you like your trip, Audrey?"

"It was the most wonderful trip I've ever had!"

"Audrey was a real trooper," Colonel Clermont said. "She even rode a camel."

"Is that so?" Mrs. Clermont smiled warmly. "That can be quite an adventure, from what I remember when I rode one."

"*You* rode one too?" Audrey could not even visualize her own mum doing such a thing. This woman certainly had a more adventurous spirit.

"Why, of course. We must try things once, yes?" She and her husband exchanged smiles as if they shared a special secret. "I'm sure you girls are hungry. But first, you must get out of those dusty clothes and take a bath! Dinner will be ready when you get cleaned up. Be sure to wash your hair well in case you brought any unwelcome guests home." As they stepped onto the marble floor of the entry, Mrs. Clermont picked up an envelope from a side table. "Audrey, you received this letter while you were gone."

Monique

Audrey clasped the letter to her chest as they went upstairs to the bedroom. Monique watched her friend's eyes light up, before a shadow passed over them as she studied the return address on the envelope.

"A letter from home?" Monique guessed.

Audrey nodded. "From Father in Cannes. I don't know if Mum has joined him there."

Audrey continued to hold the letter close as if trying to feel the contents.

"Are you going to read it now?"

"Of course." She plopped down on the bed, setting the letter to her side. "But first, I need to take a bath. And I'm starving!"

Monique cocked her head at her friend. "Why don't you want to open it? Are you afraid of what might be in it?"

"No, of course not." Audrey reached for the letter, then glanced up at Monique. "Maybe."

"But why? Aren't you glad to hear from your family?" Monique couldn't understand her friend's family. Surely, they missed each other. Sometimes Audrey seemed sad about not seeing them, but she usually acted like she didn't care. Maybe it was just an act, though. Audrey was the bravest girl she knew, but when it came to her family, she was a different person.

"I'm not sure. The news from home is seldom good, and after we've had such a marvelous time these past weeks, I don't want any bad news to spoil it."

Monique didn't want to push her friend. What if she were right and the news was not good?

"Okay, so who wants to take the first bath?" Monique opened her dresser and pulled out some clean clothes.

"I will!" Audrey jumped up, grabbed some clothes from her drawer, and then headed down the hall to the bathroom.

Monique's cat Minette strolled into the room and jumped up on the bed, purring loudly as it rubbed against her. Monique stroked the animal. "Did you miss me, Minette?"

"Meow!" The cat walked back and forth over Monique's lap, stopping to lick her hand.

Monique eyed the letter sitting on Audrey's bed. She was more curious than Audrey about it, anxious to open it.

But it wasn't hers.

A few minutes later, Audrey came back. "That was great! I never knew a bath could be so good!"

"It's my turn. You can keep Minette company." Monique strode out to the bathroom where the housekeeper was rinsing out the tub.

As the water filled the tub, Monique watched the dirt from her body float away. When the water was deep enough, she lay back and sank into the water, and let it soak into her parched skin. Finally, she soaped her body and her hair, then rinsed it off before getting out and drying off. After putting fresh clothes on, she went back to the bedroom.

Audrey's head was down, the letter open on her lap, while Minette rubbed against her back.

"You read it?"

Audrey slowly lifted her head, her eyes red as tears flowed down her cheeks. She barely nodded, choking back a sob.

Monique sat down beside Audrey and put her arm around the girl's shoulders. "Oh, Audrey. Is the news sad?"

It took several minutes before Audrey could speak. Wiping her hand across her face, she glanced up to look at Monique. "Father wants to put me in a tennis school in Cannes. He says I'll turn fourteen soon and am old enough to start training professionally. He's coming to get me and take me back there."

"When? For how long?"

Audrey shrugged. "He said he'll be here in a week. I don't know how long I'll be gone, but I won't be going to school here next year. I'll be going to school in Cannes. He wants me to play professional tennis." Tears flowed again, and she sobbed.

Monique squeezed her shoulders. "Oh no, you'll be leaving us? You won't be living here anymore?" Monique had gotten so accustomed to sharing her room, her home, and her family with Audrey that she couldn't imagine her friend not being there after living with them for a year. Audrey was right. The news from her father was indeed bad news. How could he put his daughter in a school where she knew no one? At least in Algiers, she'd known Monique, when she'd moved in with them. Monique searched for words to console her friend, but she couldn't think of anything helpful to say. "He will let you come visit often, I'm sure." She wasn't really. She had no idea when Audrey would return. Suddenly, her own tears trailed down her cheeks.

They held each other, crying, not hearing Mother until she came to the door. "Girls, I called you for dinner." Stepping into the room, she said. "What's wrong? Did something happen to your family, Audrey?"

Monique spoke up. "Her father is going to come get her and put her in a tennis school so she can play professional tennis."

"He is? When?"

"In a few weeks. Before the school year starts again."

"I'm so sorry you'll be leaving us, Audrey," Mother said. "I hope you'll come back to visit soon."

Audrey looked up at her. "I wish I could stay here forever. Your family is the best family I've ever had."

Mother came over and embraced Audrey. "Oh, dear girl, you will always be part of our family, and you will always be welcome here. You be sure to write us often, won't you?"

Audrey nodded. "I will."

Chapter 14

Nicole

Algiers, 2019

I believe if we keep going up this hill, we'll find the neighborhood where your Mimi lived," Sami said, as he drove the car on a road that wove along the hill above the city.

"This is a hill? It's a pretty big one," Nicole said, looking out toward the Mediterranean Sea as the car climbed upward.

Sami shrugged. "So you can call it a mountain. It is part of the Tell Atlas Mountains, the foothills, I think you'd say."

Mountains she was familiar with, living near the Blue Ridge Mountains. But she'd never been on one in North Africa before. "I thought the Atlas were farther away. Will we be going to other parts of them while I'm here?"

"Actually, I was about to tell you we will be going on a little camping trip tomorrow, farther away in the mountains just north of the Sahara."

Camping trip? With Sami? That could be interesting. "We are?"

"Yes, there's a dig where some students from the university are working, so we'll go there and see their work."

So they wouldn't be alone. She relaxed, thankful to find out they'd be with other people at the site. She pushed away any sliver of romanticism about the two of them. Of course, she should have realized the trip would be handled appropriately. If he wasn't so nice, not to mention good-looking, she wouldn't be so attracted. Her friends back home would call him a "hottie." She shook her head.

He glanced in her direction. "What is it? Do you have a problem with going there?"

Had he read her mind? "No! Of course not. I can't wait to go."

"Good. I think you'll enjoy it." He returned his attention to the road. "If you look ahead and up, you'll see some houses. There's also an exclusive hotel up here that began as a wealthy residence. In the early 1900's, this was Algier's most fashionable neighborhood. The street used to be the Rue Michelet, but it has been changed to an Arabic name."

Nicole's heart beat faster in anticipation. She glanced around them, trying to notice anything Mimi might have mentioned. As the road wound around, a rambling two-story white building peeked through dense foliage. Sami turned into a driveway toward the building.

"What is this?"

"This is the El Djazair Hotel, which used to be the Hotel St. George. In the 1500's, it was built as the palace of the ruling ottoman, but during the French control in the 1800's, the building was converted to a hotel. It had quite the international reputation and had many famous guests."

Sami parked in front of the hotel. "Come, I'd like to

show you something."

As they got out of the car, a black car pulled up and parked a few spaces away, probably guests at the hotel. Sami and Nicole entered the lobby with its tall ceilings and intricate mosaic floor before changing to a deep red carpet that looked like tapestries. Sami spoke to the concierge in Arabic, motioning to Nicole. The man nodded, and Sami led her through arched openings past walls covered with photos of notable people who had stayed there in the past.

Nicole paused to look at the photos, reading the names underneath. "Rudyard Kipling. Prince and Princess of Wales. Baron Rothschild. And that's Winston Churchill!" she said, pointing. "British Field Marshal Montgomery. And de Gaulle!" She turned to Sami. "Speaking of stepping back in time!"

Sami smiled. "True. The hotel has been renovated at least twice, especially after being bombed several times by the Germans during the war, but it still maintains the same atmosphere it had back in the 1940's."

"Incredible that all those people were here." One photo in particular caught her attention. "Josephine Baker."

"She was quite the sensation in her day," Sami said, looking at the photo.

"Mimi saw her perform! She told me about what a show it was."

"She worked with the French Resistance during the War. Did you know that?"

"No, I wasn't aware of that."

Sami turned and motioned with his hand for Nicole to follow. "Come upstairs. There's something else you should see."

After walking up the stairs, whose walls were decorated with mosaic tiles, they reached a hallway, and Sami walked to one of the rooms and stopped before an open door. "This is room 141, the room General Eisenhower stayed in after the Americans landed. Go on in. They've preserved it like it was then."

On the wall inside the door was a plaque that read *The landing of Allied Forces on the southern shores of Europe was planned in this room in the course of 1943.*

"Wow. So this is where it happened. I remember Mimi telling me that Eisenhower had stayed somewhere down the street from her home. But I didn't realize all that went on here. I wonder if she was ever here when he was?"

"Hard to say. But I'm sure there was very tight security. And I'm not sure they trusted the French, since they had been allied with Hitler before the Americans arrived."

"Mimi never talked much about the war. All I know is she met Great Grandpa when the Americans arrived because he was an officer who worked with Eisenhower. He was a tall, thin man from the States, and she was a pretty, petite French woman, as she says." Or said. Her heart squeezed when she remembered Mimi couldn't talk now. And this visit to Algiers had given Nicole so many questions she wanted to ask Mimi now. Would the speech therapist be able to help someone her age in her condition? That was one miracle Nicole prayed for.

After they perused the room for a while, Sami said, "So your Mimi lived somewhere near here. I wonder if we can find the place. Do you know what it looked like?"

"I've seen pictures. It was a two-story, white, not very fancy. But I know it had a view of the city from the yard.

And it was near a house that had fruit trees.”

“Well, let's drive around a bit and see if anything resembles that description. Fortunately, this area has been kept pretty natural. Most of the newer development is farther out.”

“Wait. Mimi said their property bordered a park. Is there a park near here?”

“Yes, there is. It's on the side of the hill and actually starts on this road and goes all the way down to the city street below.”

“Then that must be it!”

Sami drove the car out of the hotel driveway and turned right. “If the house were next door, it would have been on the same side of the road as the hotel. I don't remember houses up here, but maybe they can't be seen from the road.” He drove slowly as they looked for a sign of a house.

“Is that a driveway?” Nicole said, pointing to a break in the foliage.

Sami looked. “It seems to be some kind of road, but it doesn't seem to be used very much. I hope whoever owns it won't mind if we drive down it,” he said as he turned onto the hidden road.

They moved slowly as if driving through a jungle, the trees and undergrowth were so thick. Finally, they spotted a house set among the foliage, tall palm trees standing as sentinels beside it, with a small yard in front.

“Does this look familiar?” Sami said as he stopped the car.

“I'm not sure. I can't see much of the house. And Mimi talked like her yard was quite large.”

“Maybe it used to be, but the subsequent owners have

let nature take over."

Nicole gripped the door handle. "I want to get out and look around. Can we ask the owners if it's okay?"

"We can try. Let me go to the door first."

Nicole watched Sami walk to the partially hidden front door a few steps above a stone terrace and knock. A few minutes later, a man opened the door. Sami spoke to him, pointing behind him to Nicole. The man nodded, so Sami motioned for her to come. She joined him while she and the homeowner sized each other up. He was a tall, elderly man wearing the hajib and cap, but something about him was familiar. Had she seen him before, like in a picture?. He spoke to Sami, gesturing around him.

Sami looked at her and translated. "He is Amazigh. He says this home and property was given to him and his father's family many years ago after the independence."

"Did you tell him my Mimi used to live here?"

"Yes." Sami said some more to the man who spoke in return, nodding.

"He says his grandfather knew the French family who lived here."

"I hope they were friends."

"His grandfather worked for the family. His name was Matazan."

"I've heard Mimi talk about him! Would you ask him if I can look around the yard? I'd like to see the city as Mimi saw it and how she walked down the hill to school."

Sami told the man what Nicole said, and the man motioned for them to follow, then walked to a path that led around to the back of the house. Behind the house, the trees opened up to reveal a panorama of the city and the sea below.

A terrace with two chairs offered an invitation to sit and enjoy the view.

Nicole stood on the terrace staring out toward the Mediterranean, a cool breeze blowing through the opening, a refreshing contrast to the hot day. As if going back in time, she could see her great-grandmother as a child standing in this same place, crossing through time to be next to her now. For some unknown reason, she looked up and noticed a piece of rope wrapped around the limb of a tall tree that overhung the terrace.

The man who lived there stood nearby and had followed her gaze. He said something in Amazigh, pointing to the rope.

"He said there used to be a swing hanging there. His grandfather had helped put it there for the child that lived in the house many years ago," Sami said.

Tears filled Nicole's eyes. "That child had to have been Mimi."

After standing there long enough in the man's yard, Sami glanced over at their host, then back to her. "I think we've stayed long enough."

She nodded. "You're right. Thank him for me."

Sami spoke to the man, and as they walked back around the house, she spotted some flowers in the yard. Maybe those were the flowers Mimi was referring to.

"Would you please ask him what those flowers are called?"

The man answered Sami's question, calling them by another name. Sami asked him if they could be called desert roses, but the man shook his head no.

"Oh well. Strike out again."

They continued back toward the car, then Nicole paused. "But how did Mimi get down the hill to the school? That's a pretty steep cliff."

Sami asked the man how one would do such a thing, and the man answered, pointing to the side of his yard where the vague outline of a wrought iron fence could be seen.

"That's the city garden, the one your Mimi probably described. There are walkways and steps in the garden that lead all the way down to the street below."

"Of course!" Nicole looked at Sami. "Can we go over there and see?"

"I don't see why not. Let's drive over and find a place to park so we won't overstay our welcome here."

Thanking the man again, they pulled out of the driveway, then found an entrance into the garden. When they parked, a black car entered the park area. Nicole glanced at Sami. Had he noticed or was she just imagining things? After all, black cars were pretty common, and she never paid attention to the make or model.

"Sami, I think that car was back at the hotel too."

He glanced at the car. "That's possible. It is a public park. Do you think someone is following us?"

She did, but to say so sounded ridiculous. "Um, no. I just thought it was a coincidence, since it's the same color."

"You mean black?" He grinned, and she felt like an idiot for mentioning it.

They got out of the car and walked to the sidewalk, then followed it to a set of steps that descended down the hill. Did Mimi use these same steps? The garden also sloped downward, but with terraces featuring splashing fountains and flowers of all colors – pink oleander, blue plumbago, red hibiscus.

"Sami, do you think Mimi found the desert rose here?"

"If she did, I hope nobody got poisoned."

Sami walked down to an overlook. But some flowers in the other direction caught Nicole's eye, so she walked away to look at them more closely. Suddenly, strong arms grabbed her from behind and a hand covered her mouth. A gruff and heavily accented male voice close to her ear said, "Give us the ring." She twisted to get out of his grip. What ring? Mimi's? The one around her neck? She hoped he didn't know where she kept it. Where was Sami? She couldn't scream and could barely breathe. Remembering a self-defense course she took, she bit down on the man's hand as hard as she could, ignoring the awful taste of flesh and blood that ensued.

Her captor cried out with a what she guessed was a bad word in his language jerking his hand away, long enough for her to scream and yell, "Sami! Help!"

Feet shuffled behind her as Sami came running into view. "What happened?"

She spit out the taste of the stranger's hand, then wiped her mouth with the back of her sleeve. Catching her breath, she blurted out the experience to Sami. "He told me to give him the ring. He must've wanted Mimi's ring. But why?"

"I don't know, but it must be more valuable than we thought. Do you still have it?"

She touched the chain inside her shirt and felt the weight of the ring still on it, not wanting to take it out in case the stranger was still in the vicinity.

"We need to find a better place to keep it instead of around your neck," Sami said.

"Is there a safe-deposit box in your room?"

"I didn't notice. Maybe." Her heart raced, and she had trouble remembering what her hotel room looked like.

"Or you could ask the management to keep it locked up for you."

Nicole didn't want to leave it with anyone, not even the hotel management. But where else could she leave it?

Her phone buzzed, so she pulled it out of her pocket recognizing Mom's number.

"Mom? Is anything wrong?"

She listened, then looked up at Sami.

"Okay, Mom. Thanks for letting me know." She disconnected the phone.

"Is there a problem in your family?" Sami's eyes showed worried compassion.

"No. Mom just wanted to let me know that Mimi told her the pictures I sent of the desert rose were not what she was talking about. There's apparently something else called a desert rose."

So not only had she struck out finding the rose, but now someone was threatening her to get Mimi's ring. What else could go wrong?

Chapter 15

Monique

Algiers, September 1939

Audrey had been gone almost seven years, but she had continued to write. Monique looked forward to the letters that were always full of amusing stories about other players in the tennis school and their ridiculous behavior in tournaments. At first, Monique had received a letter every week or two, but as the years passed, the letters arrived less frequently, and so did their subject matter. Audrey had flings of romance with a couple of tennis pros, but they never lasted. She had traveled all over Europe, wined and dined with wealthy hosts, but hadn't been back to Algiers, slightly annoying and definitely disappointing Monique. After being like sisters for over a year, wasn't it possible for her to come visit?

Everyone's eyes were on Europe now that England and France had declared war on the German leader, Hitler, after his invasion of Poland. But all that was a long way from Algeria, even though the French were involved, so they watched from a distance, comfortable knowing they weren't close to the conflict. Besides, everyone thought the war wouldn't last long, since so many were reluctant to fight another war after the last terrible conflict.

Nineteen now, Monique attended the local university where she studied the arts. But right now, her mind was on Papá. He had been coughing more often, and his skin color had yellowed, losing its rich tan he'd had from being outside in the past. In fact, his traveling across the country had been reduced to the immediate area around Algiers with his new title of Director of Production. He oversaw the farms in the area, the vast vineyards and orange orchards that spread out south of the city. Mother's face wore lines of worry most of the time, concern for her husband a constant cause of anxiety.

Monique arrived home from school one day to find mother's eyes red-rimmed.

"Maman! What is it?"

"Your Papá. He is very ill." She glanced upstairs. "He is going to the hospital."

Alarm raced through Monique, and she grabbed Maman's arm. "Oh, Maman." Then, thinking of her mother's feelings, she said, "Don't worry. The hospital will take care of him, and he'll be home soon."

Maman gave her a blank look and nodded. "Of course, he will."

The ambulance pulled into the driveway and stopped in front of the house. Matazan went up the stairs to let Papá know. A few minutes later, Papá appeared at the top of the stairs wearing his full dress uniform with Matazan at his side and carefully stepped down each step. At the bottom, he looked at Maman and Monique resolutely. "Adieu, mon cheris'." Tears ran down their faces as Maman then Monique gave him a hug and a kiss on his cheeks. He turned and faced the door, then marched to the waiting ambulance, where he insisted on sitting in the front seat beside the driver instead of lying down on the stretcher. He held his handkerchief to his mouth as a fit of coughing shook his shoulders. Then the ambulance drove away.

That was the last time Monique saw her father alive.

Just days later, she, Maman, and her brother Rene stood side by side at the formal military procession that went from the cathedral to the cemetery. At the church, Papá's reputation for respecting different religions was displayed by the various religious leaders present in their special symbolic attire. Monseigneur Layneau, the Catholic bishop of the Notre Dame d'Afrique, Pastor Bonner, the protestant Reformed Church minister, and Father Cunningham, the Anglican priest, as well as the rabbi who led the synagogue, each had a turn to speak and offer their condolences to Papá.

Outside, the normally bright skies of Algiers were gray, fitting with all the black attire of the mourners. Monique, Maman, and Rene were escorted outside to stand while the casket was carried out and loaded onto an army caisson. As a contingent of the French Army marched by, they saluted Monique and her mother, then took up their positions around the wagon. More army troops lined each side of the street with drums beating in cadence as the wagon rolled by. Maman maintained her poise despite her grief, and Monique tried to do the same, even though her heart was so heavy that she thought it would fall to her feet.

An arm wrapped around her shoulders, and glancing over to see who it was, she found Audrey, her face full of compassion and tears. Audrey was taller, tanned with her strawberry blonde hair cut short in the latest bob. But when their eyes met, nothing had changed between them. Leaning into Audrey's side hug, her tears increased at the return of her forever friend. When had Audrey arrived in Algiers? Yet, Monique shouldn't be surprised that she would come to honor Papá, to pay her respects, and to comfort her friend when she needed her most. Monique promised herself she would do the same for Audrey as well.

A line of dignitaries fell in behind the wagon, then others followed, including the tall figure of Matazan, his own tears streaking his dark face. Another tall figure appeared in the entourage wearing the traditional dress of an important Amazigh, Chief Badis Amastan. Maman, Rene, Monique, and Audrey joined the growing entourage to escort Papá's body to the cemetery.

As Monique gazed around the crowd of mourners, she realized just how loved Papá had been. People from various tribes, cities, and settlements all over Algeria were present, all acknowledging the impact her father had made on them. There was no rivalry, anger or social separation, just unity in their grief for the loss of a special man, a man who had treated all with respect, no matter who they were. Monique made a mental promise to herself that she would carry on his legacy in the same way.

At the cemetery, Audrey stayed by Monique's side as tributes were given by several dignitaries. The Governor General of Algeria, Georges le Beau, gave a lengthy one. Another dignitary who spoke was General Charles de Gaulle, a veteran of the last war who had served with Papá, both of whom had been decorated for bravery and were good friends of Papá's. Whispers went through the crowd about his recent involvement against Hitler's advancement into Poland.

The Monseigneur gave Papá the final eulogy, recognizing him as a follower of Christ and supporter of the church.

After he finished, Maman was offered the opportunity to step forward and place a kiss on the casket. Monique choked back a sob, and her mother lovingly laid her cheek against the cold box as if she were laying it against Papá's chest. Then, lifting her head, she patted the casket and said, "Au revoir, mon amour, je te rejoindrai un jour." *Goodbye, my love. I will join you one day.* She placed a rose she'd held on top of the casket, then glanced at Monique, who stepped forward and followed suit. Rene, dressed in his uniform, stepped forward and saluted the casket.

And then it was over. The funeral. Papá's life. Their family as she'd always known it. But Monique would make sure she'd live out her life in a way that would honor her Papá's legacy.

Back home, Monique finally had the opportunity to speak to Audrey. "Thank you so much for coming."

Audrey hugged her, then said, "I had to be here. You know, I thought of him as a second father."

Numerous guests began arriving at the house to bring food and offer their condolences. Monique grabbed Audrey's arm. "Let's go out back where we can talk." They walked around to the rear of the house where the terrace overlooked the panorama of the city and the sea. Monique sat on one of the patio chairs, expecting Audrey to do the same. Instead, she strode to the old swing and settled down on it, gripping the rope as she gently swayed back and forth.

"How long can you stay?"

"A few days. I withdrew from my tournament as soon as I heard about your father."

"I'm so glad to hear that. I've missed you so much."

"And I, you. I wanted to come visit many times, but Father always had my schedule booked." She drew back and studied Monique. "Look at you, a beautiful grown woman."

"You've certainly changed as well. I mean, in appearance. You're a lovely woman and as tall as Rene now."

"Yes, I am rather tall for a woman. But that's to my advantage as a tennis player – I can reach farther." She grinned.

Monique smiled in return, imagining the life Audrey was living. "Do you enjoy doing what you're doing, never being at home?"

"Home? What is that? Certainly not like yours. Father lived in Cannes, and Mum lives in England, so naturally, I've seen Father often enough. But he's returned to England now that we're at war with Germany and has joined the Home Guard, being too old for anything else. And you, are you enjoying university? Have you a special fellow?"

Monique blushed. "No, no one special, as you say, although I have a few male friends. They were at the funeral with other school chums. You?"

Audrey laughed. "No. I've had opportunities, but most

of the men I know think way too highly of themselves. All they want to do is talk about who they beat and how well they played. Until they lose, then they're insufferable, seeking pity as if they're the only ones who ever lost. Even those who have shown interest in me liked themselves even more."

Monique tried to picture the men who surrounded Audrey. Didn't they know what an amazing person she was?

"So, you like this lifestyle? You plan to do this forever?"

"Forever? I don't think so. I finally got some semblance of approval from Father doing what he wanted, but this is his dream, not mine. It's been a fun adventure for the most part, though. Besides, even if I wanted to, my friends in Europe are warning me not to travel. I just think I'm ready to do something else. Something more exciting and worthwhile."

Monique cocked her head. "Such as what?"

"Since everyone back in England is gearing up for war with Germany, I feel like I should do something too. But I don't really want to go back to England, especially since I can't join the army. You know, women aren't allowed."

"You'd really want to be a soldier?"

"Why not? Our brothers are, aren't they? And I can drive a car and shoot a rifle, so surely I could do something helpful. I was surprised to see General de Gaulle here. He's been pretty busy lately."

"He and Papá fought together, and I believe they shared some of the same beliefs about how a war should be fought."

"I hear he and Pétain disagree on how to react to Hitler. I haven't figured out how yet, but if I can help, I will."

Monique shook her head. "You've always been so

brave."

"Brave? Ha! I just love adventure, that's all. Besides, someday you'll be brave too when you have to be."

Audrey spoke as if women should be fighting right alongside the men. Monique wasn't sure she agreed with her friend. The whole idea of being a soldier frightened Monique, and she couldn't see herself in the trenches, carrying a gun or dodging the enemy. Yet Audrey's desire for adventure would give her the courage to put herself in unpredictable situations. After all, she'd traveled all over, not staying at home the way Monique had. Leaving the comfort of her own country had never appealed to her for any length of time other than vacations with the family.

She sighed, the realization that those family vacations wouldn't be the same ever again sinking in.

Matazan appeared in the back doorway of the house. "Ladies. May I interrupt, please?"

Audrey hopped off the swing and ran over to the man, throwing her arms around him.

"Matazan! I've missed you!"

Startled by the unusual break in protocol Audrey exhibited by the physical embrace, he froze, then stammered. "Mademoiselle Audrey. I have missed you as well."

She released him, and the look of shock eased from his face.

"What did you need, Matazan?" Monique asked.

"Your maman would like you to come receive guests. I believe she is quite overwhelmed by all the people who have come."

Monique stood, guilt for abandoning her mother

convicting her. "Oh, dear. I must go see about Maman. Audrey, you'll be staying here, won't you?"

"If you'll let me. You go on, and I'll just make myself at home. I want to spend some time getting reacquainted with the place."

Audrey

Her former residence hadn't changed since she'd last been there, but she had. Once the lonely, out-of-place Englisher, she felt like she'd returned home. This is where she'd felt love, real love like a family should have. But there was a missing piece now. The colonel was gone. What would Monique and her mother do now?

She strolled over to the tennis courts where she'd played with the colonel and his friends, amazing them with a girl's athleticism. She'd never heard anything but praise for her efforts there, not condemnation for making mistakes or not playing her best. Here she was accepted for who she was, even though she was different from Monique. And Monique didn't mind either.

She chuckled to herself. Monique thought she was brave, but she thought bravery meant being strong enough to face danger. When had she ever faced danger? While innocent people were being attacked by Hitler's evil, she had been playing tennis. How absurd that she was playing games when people were dying or risking their lives? At Cannes, everyone was always on holiday. Even now that France had declared war on Hitler, it was still peaceful there. Opinion there was that Hitler wouldn't bother them. And here, it was peaceful too. Perhaps the German lunatic would stop being such a bully and leave everyone alone.

Her father and the colonel had both served in the last war. But neither would be soldiers again. Arthur Reynolds would do what he could in the Home Guard, and the colonel was gone. But seeing de Gaulle at the funeral had inspired her. He, too, had served in the last war, but now, almost fifty, he was ready to confront Hitler. In fact, he'd gotten a name for himself by challenging the elderly French leader Pétain, who preferred rhetoric, while de Gaulle insisted they mechanize for battle. Some agreed with Pétain, and others agreed with de Gaulle. Wouldn't he be a fascinating person to talk to? But when she didn't see him at the Clermont house, she assumed he was on his way back to France to prepare for battle against Hitler. Now that was bravery.

Audrey lingered on the outskirts of the yard, watching people arrive and then leave the house. Although she spent a fair amount of time among crowds, she wanted to avoid them now and have a moment of peace. No doubt Monique and her mother would like to have a moment to themselves, too. Didn't people understand that? No, they were too busy making their appearances to prove they had performed the necessary etiquette for the widow. When would they go away?

As she circled back toward the front part of the house, still keeping her distance, she noticed the Amazigh chief standing beside the front door, his eyes fixed straight ahead. She recalled the time she had first seen him, how intimidating he'd looked, tall and looking down on everyone else. He still had that aura of mystery, but he no longer frightened her since she'd enjoyed the hospitality of his home and family. His presence here at the colonel's house spoke volumes of his respect for his old friend.

Audrey remembered his stunning daughters and their friendliness. Were they married now? They probably were, since most Amazigh girls started their own homes by the time they were Audrey's age. She couldn't see herself settling down now. If she could find a man to love her with such respect as the colonel did his wife, she'd gladly be a wife. But from what she'd seen, those kinds of relationships were rare. It would take a special guy to meet her expectations.

She approached the chief, hoping he wouldn't mind. Studying him from head to toe, she was fascinated by his native Amazigh dress, the long-striped hijab with a hood, his sword slung over his shoulder, bold jewelry on his arms and fingers, no doubt made by his own craftsmen.

"Chief? Do you remember me, Audrey Reynolds? I came to your house several years ago with Colonel Clermont and his daughter."

Sober eyes looked down at her before a glimmer of recognition shone. Nodding, he said, "I do. You have grown."

Audrey offered a warm smile. "I have. And your daughters have too, I'm sure."

"Yes, they are married and have children." He glanced around. "You have husband too?

Audrey shook her head. "Not yet, I'm afraid." Was she really?

"You live with the colonel?"

"Oh, not anymore. I did live with his family for a year. I live in France now. I came for the funeral."

The chief nodded. "It is the right thing to do. I, too, am here for the family."

A flash of silver reflected off a large cross necklace just inside the man's cloak. Was he a Christian? She never expected to see that in this mostly Muslim country. Now was not the time to ask him about it, though.

"Excuse me, I must go inside," she said. "Please tell your family I said, 'hello.'"

He nodded again but did not move from his spot beside the doorway.

The last car was pulling away when Audrey stepped inside. In the parlor, she found Monique and her mother. Both looked fatigued.

"Mrs. Clermont, I am so sorry for your loss. You know I loved the colonel."

Mrs. Clermont forced a sad smile. "Thank you for coming, Audrey. You know, the colonel loved you, too."

Shock and sorrow collided in her heart, and her eyes filled with tears. A gaping hole opened like an untreated wound as the loss of the colonel registered. Never had she lost someone she cared so much for, especially someone who cared for her too. She went over and hugged Mrs. Clermont. "Thank you," was all she could say.

She gathered herself and blew out a breath. "You two need to rest. You have had a very trying day, and I know you're exhausted. Don't worry about me." She looked at Monique. "Is my bed still vacant?"

Monique gave a small smile. "Yes, unless the cat is on it. She thinks it's hers now."

"Minette? Is she still around? That's fine with me. She and I can cuddle up together."

"Audrey, there's plenty of food. Please help yourself." Mrs. Clermont stood. "I believe I'll take your advice. I am exhausted. Please excuse me."

Monique stood and hugged her mother, then kissed her on the cheek. "I'll stay down here with Audrey for a while."

Mrs. Clermont nodded. "Good night." She walked solemnly out the room and toward the stairs.

"I'm famished and would like to accept your mother's offer. Will you join me?" Audrey said, moving to the dining room table that was filled with dishes of all types of food.

"I'm not very hungry, but you go ahead."

Audrey filled a plate with food and poured herself a glass of lemonade from the pitcher on the sideboard. She poured one for Monique as well and handed it to her. "Shall we stay inside or go out on the terrace?"

"Outside, please. So many people have been in and out, the house is stuffy with the assorted fragrances of perfume and smoke they left behind. I need fresh air."

Carrying their refreshments with them, they went outside and sat down on the patio chairs. A few moments later, Matazan approached.

"Mademoiselle Monique, the chief will not leave."

"He what? Why not? Surely he does not want to speak with us now."

"No, he says he will talk to you later. But he says he must guard your house since the man of the house is no longer here."

Monique's eyes widened. "Guard? With weapons?"

"If necessary, I suppose. But he says he will sleep across

the entrance to the house to keep away anyone who is a threat to your safety."

"Oh my. What shall I do?" Monique glanced at Audrey.

"Let him. It is what he feels he should do. I don't see that there would be a problem with him doing that."

"But what if someone comes who he thinks is a threat but was a friend of Papá's?

"I'm sure he's already seen who was, since he's been watching people all day."

"How long will he stay?" Monique asked. "We should offer him food."

Matazan shook his head. "I offered, but he refused. He said he will never leave your house and leave you unprotected."

"Never?" Monique searched Audrey's face as if looking for an answer.

"Just tell him 'Thank you'," Audrey said. Nothing lasted forever.

Chapter 16

Nicole

Algiers, 2019

Are you ready to go back to the hotel?" Sami asked. "Or did you want to continue down the hill to see where the garden ends?"

Nicole nodded. "I think I've had a little too much excitement today." She glanced around the garden, then noted the stairs continuing downward. "I'm pretty sure this is how Mimi walked to school, with Matazan accompanying her." Too bad Nicole didn't have a Matazan to watch out for her too. However, it was nice to have Sami along. Would she be safe without him?

"Let's go back to the hotel and have some mint tea," Sami said.

"Sounds perfect," Nicole said. Coffee might be better, but she hadn't quite developed a taste for Algerian coffee.

It was no surprise to find the black car gone from the parking lot when they returned. Nicole was certain they'd been followed. First a camel, then a black car. What next? On the way back to the hotel, they discussed the events of the day.

"Nicole, did you get a look at the man who attacked you?"

"No, not at all. His sleeves were black, so I assume he was wearing black. But I never saw his face. I might be able to recognize his voice if I hear it again, not that I want to."

"Okay, we'll talk more about him later. Besides that, how do you feel about finding your Mimi's house? It was nice of the gentleman to let us walk around. "

"It was. I wonder how the interior has changed."

"Well, at least you saw the yard and the view of the city from it."

"You're right. And it was cool to see the remnants of the swing. Mimi said that is how she got her courage by swinging out over the edge of the hill."

"Your Mimi was an only child?"

"No, she had a brother who was about eight years older than her. She told me he was in a private military school while she was young and barely remembers him ever being home."

"Did he stay in Algiers?"

"No, I think he moved back to France during the war. I believe he was injured in the war, but he wasn't killed. Mimi corresponded with her nieces and nephews in France occasionally, but it's been a long time since she heard from them."

At the hotel, Sami accompanied Nicole into the restaurant where they found a small table in the corner. "I wanted to be able to speak with you in private, so I asked to be seated away from the others in here."

"That's fine with me."

Sami ordered two mint teas from the waiter. When they were delivered, Nicole grasped the hot mug in both hands and inhaled the scent of the tea. They say you can be stimulated by just inhaling the tea, that many chemicals evaporate from the tea when it is that hot, and you can inhale them. True or not, the beverage soothed and relaxed, just what she needed.

"I noticed there were tennis courts at the house," Sami said.

Nicole nodded. "I saw them too. Too bad they were so overgrown. I wonder if the man living there now ever played tennis. Mimi's father built them."

"Did she play?"

"I think she played a little, but she had a friend that enjoyed playing more. It was her father who loved tennis and built the court so he could play at home."

"Do you play?"

"I used to love it in high school, but I haven't had much time to play for several years now. Do you?"

"Sometimes. Maybe while you're here, we can play sometime."

The prospect sounded like fun, but Nicole knew they didn't really want to talk about tennis. There were more important things to discuss.

"Sami, be honest with me. Why would someone want Mimi's ring so badly?"

He stared down at his tea. "I've been trying to figure that out. I don't know for sure, but I wonder if there's a special message on your ring. And if there is, who would know about it? Would your Mimi know?"

"I think she would have told me if she knew something

like that. I never thought it was that valuable, just a keepsake from her childhood." Nicole sipped her tea. "I wish I could ask her, but ever since her stroke, communication has been very difficult." A feeling of uneasiness made her glance around. Were they being watched?

"I'd like to examine it more closely with a magnifying glass. I know you don't want to let it out of your hands, but if there was any way I could take it to examine it, I promise I'd return it."

She wanted to trust him, she really did, but for some reason, she couldn't let the ring get out of her sight. And she really didn't want to take it off here in a public place where eyes might be watching. But she didn't want Sami to think she didn't trust him either. Of course, she trusted him. Didn't she? Her gaze scanned the room, looking for anyone paying too much attention to them.

Leaning forward, Sami placed his hand over hers on the table. Gazing intently into her eyes, he said, "I know you're afraid to trust me. I get that. In your shoes, I might be too. After all, it is a family heirloom, if nothing else."

His eyes held such sincerity, she thought he could literally see right through her. *Lord, can I trust him*? Mimi had always taught her to pray about important decisions, and this seemed like one of them.

"I'm sorry, Sami. I don't know what to say. I don't think this is a good place to hand it over. Maybe there is some other place we could go, maybe where you can examine it with me there."

He sat back and exhaled. "All right. I have an office at the university. Why don't we go there? It should be safe."

"I feel more comfortable with that suggestion. When

can we go?"

He looked at his watch. "We can go now, if you feel like it. In fact, this might be a good time, since it's after five o'clock, and most of the faculty members have gone home for the day."

"Then let's go now. But would you mind if I go upstairs to my room for a few minutes to freshen up? It won't take long."

"Go right ahead." He held up his phone. "I'll make a call to see who's still there."

Nicole excused herself, then took the elevator to her floor. Walking down the hall towards her room, she noticed her door appeared to be partially open. Her heart thumped in her chest the closer she got. Why was her door open? She stopped in front of the door. Should she go in or just leave? Was someone in her room waiting for her? What if it was the same man who grabbed her in the park?

She glanced up and down the hall. Empty. No one was around to hear her if she called for help. Taking a steadying breath, she shoved the door open and stepped back, in case someone was waiting to grab her. The door opened slowly, revealing the disarray inside. From what she could see, everything had been ransacked, her clothes and suitcase on the floor, drawers open, bed covers pulled back.

Not waiting another second, she turned and ran down the hall to the stairs, not wanting to stand exposed in front of the elevator. She ran down the stairs as fast as she could. Relief filled her when she found Sami in the lobby.

Out of breath, she paused to collect herself before she could speak.

Alarm crossed Sami's face. "Nicole, what is it? What

happened?"

Trying to keep her voice low so bystanders wouldn't hear, she said, "Someone's been in my room! They've torn it apart!"

"Did you go inside?"

"No, the door was partially open, so I just pushed it and looked inside. When I saw the mess, I ran away. I don't know if anyone was in there or not."

"We've got to get to the bottom of this. Let's go tell the manager." Placing his hand on the small of her back, he nudged her forward.

The manager listened, although Nicole didn't think he showed much concern. He promised to call the police and investigate the break-in. When they finished speaking with them, Sami told the man they had an appointment at the university and would check in with him when they returned. As they walked away, he muttered to her, "Come on, let's get out of here."

They jogged down the front steps and got into Sami's car while the sunset call to prayer was ringing out from minarets throughout the city. As Sami drove, Nicole placed her hand over the ring inside her shirt to make sure it was still there. *Mimi, what have you given me?*

The hallway of the Archaeology Institute of Algiers University was hollow, their footsteps loud and heavy as they walked between closed classroom doors to the offices of the professors and graduate advisors.

"There are no night classes?" Nicole was amazed to find the building so empty.

"Not in this building, which is good, so we won't be interrupted."

Sami unlocked a door to the left and extended his hand for her to enter ahead of him.

The room was divided into four cubicles of equal size. Only two had windows, and Sami's was one of them. His walls were covered with posters showing archaeological sites in Algeria, and his shelves were filled with books and artifacts. One wall displayed a curved sword alongside some menacing-looking knives.

"Interesting," she said, as she scanned the room, her gaze resting on the wall of weapons. "What are these?"

Sami walked over and pointed to a long one. "This is called a 'flyssa.' It's a traditional weapon of Algeria, produced and used during the 19th century and earlier. It originated from the Kabyle tribe." He pointed to a shorter weapon. "This dagger is a traditional knife from the Amazigh. It is called 'koummya.' This shorter dagger with the short, curved blade has several names, mainly 'jambiya.'" He pointed to another, larger sword. "This is the type that was in a scene in 'Raiders of the Lost Ark.' It's an oversized scimitar."

Nicole remembered the scene and how Indiana Jones handled the threat. "You found all these yourself?"

"No, they were gifts. No problem with having them since they are so prevalent in the country and there are many modern copies."

Sami approached a door between his cubicle and the next and unlocked it. As they walked in, he flipped on the light.

"Welcome to my lab."

The lab had tables, equipment, and artifacts lined up beside them. He walked to an optical microscope like Nicole had used in her college lab and sat down in front of it.

"May I see the ring, please?"

Nicole pulled the chain over her neck and handed it to him. Sami placed it on the microscope stage beneath the lenses, then switched on the light below the stage and placed his eyes over the double eyepiece. Turning the focus knob, he studied the ring. Then he turned the ring upside down and repeated the process.

"Yes, that's what I thought." He lifted his head from the microscope.

"What?" Nicole said, glancing from Sami to the ring.

He moved from the chair and pointed to the microscope. "See for yourself. What does it look like to you?"

Nicole looked through the eyepieces. "A face. And some kind of writing or letters?"

"Yes, I believe it is, but I'm not sure what type of writing it is. It looks vaguely familiar, but I can't place it."

Nicole had the same feeling. "So you think there might be a message on it that someone wants to see?"

He nodded. "I do, because there isn't enough gold in the ring to make it that valuable. There must be another reason someone wants to get their hands on it."

Why hadn't she ever thought of looking at the ring through a microscope? She'd honestly never considered it to be important enough to examine. It was just a ring Mimi gave her. Did Mom know if it had any words on it? Nicole would text her and ask.

"So you don't know what language it is?"

"No, it's not a language used today. It's ancient, so I'll have to research it."

"So we won't know what it says until we find out what

language it is."

"That's correct."

"Do you think whoever wants the ring knows the language?"

"Sounds likely." Sami moved back in front of the microscope and looked at the ring some more, twisting the focus knob back and forth. He scribbled something on a notepad beside the microscope. "I'm trying to copy this so I can compare it to various writings we've found." He paused. "Wait. I see some more images. Over the top of the person's head, it looked like small triangles which could be mountains. And, yes, there's a cross on it too. Very interesting."

He handed the chain back to Nicole, and she slid it over her head again, dropping it inside her shirt. Footsteps sounded outside the door. Nicole froze as she exchanged glances with Sami.

"Sami, are you in there?" A male voice came from the office.

Sami quickly stood and stepped away from the table. "Yes, Nadir. I'm in here."

A bearded man wearing a fez and American clothes stepped into the room. "Ah! I wondered why the doors were open." He glanced at Nicole and smiled. "What are you doing, my friend?"

"Nadir, this is Nicole Bennett from the US. She's the one doing graduate studies here. I was just showing her around here. Nicole, Nadir is one of our professors."

Nadir nodded. "Nice to meet you, Nicole. I hope Sami is treating you well." He glanced at Sami with lifted eyebrows.

"Nice to meet you too." She offered a friendly smile, trying not to appear nervous like a child caught with her hands in a cookie jar. "Yes, Sami has been a very helpful guide."

"So where to next?" Nadir glanced between them.

"We'll be going to the dig at Beni Hammad tomorrow."

Nadir pursed his lips. "Ah, Yanis' dig. It's a long trip, but definitely worth it. We have many important ruins to see in our country, Nicole, so I hope you'll have time to see them all."

"I'll be here three months, so I'll try."

Nadir glanced toward the microscope. "You were examining something?"

Sami and Nicole glanced at the microscope, the light still on. Nicole swallowed a lump in her throat. Would Sami tell him about the ring?

"Ah, yes." Sami grabbed a coin from a box of miscellaneous artifacts near the microscope. "I was showing her one of our ancient coins." He switched off the light.

"Umhmm. We have found quite a few of those," Nadir said, his tone doubtful. Or was it Nicole's imagination.

"Well, we were just leaving," Sami said, moving toward the door. "We need to get an early start tomorrow." His eyes beckoned Nicole to follow.

"Yes, you do." Nadir followed them out of the lab, closing the door behind him. "Don't worry, I'll lock up here. I just came back to the office to grab my notes for tomorrow's lecture." He picked up a leather journal from one of the desks and held it up. "You two have a productive trip tomorrow."

"We will. Good night." Sami escorted Nicole out the

door and down the hall. It wasn't until they were outside the building that either of them spoke.

"What a coincidence that Nadir arrived while we were there," Nicole said.

"Yes, it certainly was. He is not in the habit of showing up after hours. He usually is quick to leave and meet friends for dinner at his favorite restaurant in the Casbah."

"I'm glad we had put the ring away before he showed up," Nicole said.

"Yes. I'm sorry about leaving the light on the microscope."

"It wouldn't be unusual for you to show me an artifact, would it?"

Sami rubbed his chin. "No. But I do find his reason for being there a bit questionable."

Nicole paused and studied his face. "Why?"

"For one, his notes are in his computer, which he can access anywhere. Plus, the lecture he is giving is one he's given many times before because he's taught that class for years. And three, the journal he picked up? It wasn't his."

Chapter 17

Monique

Algiers, October 1939

Monique stepped into Cohen's Jewelry Store in the Casbah. Her friend Sarah stood behind the counter.

"Hi Sarah. I need to get my watch repaired." She laid the watch on the counter.

Sarah's usual cheerful expression was missing, replaced by one of immense sadness.

"Sarah, what is wrong?" Monique reached out to touch Sarah's arm.

Tears welled up in her eyes, and she glanced to the back of the shop where her father, Samuel Cohen, was bowed over a table while he worked with a small screwdriver.

Sarah motioned for her to come with her. "Papá, I'll be back in a minute. I'm just stepping outside with Monique."

Her father's head bobbed up, and he glanced over at the two of them, then returned to his work.

"Monique, haven't you heard about Hitler invading Poland? He broke the Munich agreement, and now he's taking his hatred of the Jews out on the Jews in Poland! Did you know about that?"

She had heard some things, but didn't comprehend or didn't want to. She knew Adolf Hitler was anti-Jewish, but could he be as bad as the stories?

"But Sarah, he's in Germany and nowhere near us."

Sarah gripped Monique's arm and fixed her with a glare. "Monique, he's taking away all Jewish rights, property, and business! They have nothing and can't get away. Instead, he's rounding up Jews like cattle and sending them to death camps."

"But you're safe here. And Hitler agreed to not go any further. Remember, we have the Maginot Line."

"Monique, open your eyes. I have relatives in Germany. My father has not heard from his brother or sister that live in Germany. Those are my people, my aunt and uncle, and their children are my cousins. And now, Hitler has invaded Poland and is treating the Jews there as badly as in Germany. And nobody's doing anything about it. Nobody's stopping him. No one is standing up for the Jews. Instead, other countries like Italy have passed antisemitic laws, too, and Italy is not that far away from here. The Maginot Line in France isn't doing anything to stop Hitler's treatment of the Jews. Even though we declared war on him, he hasn't stopped. What if France loses and Algeria does the same thing? What if they take away our business? How will we live?"

Shock rippled through Monique. Could France lose to Hitler? So what she'd heard wasn't just stories. Real people, people she knew, were being affected by that awful man in Germany. But what could she do? She began to list all the people she knew who were Jewish, people who'd always been part of her life. The banker Joseph Levin handled all her family's finances. He was the person who took care of her and her mother's affairs since Papá died. He and his family of five were Jewish, too. And Mr. Kaplan, who ran the shoe store. Were all these people in danger?

She did know some French people who were antisemitic, but she didn't understand why. Her father had taught her to treat all people with respect, regardless of their religion or skin color, and she had always tried to do the same. Maybe she needed to pay more attention to the news in Europe and not pretend it didn't affect her.

"I'm so sorry, Sarah. I didn't realize…what can I do to help? "

"You can pray for us. I know you're Christian, but I believe we pray to the same God. Pray for the Jews everywhere."

"And you? I don't know how else I can help, but let me know if there is a way."

"I will." Sarah looked over her shoulder. "I'd better get back inside. You can pick up your watch tomorrow."

Monique couldn't fully comprehend what Sarah had told her, couldn't believe Hitler's actions were affecting people she knew. What could she do about it? Sarah asked her to pray, but she wanted to do more. When she got home, she found her mother on the patio. "Maman, have you heard what Hitler is doing to the Jews?"

Maman slowly nodded. "Yes, I have. It's terrible."

"Do you think that will ever happen here?"

Manam shook her head. "Here? We're not even close to where Hitler is."

"Well, we mustn't let it! These are our friends!" She

told her mother about her conversation with Sarah Cohen and how Hitler's actions affected her family.

"I'm so sorry to hear that," Maman said. "The Cohens have always been our friends."

"And what about all the other Jews we know? They are all affected, and I'm sure worried about their future."

"But what can we do about it?" Maman lifted her hands as though she had no answer. "I feel so bad for them, but none of that is within my power to correct."

"Are they? I'm sure Papá would have something to say in the matter if he were here." But what would that be? What would he do?

"Yes, I'm sure he would."

"Maman, do you really think France could lose against Hitler? What would happen to us if they did?"

"Monique, I can't see how we would be affected. We're not in France, and Germany is not invading Africa."

Much as she wanted to take comfort in what Maman said, Sarah's words echoed in her mind. Maman said they were safe here in Algeria, but were they just being naïve?

Matazan stood nearby like a sentinel who could not speak. She glanced at him. He knew what it was like to be treated like a second-class citizen just because he was from a local tribe and assumed to be inferior. Wonder what he thought about the declining treatment of the Jews? If Algeria got involved in the war, would he be willing to fight the Germans?

For six months, Algeria was untouched physically by the war in Europe. But in April of 1940, Hitler's army invaded Denmark and southern Norway. One month later, they invaded the Netherlands, Belgium, and Luxembourg, the countries falling like dominoes under the Nazi army. Then Hitler did the unthinkable. He broke through the Maginot Line and invaded France by driving tanks through the Ardennes, a dense forest in Belgium that the French thought could not be penetrated. By going through Belgium, he was able to get around the northern end of the line, making it useless. And on June 14, Hitler's army rolled into Paris.

Monique and her mother and the rest of Algiers listened to the news on the radio in horror as France fell to Germany. One week later, they sobbed as French Prime Minister Marshal Henri' Pétain signed an armistice with Hitler, even though de Gaulle, speaking over the radio from England, urged his countrymen to keep fighting against the Nazis. After Pétain's surrender, half of France was occupied by the Germans. Pétain took office as "chief of state at Vichy, a city in unoccupied southern France. The Vichy government, as it came to be known, collaborated with the Nazis. And Algeria came under Vichy control.

After France caved in to Hitler, he began bombing England. But England didn't surrender like France did. Monique hoped England would be able to retaliate and help France, but they were fighting to survive themselves. Where was Audrey? Was she in England being bombed?

Was she safe?

Life began to change in Algiers. The Vichy-controlled government tried to implement the Nazi policies, and everyone was suspicious of everyone else. There were Germans, French collaborators, and Allied sympathizers, but the latter kept quiet to stay out of trouble. Monique was especially angry to discover people who had previously been friends of her family had aligned themselves with the Vichy. She had to be very careful what she said to whom and find out who her true friends were.

Even Maman's activities changed. Her normally full social calendar was empty now. Her charity work dwindled, and she no longer hosted tea parties. Nor was she invited to any. Maman said part of the reason was that now that she was an army widow, she was not included with the wives of the officers anymore. Those women she used to consider friends and invited her for tea parties quit calling. "I have become like a persona non grata," Maman said stoically, but Monique knew her mother suffered the sting of betrayal. "It is just as well, though," Maman continued. "Most of them are now with the Vichy government, and I do not care to associate with anyone involved with the Nazi regime."

One of the side effects of the war for Monique was the end of being paraded and invited to parties for the purpose of meeting young men. Much as she enjoyed parties, Monique felt awkward trying to make conversation with people she didn't know, feeling like she was in some competition with the other girls for attention. The goal, of course, was to find a husband. But the war changed that goal. Now she had more in common with the other girls her age, sharing their mutual concern for French soldiers.

Her beautiful mother's face had lost the light that used to shine from it, and Monique hated the situation they now lived in. However, up here on the hill overlooking the city, they could pretend they were not connected to the rest of the world unless they listened to the radio. However, most of what they heard on the radio was Nazi propaganda, but they listened, hoping to hear that the Allies would come to their rescue and liberate the country.

One of the first things Maman did after learning Algiers would be controlled by the Vichy government was to pack a trunk full of important, valuable family items and take it to the farm outside the city, where Papá had an interest, and bury it in an underground tank. Monique heard that other families did the same, like families had done in previous wars. Everyone had a relative in the army, navy, or air force, and most of them were in Europe like Rene.

Monique and Maman knitted scarves and socks to send to the soldiers, and Monique took a course in first aid at the Croix Rouge. But for now, they had to tolerate the inconvenience of the German checkpoints that were set up and the guards who stopped people at random to check I.D.'s and question who they were and where they were going. Despite the nausea she felt by doing it, Monique learned to use her feminine ability to flirt and distract the young men so others could get past without being questioned.

Blackouts were ordered, so curtains were required to cover the windows. Cars and buses used dim blue lights to get around, if they had gas to do so. But gas restrictions were severe, so most people did without. As a result, the whole city was dark and rather spooky.

One day, Monique arrived at Cohen's Jewelry Store to find it boarded up. What had happened to the Cohens? Knowing where they lived, she went straight to their house. After knocking on the door for several minutes, Sarah slowly opened it.

"I went by the shop. Sarah, why is it closed?" Sarah glanced both ways, then pulled Monique inside.

"It is as we expected. The Vichy regime has taken away all Jewish citizenship, so we can no longer serve in government positions or be treated with equal status to the French. Jews can't even serve in the army now." Sarah lowered her voice. "As they did in Germany and everywhere else they've been, there are now orders that forbid Jews from continuing to work in their professions. Mr. Levin from the bank, and others—Jewish pharmacists, teachers, and nurses in hospitals have been forced to leave their jobs. Even Jewish children have been forced to leave the education system because now that they're not citizens, they're no longer entitled to it. So now, the teachers who have been expelled are the new teachers for our own Jewish schools. Sarah clasped Monique's hand. "Monique, you should not come here. You could get in trouble for being at a Jewish house."

Monique waved her off. "Nonsense. I'll see whoever I want to."

Brave words, but Monique began to pay more attention to whoever might be watching her as she realized the danger. Jewish sympathizers were considered partners with the undesirables, so most people just ignored the Jews and pretended they didn't exist. Maman worried every time Monique left their house, hearing stories about the mistreatment of even innocent people in other countries. She did not trust the Nazis or anyone associated with them. But the situation for the Jews in the city grew even worse. The next time Monique checked on the Cohens, they were dealing with another Nazi policy to limit their freedom, this time to require them to register their property with the intention of nationalizing it.

Soon, Jews who engaged in "political activities" were arrested and sent to labor camps in the desert in the south of the country. No one knew what kind of political activity caused their arrest, and Sarah's family and others cowered behind closed doors, wondering who the Nazis would come for next.

Without an income, the Jews had a hard time buying necessities, including food. Monique and her mother had problems as well because the Vichy government installed rations for everyone. But Monique couldn't stand by and see her family and friends treated the way they were. She certainly couldn't let them go without food. But how could she and her mother share enough of their food to feed Sarah's family of five?

When Mr. Alexis, a good friend of Papá and overseer of the area's agricultural farms, showed up at their house, he brought news about how he was "fooling" the Vichy government by misrepresenting the production of the farms. Even though he often had official escorts to the fields to survey productivity, he was able to set aside part of the production to help civilians.

Mr. Alexis could be trusted. As a result, he arranged for Monique to go to the farms with him and smuggle vegetables and fruits back to the city. Since she and Maman didn't need much to eat, she made trips to Sarah's home with their extra. Sarah was then able to share with other Jews who needed food. Gas was unavailable, so there wasn't much car traffic. Monique had to use her bicycle for the deliveries or walk. Going up and down the hill behind her house proved challenging in more than one way. Besides carrying the extra weight, she sometimes had to dodge checkpoints to get where she needed to go.

She varied her route from time to time in case she was being watched but hoping they only thought of her as just a student at the university. Going to the city by way of the park was one of her favorite ways to travel, the aroma of flowers distracting her from the weight of the food she carried in her knapsack.

Matazan approached her one day. "Mademoiselle Monique, I know you are helping your friends by bringing them food. Let me help you so you won't get caught."

"I am careful, Matazan. Don't worry, I'm not Jewish so the Nazis don't bother me."

He frowned, but did not respond, instead eyeing her with a lifted eyebrow as if he questioned the truth of her statement.

"And what about you? Couldn't you be caught, too?"

"If I am stopped, I will tell them I am going to see family. I do not think the Nazis would suspect me, a native, of helping the Jewish people," he said.

"I will think about it," she said, trying to appease him.

Later that day, she was heading down the steps of the garden when she ran into two Vichy guards stopped on the sidewalk. Acting nonchalant, she gave them a flirtatious smile and said, "Bon Jour." She continued to walk past them when one of them grabbed her arm.

"Where are you going?"

"I am a student at the university. I am going to school."

"Then you will not mind if I check your knapsack."

She couldn't let him see all the food she carried. Besides

being more than the rationed amount, it would be obvious she was taking it to someone. And what if they found out who? What could she do? Run? They would chase her and would certainly catch her. From the dense trees in the natural area of the park came the cry of a wild cat.

The two guards glanced at each other with widened eyes. "What is that?

Monique suspected the source but played along. "That is one of the wildest big cats in all of Africa. They are very hard to see because they hide in the forests. They've been known to eat a grown man."

One of the guards raised his rifle to shoot into the trees as the noise repeated.

"I wouldn't do that if I were you," she said, keeping a serious demeanor. "They just get very angry at loud noises, and if you fire and miss, they will certainly attack. After all, they can see you even if you can't see them."

"How do you get out of here?" one of the guards said.

Monique pointed down the steps. "That way. The closer you get to the city, the safer you'll be because they hate all the city noise."

The soldiers quickly forgot about her and hurried away. She stood watching with a smile on her face, waiting until they were out of sight before she moved. "Okay, Matazan, they're gone. You can come out now."

Rustling behind her caught her attention, and she turned as Matazan stepped from the tree cover.

"I see you have not lost your gift for making animal sounds, nor have you quit following me since I was a little girl," Monique said.

"Mademoiselle Monique, you must let me make the

deliveries for you. I might not be near to help you someday."

It was hard to believe he wouldn't be. Ever since he'd come to work for her family, he had been her shadow, always appearing when she needed him. But she had to admit today's experience had frightened her.

"We'll take turns then. I cannot let you take all the risks. Besides, Sarah and I plan to change our meeting place."

When Matazan returned later that day, he brought more bad news. "She cannot meet you, she said. Her parents do not want her to leave the house because they are afraid she will not return. They think their house is being watched.'

Chapter 18

Audrey

France, 1940

Mother and Father didn't particularly seem to care if Audrey stayed in France. At the chateau of Jeanette Rousseau, a wealthy widow and friend who had been a patron of Audrey's tennis career, her parents thought she was safe. The chateau was in the south of France, far away from any battles. Her parents knew Madam Rousseau and did not worry about her, saying only "stay in touch, dear," in their letter. Besides, if she went to England, she'd give up the independence she'd enjoyed for years. But Audrey was bored. With international tennis tournaments suspended, the social scene coming to an end, and all able-bodied French men leaving to sign up for the army, including the staff of the chateau, life was dull.

"Jeanette, what can I do? Surely, I can contribute in some way to the cause."

"I heard in town that other young ladies of your social status are signing up with the Croix Rouge, the French Red Cross. All the young girls from the right families are doing just that." Jeanette sipped her daily glass of champagne.

"And your friend Claudette says the uniforms are quite becoming. And just think of all those grateful young men you'll meet." Jeanette winked and gave her a mischievous smile.

With the Croix Rouge her only option, Audrey marched down to the local station and volunteered to drive an ambulance. Since she was one of the few women who could drive, her services would be greatly needed. However, the stern-looking woman at the desk informed her she'd have to have a nursing diploma to ever qualify to drive an ambulance. "You might well have to give emergency medical attention to wounded soldiers," she said, adding, "You'd hardly be any use if all you could do was drive."

Audrey reluctantly signed up for a three-month nursing course, the only English woman among the thirty volunteers. She moved to the town of Poitiers, a medieval hilltop town overlooking two rivers, taking a room with an English woman married to a French army officer who had gone to join the fighting. As she unpacked, she examined her new nurse's uniform, which consisted of a starched white overall, an apron, and a cap. It was indeed very becoming, although Audrey still struggled with her decision. Did she really want to be a nurse?

She began her nursing course with great reluctance as she learned the basic principles of health and hygiene in the gloomy Poitiers hospital. The ward smelled of disinfectant and carbolic soap, and her tasks were menial and humiliating. Unused to manual labor, her hands became raw and her manicured nails split. After a month of scrubbing floors, washing sheets, and dressing minor wounds, she was finally asked to spend time with patients. Her time was divided by spending two weeks on a ward with the seriously ill and then two weeks nursing those who were not so ill.

The nursing course dragged on and on, but Audrey sucked down her pride while performing the tedious tasks to reach the goal of driving an ambulance someday. What a waste of time and money, since she was hopeless as a nurse but already experienced as a driver. She had no patience with the ill and resented having to take care of them.

Doctors appeared to be overly eager to operate on the patients, and Audrey often had the task of administering the chloroform and ether by mask connected to a contraption. Her job was to push down to increase the dosage, and the Matron in charge of her training warned her not to administer too much, lest she kill the patient. Afraid she'd kill someone, Audrey barely pushed down on the contraption and the patient woke in the middle of the operation, clutching the mask and trying to get up. The quick-thinking doctor gave her a furious glance, then shoved the mask down on the man's face, and the patient slumped back. Her reputation quickly traveled through the hospital so that she was no longer asked to assist in surgery.

In March, the war escalated in Scandinavia where they were under attack by the Russians, and they appealed for help from the rest of the world. Audrey jumped at this opportunity to get to the front lines as a driver. She volunteered but was told her chances of being chosen were minimal, based on the other women who had volunteered only to be otherwise engaged when summoned. As it turned out, Audrey was accepted for her nursing skills, not her driving ability. The French Expeditionary force she joined included six ambulances, several drivers and six nurses.

She traveled to Amsterdam by train, stayed overnight, then continued by air to Copenhagen and Stockholm, avoiding German airspace. She was finally going to experience the excitement of the war. But her dreams of high adventure in a distant land soon ended. As they landed in Stockholm, they received the news that the Finns had surrendered after fourteen weeks of fighting in subzero temperatures. More Russian soldiers died than Finns, but the Finns had run out of energy. While waiting in Copenhagen for their next orders, the Germans invaded Denmark and Norway, planning to attack British shipping in the North Atlantic. The Germans mined the waters off the coast of Norway, and all lines of communication with England were cut.

Audrey and her team were stranded in Copenhagen. When a hospital in a small town heard they were nearby, they asked if the French medical group would come help with the wounded Finnish soldiers. Many of the wounded had lost some fingers and toes to frostbite, while others suffered from exposure, and a few had been shot or hit by shrapnel. The men spoke perfect English and told horrific tales of fighting the Russians in the bitter cold, many of their comrades freezing to death. Audrey couldn't imagine the horrors they'd witnessed and was grateful she had not been present where the fighting had occurred.

While Germany invaded Holland, then Belgium, Audrey waited anxiously to get back to France. Now that Italy had joined Germany and declared war on the Allies, the aged Commander-in-Chief of the French Army Philippe Pétain was invited by the Germans to form a government in the spa town of Vichy. Many French people supported the new Vichy government, afraid that France would not withstand a German attack.

Audrey and her fellow nurses listened on a crackling wireless to an emotional and powerful broadcast by General de Gaulle, who'd gained the backing of Winston Churchill in England. In defiance of the new Vichy government, he invited all French soldiers, and any others who wanted to help in the fight for France to join him and his "Free French" against the Germans and Vichy France. With England's support and the expected aid of the United States, de Gaulle declared the war a "world" war.

When Audrey heard de Gaulle say, "Whatever happens, the flame of the French resistance must not go out, and it will NOT go out," her heart was stirred. Her second home, France, was in enemy hands, and she had to fight for its freedom. After a treacherous voyage through mine-filled waters, Audrey's ship finally docked in England in July. She went straight to her Aunt Gertie's house in Kensington. When her aunt opened the door, Audrey said, "Any chance I could have a bath?' Taking one look at Audrey's crumpled attire and small suitcase, her shocked aunt threw her arms around Audrey and ushered her inside.

Aunt Gert was eager to hear about Audrey's adventures and what she planned to do next. Audrey wasn't sure. But she knew she didn't want to be in London. She desperately wanted to be in the action in France, but then her aunt told her what had happened at Dunkirk when the British Expeditionary Force, along with French and Belgian troops, had been driven back by the Germans when trying to invade France. It was only a matter of time before England fell.

Audrey couldn't sit still and wait for that to happen. In

July, news came that de Gaulle had set up his headquarters in the former government offices in Carlton Gardens in Central London. He was enlisting help for volunteer nurses, drivers, and soldiers, hoping to take the campaign to French Africa. "Do you think he'll take me?" Audrey asked her aunt.

"Why not go up there and see?" she said. "It could be just the opportunity you're looking for."

Audrey kissed Aunt Gert on the cheek before jumping on to the next double-decker bus. When she reached the grand building, she walked up the stairs with an optimism she hadn't felt in a long time. People were rushing everywhere, secretaries with documents, soldiers in greatcoats, women in feathered hats. Military police stood guard at the doors, refusing to let anyone enter, especially now that de Gaulle had been convicted of treason and sentenced to death by the Vichy government.

After asking someone which way to go, she was pointed in the direction of a Miss Ford, a woman she'd met once in Paris. Clad in a gray suit, Miss Ford stayed professionally aloof while organizing the nursing services. Audrey introduced herself and explained her experience.

Not wasting any time, Miss Ford replied, "Yes, Miss Reynolds, General de Gaulle has been given the use of twenty ambulances, and we need nurses, so you can be of some assistance. You'll need a complete medical and have to supply your own uniform and belongings suitable for the tropics." She handed Audrey some papers. "Here are some forms to fill in and a list of the inoculations you'll require. If you pass the medical, you'll be taken on at the rank of sergeant on two-thirds of a regular sergeant's pay. Report to headquarters 30 August."

Forms completed and tests passed, she had two weeks to kill until reporting for duty. Enough time to see her parents. It was the right thing to do, of course, but the prospect of seeing them again was a mixture of dread and the tiniest bit of hope. But true to form, nothing had changed. Mother was still distant and difficult to talk with, not interested in any of Audrey's adventures but only inquiring after Aunt Gertie.

Father was more animated. He strutted about in his khaki uniform and regaled her with stories of how he was introducing military discipline to the local volunteers in the Home Guard. He was doing such a good job, in fact, that he'd already received a promotion to senior officer. While she was there, Audrey and her family, including the two Corgis, fled nightly to the cramped Anderson shelter in the garden when the air raid sirens droned as Nazi planes headed for the harbor. Every day, German planes flew over England and were engaged by the Royal Air Force, the RAF. One early evening, she and Father stood mesmerized as they watched a dogfight between an RAF plane and a German Luftwaffe in the sky above the harbor.

Later, they listened as Churchill paid tribute to the RAF in a speech to Parliament which was aired over the radio.

"Never in the field of human conflict was so much owed by so many to so few," said the prime minister.

When Audrey returned to London by train, it was during the first massive bombardment of the city. Air raid sirens rang every night while German planes soared over the city dropping bombs at will. The next day, firefighters would be putting out fires in buildings that had been hit while others searched for victims. The air was full of smoke and burning rubber, and the streets were full of rubble. Every window was covered in black tape, and with so many people losing their homes, more and more people slept in the Underground station and tunnels. Amazingly, life continued as normally as possible, showing a resistance that made Audrey's British heart soar.

But despite the show of patriotism, Audrey still didn't feel as English as she did French. After years elsewhere, she felt sorry for those whose homes had been damaged, yet she was ready to go back to France to help her comrades there. She purchased a canvas bag, a folding bed, and suitable clothes for the tropics and reported to headquarters. Afterwards, she boarded a bus, then a train to Liverpool. As she gazed out the window at the suburbs of London speeding by, she caught her own reflection in the glass. A young woman with short, strawberry blonde hair and piercing blue eyes, wearing a simple black felt hat and plain grey jacket, looked back at her. She liked the new person she saw, a person ready for the adventure of a lifetime.

Chapter 19

Nicole

Algiers, 2019

What did the hotel management say about the break-in of your room?" Sami asked when he picked her up the next morning.

Nicole wrinkled her nose. "Well, first he apologized. Then he asked if anything *of value* was missing. And then of course, he offered to keep my valuables in the hotel safe."

Sami nodded. "That sounds typical."

"Probably, but I felt like he was inquiring about a specific valuable. Or maybe I'm just paranoid now."

"So did you leave anything with him?"

Shooting him a glare, she said, "Of course not! For some reason, it seems like everybody wants to get their hands on Mimi's ring. Maybe it's my imagination, but too many weird things are happening."

"I understand why you don't trust anyone. I hope that doesn't apply to me, too." His face saddened with a scolded puppy look.

"What? You're the only person I DO trust!" Even while

saying the words, she questioned herself. She wanted to trust him, but was her attraction to him blinding her from using common sense?

"Thank God for that. I try to maintain a reputation for integrity."

They walked to his car, and she tossed her full backpack in.

"Let's put that in the trunk, just to be safe," Sami said.

She retrieved the bag and handed it to him, where they stood behind the car with the trunk open.

"Is that going to be enough for several days on the road?"

"I hope so. I've been on digs before and learned to pack light. I have my own special trowel, a couple of brushes, a measuring tape, a few resealable plastic bags, a pen, a pencil, a toothbrush for the dig, and one for my mouth too. Plus other personal stuff and a change of clothes."

Sami's smile lit up his face. "Good for you."

Soon they were heading southeast toward the Hodna Mountain range, part of the Atlas Mountains.

"So tell me about the place we're going."

"All right. Beni Hammad was called Al Qal'a of Beni Hammad when it became a World Heritage site in 1980. It is described as 'an authentic picture of a fortified palatine city from the eleventh century and served as the first capital of the Hamadid dynasty.'

"Okay, sounds interesting. Tell me more."

"Well, the town has about four miles of walls that enclose four different residential complexes and the second largest mosque in Algeria."

"How far is it from Algiers? "

"160 miles, about two and a half hours."

"I've always wondered why they built cities in certain places. I mean, it's obvious why a city would be built by water, since it provides easy transportation of goods, but out in the middle of nowhere, I don't get it."

"In the year 1007, when the city was built, it was a military fort as well as a city and was located on a colonial trade route from Egypt, Iraq, and Syria. In its heyday, it was a huge center of commerce and a destination for caravans carrying all kinds of goods."

"And it's still being excavated?"

"Yes, the initial excavation began in 1908, but it was stopped by World Wars and the Algerian Civil War. It was restarted in the 1950's and still continues. There is still much to be discovered, since it was a well-developed city."

"I'm looking forward to seeing it." Nicole's mind wandered as the rolling terrain of the country passed by. So far, her trip hadn't turned out exactly as she'd planned. She'd wanted to find the Desert Rose for Mimi, but instead, people seemed to be after Mimi's ring. She thought back over the last events, trying to piece them together.

"Are you all right?"

She glanced at Sami, who was eyeing her with concern.

"Yes, sure. I'm just thinking about everything that's happened, and wondering about Mimi's ring."

"I did a little more research last night, and I think the writing is ancient Numidian."

Monique sat up and turned toward him. "Oh? Can you translate it?"

"Not yet. The Tamazight language was derived from it, but it's been blended into five different dialects in the country now."

"Tamazight. That's what the Almazighs speak, right?"

"In one of the dialects, yes. There is one special script called Tifinagh that is derived from it, but few people use it these days."

Her interest piqued. "Who uses it?"

"Only the Tuaregs still do."

"The Tuaregs. Aren't they the people that live in the Sahara?"

Sami nodded, glancing over at her.

"Wasn't that what you said the man with the camel was?"

"Yes, he was dressed in the traditional Tuareg garb."

"Do you know anyone who can read the Tifinagh script?"

"As a matter of fact, I do. Nadir."

Nicole jerked her head. "Nadir? The professor you work with? The man who just showed up unexpectedly last night?"

"Yes. Strange, isn't it?"

"I'll say." She paused to let the information sink in. "But we don't want him to decipher the ring, do we?"

"I don't think so. Something's going on, and now I think he may be part of it."

Nicole blew out a frustrated breath. "Is there anyone in this country you can trust?"

Sami laughed. "Let me think…"

She slapped him playfully on the arm. "Surely there's someone else who knows how to interpret the language."

"There is. I just have to find the right someone."

Sami glanced in his rear-view mirror and frowned.

"What is it? Are we being followed?"

"I don't know, but it's possible."

Nicole twisted left, then right in her seat, trying to see behind them.

"You told Nadir where we were going, didn't you?"

Slowly nodding his head, Sami said, "I did."

"Oh no. Now what? Can we change our plans?"

"Not now. Look, I don't think anyone wants to hurt you. There must be a reasonable explanation," Sami said. But he didn't sound very convincing.

"Is there someone you could report this…this harassment to? Like police or something?"

"What would I report? Who would I say is doing it? We don't know."

"Lord, please keep us safe," Nicole said. Sami didn't seem as concerned as she thought he should be, but who else could help in this situation?

Sami patted her arm. "Yes, praying is a good idea. So let's not worry, okay?" The black car that was behind them zoomed past. "See, that car isn't following us. It just wanted to get around us."

Nicole didn't know cars that well, but it sure looked like the one that had followed them before. But maybe the presumed threat was gone. Now, if she could just relax. The road was flanked by rolling hills planted in rows and rows of grapevines, seemingly without end. "These fields go on forever!" she said. "I didn't know Algeria produced wine."

"Yes, it used to be a huge export crop for Algeria. It was brought here by the Spanish in the 1700's, but the French were the ones who really cultivated it. In fact, in the 1930's, there were almost 400,000 acres of vineyards, making

Algeria the largest prewar exporter of wine. But unfortunately, it's not what it used to be since then. After the civil war, the French left, and subsequently, there was a lot of mismanagement."

"What a shame. I haven't seen anyone here drink wine. I thought all they drink is mint tea."

Sami chuckled. As the car climbed higher, the mountains drew closer, but Nicole kept looking for suspicious cars. This trip was supposed to focus on the country's archaeology and what she could learn. She was not supposed to be the focus. If only she could talk to Mimi about the ring and find out what she knew about the inscriptions.

Chapter 20

Monique

Algiers, 1940

Meat was becoming scarce, so everyone who could, fished or bought from fishermen. The cook tried many ways to prepare the seafood, but eventually, Monique tired of it. She hated to complain, but on her next trip to the farm, she told Mr. Alexis how much she'd like to have fresh eggs.

As was his usual jovial way, he got a twinkle in his eye before he answered. "I think we can fix that problem."

When they arrived at the farm, they went to the storage cellar where he had hidden fruit and vegetables. She filled a basket with oranges, grapes, olives, and dates, then filled another with tomatoes, cucumbers, and potatoes. After gathering all she could safely carry back with her, she and one of the farm workers loaded the baskets into Mr. Alexis's truck. She climbed in to wait for him to finish his business, meanwhile trying to figure out how to get most of the food to Sarah's family.

Mr. Alexis returned with a small wooden crate and placed it behind the seat of the truck.

She thought nothing of it, but noticing his grin, she had to find out what was so funny. Her question was answered as soon as they bumped down the road when something in the box squawked.

"Mr. Alexis, is there a chicken in here?"

Laughing, he said, "Why yes, there is, as a matter of

fact. Mademoiselle Poulet is going home with you. You said you wanted eggs, yes?"

"Yes, but a chicken? How do we hide her?"

"You don't. You let her roam in your yard, but keep her fenced in so she doesn't roam too far. She is a good layer, so you'll have plenty of eggs."

Monique's mouth watered at the thought of an omelette using fresh eggs and the vegetables she had gathered. And now she would have eggs to share with Sarah. Her mind began devising ways to get them safely to her friend.

"You know we had some special visitors last week," Mr. Alexis said.

"Visitors? Who?"

"A delegation of German and French collaborators came over from Paris to investigate our alcohol production. They don't think we're making enough." He laughed. "What they don't know is we're making plenty, just not for them."

"How did you keep them from finding out?" Monique worried that Mr. Alexis would get in trouble with the Nazis.

"Underground tanks. They walked all over the fields, those important men in their suits, and didn't know they walked over the tanks."

Monique eyed Mr. Alexis, his strong, tanned arms visible in a short-sleeved shirt. She couldn't imagine him working in a business suit. "Oh my. Weren't you afraid they would be found?"

"No, I can play dumb really well. They were calculating what our production should be and told me it should be much higher."

"What did you tell them?"

"I said we'd try to do better." He pushed his straw hat

back from his forehead. "Try harder to keep our production out of the hands of the Germans, that is. Of course, that I did not say. Besides, Algeria has always been the world's largest wine producer, but now the Nazis are getting most of that!"

How advantageous it was to have a friend like Mr. Alexis. Not only did he help them, but he also did not take the pro-Nazi side of the Vichy government. He still yearned for a free French country the way it had been before and worked secretly to undermine the current regime. She was proud of him for standing up for what he believed. How many others did she know who were as well?

The realization that she was doing the same thing by getting food to the Jews surprised her. Were there people she knew who were helping the Jews, too? No one dared admit it and risk getting caught, but perhaps they could work together. Surely, Sarah knew who they were. But would she share that information with those opposing the Vichy government in danger of arrest?

Maman's introduction to Mademoiselle Poulet was a surprise, to say the least. Monique's mother covered her mouth at first sight of the chicken. "Un poulet?" A slow smile eased across her face, and then she laughed.

"Maman, now we can have fresh eggs," Monique said. It was good to see Maman laugh again. "Mademoiselle Poulet will give us fresh omelettes."

"She will lay omelettes? Now that is a very special chicken."

They all laughed, and Monique felt as if she'd won a small victory by acquiring items they needed despite the Vichy government's rationing. Drawing strength from Mr. Alexis and his efforts to defeat the enemy subversively, she was eager to do more. Her family was still respected by the French, even those who collaborated with the Nazis. No one would suspect them, especially her, the daughter of an esteemed French officer. Here in their home above the city, removed from the eye of the officials, they were safe.

Over the next few days, Mlle. Poulet fulfilled her role of providing eggs for them. Monique swooned at the first bite of omelette the cook prepared, but in the same instance was pricked by guilt that she was allowed this luxury denied to others like Sarah's family. Not only did they have omelettes, but they also boiled eggs to keep for other meals. Perhaps that would be the best way to share the eggs with Sarah, since unboiled eggs would easily crack. She shared her plan with Maman, who agreed but warned her to be cautious. Once they had accumulated a supply of the boiled eggs in the refrigerator, she would take them to Sarah.

When they had a dozen, she wrapped the eggs in a colorful scarf and tucked the scarf in her backpack among a few books. She tossed in a couple of oranges as well, which shouldn't be suspicious since they could be a snack for her. A thought occurred to her that the guards might enjoy an orange too, so she packed more to share. She remembered Papá saying to "keep your friends close and your enemies closer." She'd only thought that referred to classmates, but she'd never had any real enemies before the war. Now she saw the wisdom of that practice. If she were asked to stop and show her identification, she'd offer oranges to the guards.

Her bike ride down the hill was uneventful until she reached a street that led into the Casbah where two guards stood post. One raised his hand to stop, so she did. She did not recognize this guard. Was he new to the city? Had the Germans sent more troops to their area?

She sucked in a deep breath, telling herself to remain calm and praying silently for strength.

The new guard extended his hand. "Papers."

Not even a "please"? At least the other guards were polite and liked to flirt with her. This new guard wore a no-nonsense frown.

She handed him her identification papers, which she kept in her pocket to avoid opening her backpack.

He studied them, then looked up at her. "Where are you going?"

"I am a student at the university. I'm going to my classes." She fought to keep her voice steady, although uncomfortable with his probing eyes. She was, in fact, telling the truth. She was just taking a detour on the way.

"Why do you want to go through the Casbah? The university is on the other side."

"It is a shortcut and out of traffic."

"A shortcut? With all the twists and turns? "

She shrugged. "I've just always gone this way. I rather enjoy it."

He scanned her and her bike, settling on her backpack. "What is in your backpack?"

A tremor of fear raced through her. "My books, of course. And a couple of oranges in case I get hungry. Would you like one? They're very good."

He frowned. "Are you trying to bribe an officer?"

Shocked by the question, Nicole felt her grip on the handlebars of her bike loosen as her palms sweated. She glanced at the other guard, one she was slightly more familiar with, in a silent plea for help.

Her heart raced. "Why no, why would I do that?"

The other guard stepped forward and extended his hand. "Mademoiselle always has the most delicious oranges. I have enjoyed them myself."

The intimidating guard glanced at him, his attention averted from her. "Is that so?" Now Monique was afraid she had put the nice guard in trouble.

"Yes. Hans, it's just an orange. You should try one."

Monique grabbed her backpack and quickly retrieved two oranges, extending them to the guards.

The nice guard took one, but the other guard hesitated.

"Where did you get these?"

"We have an orange tree in our yard." She hadn't really answered his question, since the orange tree in their yard didn't produce as many as she got from the farm outside of town, but she hadn't really lied either. They did, in fact, have a tree in their yard.

Finally, he took an orange, and she closed the backpack and pushed it behind her.

He nodded, lifting the orange as if thanking her. "You may go."

She smiled, sending a thank-you through her gaze at the nice guard. Then she proceeded through the Casbah, but took a circuitous route in case anyone watched her before going to Sarah's house. Her pulse raced, her hands sweaty on the handlebars of the bike, as she rode, trying not to look over her shoulder in case the guards changed their minds.

Sarah opened the door and pulled her in. "Were you followed?"

"I don't think so." She didn't want to share her

encounter with the new guard and frighten Sarah even more. "I brought you a surprise." Monique opened her backpack and unwrapped the scarf, revealing the eggs.

Sarah reached with both hands. "Eggs?"

Monique told her about the chicken. "They had to be boiled, because I was afraid they wouldn't make it if they weren't."

"Oh, I am so thankful for these. We will enjoy them so." She paused. "Do you know if they are kosher?"

Kosher? Monique hadn't thought of that. To be kosher, the chicken was supposed to be blessed by a rabbi.

Sarah's father appeared in the doorway. "I'm sure God, king of the universe, has blessed those eggs, and He is greater than a rabbi." He smiled and nodded toward the eggs. "Perhaps the hen is a Jew too?

Monique smiled too, happy to see her gift was received.

"Sarah, there must be others who are helping you and your friends. I cannot do enough for so many. Do I know any of them? Perhaps we could work together."

Sarah glanced at her father. "We dare not speak their names and put them in danger, even though I know you mean well."

"We will let the others know what you suggested, and if they want to, they will contact you."

"All right. That's fair." She turned to leave when Sarah's eleven-year-old brother burst in the door.

Panting, he leaned over to catch his breath. Sarah rushed over to him, bending over with her hand on his back. "Levi! Are you okay? What is wrong?"

With tears in his eyes and trembling, he said, "It's Isaac. They've arrested him."

Sarah covered her mouth, hearing the news about Sarah's brother. "No." She plopped down in the closest chair.

Panic gripped Monique. "Why? What did he do?"

"The police said he was a subversive," Levi sobbed. "What does that mean?"

"It means he is accused of working against the government," Sarah's father said as he entered the room. "He didn't have to do anything to get arrested for that. Just the fact that he is Jewish is excuse enough for them, but they call it something else."

"What will they do with him?" Monique asked.

"He'll be sent to the labor camp at the edge of the desert. He is considered a political prisoner."

"But can't we get him out? Will he go to a trial?"

Mr. Cohen shook his head. "There is no trial for Jews. The only way he'll get out is for the war to be over and the Allies to win. We can only pray that happens soon."

Monique looked from one of Sarah's family members to another. She was so out of place because she wasn't Jewish and would not suffer as they did. What could she do for them? "I'm so sorry," was all she could say.

"You'd better be careful, Monique. They are watching the houses of the Jews. If you're caught here, you could be arrested for helping us. You know that is a crime, don't you?" Mr. Cohen said. At that moment, Mrs. Cohen walked into the room.

"What is it? What has happened?" She looked from one to another. "Where is Isaac?"

Their solemn faces answered her, and she collapsed against her husband, moaning.

Monique quietly walked to the door and left. A few boiled eggs would not solve this situation.

Chapter 21

Audrey

England, 1940

The summer night was moonless as their ship pulled out of the Liverpool docks, the ship's lights out as German planes swept in overhead to pelt them with gunfire. Confined to quarters below deck with a blackout enforced, Audrey, along with nine other nurses, was assigned to an unarmed Dutch liner. Their ship would join the sister ship, which carried a thousand men of the French Foreign Legion.

They flew the flag of the new Free French, the tricolor of France, and the Dutch flag. General de Gaulle was onboard, along with his advisers and several British liaison officers, including Major General Sir Edward Spears, Churchill's personal representative. Ahead and behind them was a fleet of some thirty ships of various types.

Accompanying the ship was a fleet of British ships. Altogether, the combined forces totaled more than 1500 men making their way to West Africa to convince the Vichy

French in the area to join them against the Germans.

Of the ten nurses, six were English, and the others were either Belgian or French. Audrey made friends with the English head nurse, a young French nurse, and a Belgian nurse. The journey took several weeks because they had to detour to avoid German U-boats and aircraft. Two days into the trip, they were all lined up to be formally introduced to de Gaulle, who greeted them with a stiff, but courteous smile, a firm handshake, and a steel gaze.

Across the room, one of the French officers stood at attention, watching the scene. He was tall with dark hair and incredibly handsome. When his gaze met hers, her face heated. Had he known she was admiring him? He smiled, and she couldn't help but smile back. After the general and his entourage left the room, those remaining were invited to enjoy the refreshments. Audrey approached the table while speaking to one of the other nurses. As she reached for a plate, someone handed her one. "May I be of service?"

Audrey looked up and found herself face to face with the officer she'd noticed before. "Thank you," she said.

"You are welcome. You speak French, but I detect another accent. Are you British?"

She nodded. "I confess." Smiling, she said, "But can we still be friends?"

He laughed out loud. "Absolutely. My name is Phillippe Fontaine."

"I'm Audrey Reynolds. I am from England, but I have spent many years in France."

"I think I've heard of you." He paused and studied her, causing her pulse to quicken.

"You have?" She moved on down the food line, taking

a small sample of each dish.

"Ah, I think I know. Did you play tennis?"

Audrey was shocked to discover he followed women's tennis. "Yes, I did."

"I was at one of your tournaments. You play very well."

Blushing, she said, "Thank you. Do you play?"

He selected some food. "I do. Or did. It's been a few years."

At the end of the line, he motioned to one of the tables. "Would you join me?"

She nodded, and they sat at a large table where four other people were seated. Audrey wished they could sit alone so she could learn more about this man. But as it turned out, they only spoke to each other at the table, and she soon forgot anyone else was there. They shared a delightful rapport, more so than any conversation she could remember with a man. He had no ring on, but he must have a girlfriend somewhere. But they didn't discuss that, so she was left to dream. Even though she knew they would soon part ways, she would remember tonight as the highlight of the trip.

The ship stopped at the British naval base of Freetown in Sierra Leone for a week before moving on to Dakar. Two days later at dawn and in the middle of thick fog, they found themselves a quarter of a mile from the target. The nurses had been ordered to stay below, ready to disembark at all times. Looking through the portholes, Audrey could see nothing. That evening de Gaulle broadcast a rally call for the French-speaking people of Dakar while British and French planes swooped in to drop propaganda leaflets. He then sent a delegation of three officers in two small, unarmed planes. Those officers were arrested on landing.

Next, de Gaulle sent another delegation of five officers by motor launch bearing a white flag. The French governor-general made it clear he had no intention of cooperating with the Free French. On landing, the officers were threatened with arrest for treason against the Vichy Government and fired on by machine guns, so they fled. Two of the officers were seriously injured and were carried into the dining room, which was the makeshift sick bay. While the ship was being fired upon, Audrey and the other nurses set to work bandaging and tending their wounds.

"What is your name?" one of the officers asked her as he squeezed her hand, his face pale.

"Audrey," she said, mopping his sweating brow while darting glances toward the porthole.

"Don't be afraid, Audrey," he said. "They are just bluffing."

The bluff went on for a very long time, but the Free French ship did not return fire and instead sent a message to the city asking them to stop the attack. They replied with more shelling, so Audrey's ship opened fire as well. The men on the ship regretted having to fire on their fellow countrymen. After more damage to the Free French ships and the British ships, de Gaulle ordered them to cease fire and return to Freetown, a small town on the shore of Sierra Leone. De Gaulle was gravely disappointed, but the troops still supported him.

In Freetown, the nurses visited the sole, dirty hotel where they ate unpalatable food served with rice. Due to the unbearable heat, the women sought respite by swimming in the sea. For Audrey, the ordeal meant a huge adjustment. Living in a cramped room on board with two other women in the terrible heat and without the luxuries she had enjoyed in her previous life, Audrey had never been so uncomfortable.

Strolling through the town, Audrey had the chance to study the Legionnaires, the men who were her allies. They were all very handsome and confident, despite the recent setback. Availing herself of some local mangoes, she wandered among the soldiers, offering mangoes, while admiring their patriotism and perseverance as they discussed de Gaulle and their belief that he would succeed in freeing France of its enemies. Seeing their commitment sparked an attitude of pride in herself as part of their joint effort.

Thankfully, Churchill continued to support de Gaulle's efforts publicly but withdrew the British fleet after they arrived at the next port in French Cameroon. The French colonists, natives, and troops gave them an exciting welcome, providing the needed encouragement for de Gaulle to press on. Much as Audrey wanted to accompany the troops, the nurses were held back out of danger before being sent on to a remote town in the Congo with five other nurses to set up a hospital.

The town was one of the most inhospitable places Audrey had ever been. The homes and gardens appeared to be neglected, and the local colonists were mainly pro-Vichy and anti-English. They didn't appear to like each other either, with the social orders divided into cliques. The marketplace was, oddly enough, run by Portuguese and Syrians, and in the stalls one could find an unusual mix of goods and foods such as coconuts, bananas, and smoked catfish, among other strange items Audrey could not identify, so she steered clear of them.

In addition to the unfriendly people, there were no roads, so boats ran through mangrove swamps, sometimes running out of gas and needing to be towed out. To her dismay, Audrey and the nurses were assigned to a humble clinic for mothers and their babies in the poorest section of town. She was shocked by the inferior dispensary available to the natives as compared to the fully stocked and pristine clinics for the colonists. She and two of the nurses shared a bungalow, which Audrey was certain was the only thing that preserved their sanity.

Audrey had never been so hot, and despite storm clouds gathering each day, rain did not come, only lightning and thunder. The local witch doctors did their best to provoke the African spirits to make it rain as well, but the spirits would not comply. The only respite was to swim in the beer-colored Congo River among the water hyacinths, avoiding the large hippopotami glaring at them from the opposite bank. The water cooled them, but unfortunately, once their skin was exposed to the air, swarms of mosquitoes attacked, so much so that they could not sleep at night due to itching. As a result, they gave up swimming.

When the rains did come, the water clattered on the tin roof day and night, but it was still hot. Along with the rain came unwelcome guests into the shelter of the house. Goats and chickens, geckoes, snakes, and other creepy-crawlers decided to move in with them. Audrey thought she would go insane; she was so distracted by how uncomfortable her surroundings were. At the clinic, she spent her time treating infected insect bites on the children, an unending, hopeless chore.

Within two weeks, two of the nurses were ready to quit,

so when a British official arrived looking for girls who could type, they jumped at the chance, preferring clerical work in an office with a fan to being a nanny in the middle of the jungle. Audrey couldn't type, so she couldn't avail herself of the opportunity. She bought a grey parrot she named General from a child in the market, and it became her only friend. After a while, she couldn't stand the boredom of her situation anymore, so she went to see the French Inspector General of the town and asked if there was any way she could rejoin the Free French troops.

"I don't know what they'll be doing or where they're going, but I want to be with them wherever the war is," she told him.

He initially shook his head, his hands clasped on the desk. "It is too dangerous for women."

But she was persistent. She had to get out of this dismal place and return to where the action was. "It is dangerous here, but in a different way. I need to be with the soldiers."

He sighed. "Very well. I see you are a determined woman. They may not take you, but there is a boat coming with supplies for the brigade. Perhaps you can get on the boat to where the troops are." He signed the papers and waved her off with a smile, seeming to be happy to be rid of her.

Her fellow nurses were shocked to learn of what she planned to do and tried to talk her out of it, but she would not listen. She fully intended to be with the army because that was what she came to do.

Leaving her parrot with one of the local staffers in the clinic, Audrey began a month-long, arduous journey on a grimy cargo ship. When the ship stopped at the port of Durban, she was thrilled to see a troop ship pull into the port.

Receiving permission to join the troop ship, she had never been so happy to see familiar faces in her life, as many of those onboard were the Legionnaires she'd traveled with before. Audrey was delighted to learn she also knew the other four nurses she'd be working and bunking with. She couldn't be happier to be back where she thought she belonged.

Sleeping was difficult due to the blackout curtains and the inability to open the portholes for some air. Waking every night in a sweat, Audrey decided to sleep on the deck in the open air instead. Each morning, when she was awakened at sunrise by the sailors cleaning the deck, she'd scramble back to her room for a shower before breakfast.

The only people the nurses treated suffered from seasickness, so her medical knowledge was not tested, for which she was thankful. And the young military men who were their patients were always appreciative of their efforts. She admired in particular the way the officers handled themselves. They were from various backgrounds— Belgium, France, and one from Russia—but they were all handsome in their own way, and each was polite, friendly, and impeccable in their uniforms. It wasn't a surprise that each of the nurses ended up in romantic involvements with them.

Audrey liked them all, but she wasn't vying for attention. She could appreciate them from a distance, respecting their authority. Lieutenant Colonel Cantrell was the only officer onboard that was not attractive. In addition to his wearing a perpetual frown with his dark bushy eyebrows knit together like the V on an owl's face, he had foul breath and a habit of belching. He never had anything positive to say either, so everyone tried to avoid him. Unfortunately, he developed some type of interest in Audrey. At night after dinner, the crew, officers, and nurses would play card games, bridge being the favorite. Audrey had learned the game from an early age, one of the few "fun" things her family did together. At home, the game was very competitive as she, her brother, father, and mother tried to best each other; therefore, it didn't take long for her shipmates to notice her prowess in bridge.

Lieutenant Colonel Cantrell always managed to interject himself in the game Audrey was playing, sneering at her every move. If he was supposed to be flirting, Audrey didn't feel it. However, his constant presence made her want to slip out. She just couldn't figure out his interest in her. Perhaps it was because she was the only British nurse among the predominantly French population of the ship, and he, like many Frenchmen, did not like the British.

On their final night onboard the ship, Cantrell changed the mood of the evening by mentioning the dangers they would soon face. He was seated beside Audrey and announced the fact that they would be entering a dangerous area, closer to the conflict, a fact that everyone knew was inevitable. He said that since Italy, Germany, and Britain were all vying for success in the Mediterranean, North Africa would soon become a hotspot of activity. Germany's Major General Rommel was leading a specially trained force in desert warfare into Tripoli, increasing the threat of future conflict. Called upon to be an interpreter between Cantrell and the captain, Audrey was trapped at the table.

As if determined to ruin her day, Cantrell turned to her. "I've been advised that you might not be allowed to continue with the Legionnaires."

Audrey couldn't sleep that night and lay awake wondering how to sneak ashore.

Chapter 22

Nicole

Algeria, 2019

The high walls of the archaeological site caught Nicole's attention from miles away. As the car approached the area, she was amazed at how large the site was.

"How far did you say those walls go?" She shielded her eyes to look up at where they ran along the mountain base.

"Four miles," Sami said. "They're part of the fortifications, which is why some people refer to this place as a 'fort.'" He drove into the site along roads between a vast array of building foundations.

"Wow. I've never seen anything like that." She lifted her phone to snap a picture.

As she turned her head the other direction, she saw a tall rectangular tower. "What is that?"

"A minaret. It's a little over seven stories tall and was part of the mosque that was here. From what we can tell, this was the largest mosque built in North Africa before the twentieth century."

"Fascinating." She took a picture of the minaret.

"Seems to be made of stucco and bricks."

"That's right, like most of the structures around here. Some of the residences contained marble as well. He drove around the area, pointing out various places archaeologists had identified before stopping in front of one. "We have found evidence of five palaces built for the emirs who ruled this area."

He climbed out of the car, and she followed suit. They walked along a path between sections that Sami pointed out as rooms of a former palace.

"Is that a fountain?" Nicole pointed to a mosaic-covered object.

"It is. There are several. Situated here at the foot of the mountains, they were able to have water running downhill."

"Interesting." Nicole looked around the area and noticed a few cars scattered throughout with people strolling around the ruins. "Are those tourists or students?"

"Tourists. As a World Heritage Site, it's on travel itineraries for those who want to see the whole country. However, due to its remote location, it is not visited nearly as much as the sites close to the cities."

She scanned the expanse of the site again, thankful she didn't see anyone suspicious, but she didn't see any students either. "Where is the dig?"

He motioned ahead, and when they turned by a wall, they found a depression where about a dozen people sat on the ground, raking through the dirt with hand trowels. Low canopies supported by poles helped to keep the hot sun off the students.

"Hey, everybody," Sami said. The students looked up. "This is Nicole. She's from the United States and will be working with us for a while."

The students smiled, and some raised their hands to wave. Nicole smiled back.

A man who looked a few years older than Sami stepped forward. He wore a head scarf wound around his head and neck, barely showing bushy black eyebrows, a mustache, and beard underneath. He pulled down on the scarf to reveal his mouth.

"So this is our graduate student from North Carolina?" He smiled at Nicole. "Welcome."

"This is Yanis. He is the director of this dig," Sami said.

Yanis waved his hand over the site. "This area is the garden of one of the palaces. It has not been excavated yet." He motioned to another area. "In another garden, we discovered a fountain, so we think there is one in here too."

"Great! Put me to work." Nicole looked at the other students, most of whom appeared to be her age. "I should go back to the car to get my backpack. I'm sorry, I didn't know we were so close to the dig. My tools and my water are in it."

"I'll go back and get it in a few minutes," Sami said. "We have extra trowels you can use in the meantime. Come." He motioned to her to follow him. They stopped by a young girl with dark olive skin and black hair in a long braid down her back. She wore a scarf over the rest of her head. She looked up and grinned. "Aisha, this is Nicole. She'll be working with you."

Aisha stood and brushed off her hands. She was shorter than Nicole, probably close to five feet tall, about the height of Mimi. "Hi. Welcome."

"Thank you. It's good to be here. So tell me what you're

working on," she said.

"Sure."

Sami said, "I'll leave you two here. I need to see what progress we've made."

As he walked away, Aisha explained to Nicole the section of the garden where she was working and what she hoped to find. "I've found some pieces of mosaics, so I hope to find what they were connected to."

Aisha sat down on the ground, and Nicole sat beside her. "How long have you been working at this site?"

Aisha handed her a pointed trowel. "Two weeks so far, but I think we plan to be here all summer. It's slow work, you know." She batted a fly away from her face.

"Yes, I know. I've been on a few other digs, but not in this country. So do you stay here the whole time? Where are you from?"

"Constantine is where my family is. It is about a three-and-a-half-hour drive from here. We are free to go home on the weekends if we want or we can stay here. Most of the time, we want to go home, though, to get some good food and take a shower."

Nicole smiled, liking Aisha right away. "I can understand that. I think I would too."

Aisha used her hands to lift a small pile of dirt and placed it on a sieve that covered a bucket. She carefully ran her hand over the dirt to make sure she hadn't missed something.

Nicole carefully poked holes in the ground, watching for anything that wasn't part of the dirt. "Is Sami your professor at college?"

Aisha nodded. "He's one of them, probably the nicest."

She lowered her voice. "And all the girls have crushes on him."

Nicole felt a blush, since she might be classified with those girls, too. "I'm not surprised," she said. "My college professors didn't look anything like him."

Aisha giggled. "Yanis is nice, too. But he's older. And married. And not nearly as handsome as Sami."

Nicole needed to move the conversation away from Sami. "So where do you stay out here?" Nicole glanced around.

Aisha pointed toward the high walls of the city. "Over there by the walls. We have tents."

"I'm sure you're glad to have company out here. It might be a little spooky by yourself," Nicole said.

"Spooky? What does that mean?" Apparently, spooky wasn't a word usually taught in English classes here.

"Scary, frightening."

"Oh yes. No, I wouldn't want to be here by myself. The university makes sure we are safe on our digs. There are always at least two professors with us. And we have equal numbers of girls and boys so we can have tent-mates."

"Are there any wild animals out here?"

"Not too often. People have scared them away. There are jackals, gazelles, and wild boars that live around here, but they pretty much stay away from people."

"Wild boars? They can be pretty dangerous. We used to have them in the woods back home, and I've heard of them attacking people," Nicole said.

"The professors carry guns for a reason."

Guns? She'd feel safe if she could trust whoever had the gun. But she wasn't sure she would trust Nadir, if he was with them. "At least they wouldn't be shooting at people," she said.

Aisha eyed her curiously. "Hopefully not. But there's always a threat of thieves in remote areas like this. Even though the valuables like jewelry and gold that were found here have been moved to a museum in the city, there's still a chance we'll find something else valuable and word travels fast, you know. Plus, there's the risk of kidnapping."

Nicole jerked her head to look at Aisha. "Kidnappers?"

"Yeah. They usually kidnap tourists who are dumb enough to travel alone."

Sami walked up, a serious expression on his face. Something was wrong.

"What?"

He ran his fingers through his hair. "I went back to the car to get your backpack, but it's gone. They stole it from the trunk, got it open somehow."

Nicole scrambled to her feet while Aisha glanced wide-eyed at Sami, then at Nicole. "Why would anyone do that?"

Sami shrugged but sent a knowing look to Nicole. "Someone intent on looking for valuables, I suppose."

"I haven't heard of anything like that happening around here lately," Aisha said.

"It's rare, I admit, but there are thieves everywhere." He looked at Nicole, who was still trying to wrap her head around his announcement. "Too bad we don't have cameras installed here like they have at other UNESCO sites."

Nicole found her voice. "Sami, I need those things. My clothes, everything."

"Everything?" He raised his eyebrows. "Nothing very valuable, I hope."

Nicole knew he was referring to the ring.

"Valuable to me." She thought he knew the ring wasn't in the backpack. Still, another invasion of her privacy was unwelcome, not to mention annoying. Something had to be done. Whoever was tracking her had to be stopped.

Sami motioned to her. "Come with me. Let's tell Yanis, then we'll go find the site manager and report it to him."

"Aisha, I'm sorry. I'll be back. Don't discover anything cool before I get back," Nicole said, smiling.

Nicole joined Sami. "Wait here," he said, then jogged over to Yanis. In a few moments, Sami came back to her. They walked far enough away to put hearing distance between them and the students. Nicole placed her hands on her hips. "Sami, this is ridiculous. We've got to stop them."

"I know. I have an idea."

"What's that?"

"We can let them find the ring."

"What? No way!"

"Not the real ring. I'll find one that's similar, and we'll let them steal it. That should keep them away for a while."

"Okay…how will that work?"

"I haven't figured that part out yet. But I'll come up with something." He glanced around. "But we do need to report it just in case it's a random thief looking for something to steal."

They returned to the car and drove over to the small office near the entrance. Inside, they told the lone manager about the theft.

"Haven't had anything like that reported lately." He looked at Nicole. "Can you describe the backpack and the contents?"

She nodded. "Yes." She listed everything she'd put in the backpack.

He wrote it down, folded his hands on top of the paper, then looked up. "I can't promise anything, but we might find something on camera."

"You have one?" Sami asked.

"We do. There's one on top of the minaret that scans the area. If you're lucky, it might've caught something."

"Please let me know if you do," Sami said.

Once outside, Sami said, "I didn't realize they had a camera. Let's hope and pray it shows something."

A dark-haired boy around the age of ten ran up to the building carrying a backpack.

"Hey, that's mine!" Nicole said, pointing to it.

The boy looked confused. "It is? I just found it over there. I was going to turn it in to the manager."

"We'll go in with you," Sami said.

The boy entered the building with Sami and Nicole following. He handed the backpack to the manager. "I found it, but I didn't take it."

"Where did you find it?"

"I'll show you."

They all followed the boy outside, and he pointed to the location. "Let's see what else is there," the manager said.

"There was some stuff on the ground by it, but I didn't touch it. Looked like girl stuff."

Several "streets" away from the manager's building, he showed them where he found the backpack, and sure enough, there were Nicole's belongings. The manager handed the backpack to Nicole. She bent down and picked up each item, shaking the dust from it before putting it back into her bag.

"You can take it," the manager said. He turned to face the boy. "Did you see anyone near it before you found it?"

The boy twisted his mouth and frowned. "Well, maybe. I mean, I was a ways off, but I did see a guy run that way." He pointed in the opposite direction.

"What did he look like?"

The boy shrugged. "Nothing special, regular pants and shirt, but he was wearing a keffiyeh."

Nicole looked at Sami for an explanation.

"A headscarf," he said, using his hands in a motion around his head to describe it.

"What color was the keffiyeh?" Sami asked, looking at the boy.

"Red and white, like the Bedouins wear," the boy said. "That's all I remember."

"All right. Thank you for being honest," the manager said.

The boy looked from one person to the other, as if expecting something. Sami dug into his pants pocket and pulled out some coins. Handing them to the boy, he said, "You did the right thing."

The boy smiled and ran off. They watched him until he was united with a group of Arab tourists.

"Well, that's that," the manager said, turning to go back into his office. "Glad you got your bag back."

"Thank you for your help," Sami said. "And if you do get anything on camera, please let me know. I'd like to know how he got here—car, etc. "

"What's the point? You have what you lost," the manager said.

"True, but we need to know if he's related to another theft we experienced this week."

"I see. Well, then, I'll take a look."

Sami gave the man his card. "You can reach me here. I'm a professor at the university."

"You're over the dig here?"

"I am. Are the students behaving themselves?"

"They are. I never have a problem with the ones from the University of Algeria. Other groups?" He shrugged, then went back inside.

"Are you missing anything?" Sami nodded to the backpack.

"Doesn't look like it. I think he rummaged through it quickly and tossed everything on the ground when he didn't find what he was looking for."

They climbed into the car and drove back to where the dig was. "I wouldn't mention the ring to anyone," Sami said.

Nicole frowned. "As if I would. I still don't trust anybody here. Remember?" When they reached the dig, they got out of the car and began walking back to the place Aisha worked. "I'm just glad I don't have to worry about my backpack being stolen again,"

"Not here, at least."

"So we can sleep better tonight, thank God."

Sami paused, stroking his chin. "But if they know the ring wasn't in the backpack, and they think you still have it…"

"They might still come after me?" Uneasiness crawled up her back.

"I'll make sure my tent is near yours, just in case."

Chapter 23

Monique

Algiers, 1941

The next time Matazan came to the house, she asked what he knew about the place where political prisoners like Sarah's brother were sent.

"Matazan, have you seen the prison camp the police are sending people to?"

Matazan slowly nodded his head. "I have. It is not a good place."

"Tell me what it's like. Please. Isaac Cohen has been sent there." Her heart ached for Sarah's family.

"It is in the desert and is hot, very hot during the day. At night, it is very cool and there is not much to keep them warm."

"What do they do there?" Monique asked.

"They move dirt and rocks. That's all. They're supposed to be clearing the ground for a road. But I don't know what road it will be."

"Do you know anyone there?"

He looked down at the ground. "Yes, mademoiselle, I do."

"Are they Jews too?"

"Some are, some aren't."

Matazan averted his gaze, perhaps because he had friends or even family who had been sent to the prison

"Do they…they…hurt them?"

"Not much. They stand guard with guns so they won't escape. But the men there don't have enough to eat. They are starving."

Monique's heart twisted in her chest. This kind of treatment wasn't fair or deserved. "How can we help? Can we bring them food?"

Shaking his head, he said, "No, you cannot." His eyes deepened with intensity, daring her to question his stance on the subject. "And you cannot visit them either."

"So it's like the concentration camps I've heard about in Germany? How awful."

"It may not be quite as bad, just because they are not killing them outright. But they are killing them slowly."

"There must be a way to help. There has to be." Monique had stayed away from Sarah's house for a few days, hoping the house wouldn't be watched when she returned. But she was itching to bring them more food, to do something more, especially now.

"Next time you go there, do not bring anything," Matazan said.

"Not bring them anything? Why? They need food."

"But if you're stopped next time and your bag is searched, you will have nothing to incriminate you. You must do it this way for now."

Begrudgingly, she agreed. "I suppose that makes sense. But it seems like a waste of time." Was there any point in visiting them if not to help them?

"It will be better in the long run. All right?"

She nodded. Although she didn't know all Matazan did, she assumed he was helping undercover as well, so she thought she should take his advice.

When she packed her bag, she placed her books on the bottom and two oranges on top as usual, just so nothing was new if she got stopped. She climbed on her bike and headed toward the city. This time, the nice guard she was familiar with wasn't at the checkpoint. Instead, it was the grumpy guard and another guard she did not recognize, but his emotionless face was as frightening as the grumpy guard's.

When they made her halt, they asked for her papers as usual. Grunting as he looked at them, Grumpy Guard number two said, "What's in the backpack?"

"Books. I'm a student."

He extended his hand. "Give it to me."

Surprised by his curtness, she did as he requested. He unzipped the bag and rummaged through it. He held up an orange.

"What is this?"

She bit her tongue to keep from saying something sarcastic like, "It's an apple." Instead, she forced a smile. "My snack. I get hungry at school. But you can have it if you'd like."

"You dare to bribe me?" He practically yelled at her, and several passersby looked over at them.

She cringed but tried to stay calm. Now she knew what it felt like to be interrogated, especially when doing nothing wrong. "Why no, I'm just trying to be nice, the way my parents taught me." She glanced at the other guard, who had taken an orange from her last time, but his expression was stoic.

The guard huffed, then handed the orange back to her. "Why do you go this way? It is more difficult."

She shrugged, trying to hide her shaking. "It is a habit, and I enjoy going through the Casbah. Always have, since I was a child."

"Well, this time, you go around it."

She tried not to glare at him, even though she wanted to. Thank God, she had not packed anything for Sarah's family this time. Matazan must have known the guards were getting more difficult. She complied with his command and went around the Casbah to get to the university. But she didn't plan to return that way. Was there some reason the guards did not want her in the Casbah?

After she got out of class, she went to the other side of the Casbah to go through it. If there was something going on, she had to find out what it was. She'd heard about roundups of Jewish people in Nazi-occupied countries. *Please, Lord, don't let them do that here.* She carefully rode or pushed her bike through the dark alleys, feeling so much darker now. Pausing at an intersection, she looked both ways to make sure there weren't any guards nearby.

Without warning, a strong hand covered her face. Her heart leaped to her throat.

"Do not make a noise," a male voice whispered in her ear.

She nodded her head to show compliance while her body trembled from fear.

"We heard you were looking for a contact to work with to help us."

She nodded again.

"Good. I trust you know the dangers. I will tell Matazan to include you in the work. Do not do anything we do not ask you to do, and do not tell anyone what you are doing. Do you understand?"

She nodded.

The hand moved away from her mouth, and she didn't hear another word. After a few minutes, she took some breaths to slow her heart, then looked around. No one could be seen. But now she knew two things. Matazan was involved in the resistance, and now so was she. She hurried home, eager to find Matazan.

"Maman, where is Matazan?"

"I don't know, but we need to talk. Sit down."

The look on Maman's face was hard to read, but she was serious. Had something happened to Matazan? Someone else she knew?

Monique took a seat on the sofa. "What is it, Maman?"

Maman sat beside her and studied her hands before glancing up at Monique. Her voice trembling, she said, "We have to move."

Monique gasped. "Move? Where? Why?"

Maman's tone seethed with anger when she answered. "Apparently, one of the new Vichy officials wants our house. With your father gone, we are no longer officially connected to the government and don't deserve such a nice house."

"Can they do that? Can they take away our house? I won't let them!"

"Monique, there's nothing we can do about it. Your father owned this house, and it belongs to us. But we cannot fight the Vichy government. We will be considered subversive.”

“But where will we go?”

“They said we will have a nice apartment in the city.”

An apartment in the city? No trees? No lush green gardens? This couldn’t be happening.

“What about our things? Can we take them with us? Will our furniture even fit in an apartment?”

“I guess it depends on how large the apartment is. Look, the official who wants our house does not know everything we have. We can take what we need and find someone to keep the other things for us until we can find a larger place.”

“Or move back.”

“Or move back.”

“How soon do we have to leave?”

“They said we have a week.”

“A week? That’s impossible. How can we move that quickly?”

“They said they’d help us. But I think we need to hurry and get our large furniture out of here before the official sees it and decides he wants to keep it. I have contacted Mr. Alexis, and he will bring a truck tomorrow with some workers from the farm. Matazan will help as well. Mr. Alexis said he can hide the furniture somewhere on the farm.”

“Let’s go through the house and decide what to take and what to send away.”

“Will we get to see the apartment first?”

“Not before tomorrow morning. However, Matazan said he is familiar with those apartments, and they’re pretty nice, but smaller than our home, so he can advise us on what to take."

"And what of Minette? And Mademoiselle Poulette?"

"We will take them with us."

"Where will we keep the chicken?"

"On the balcony. We can put her in a cage out there and feed her chicken feed from the farm. She might not like not being able to roam freely, but she'll adjust. At least, Mr. Alexis says she will."

"Oh, Maman." Monique stood and looked around her home. She must be in a bad dream. This was her home, where she'd lived all her life. And she had to move because some Nazi wanted her house? So this was what Sarah's family was faced with every day. However, when the Jews were forced out, they weren't given a nice place to move. Maman stood by her and wrapped her arm around Monique. Monique leaned against her mother, fearing her legs would not support her otherwise.

"It will be all right, Monique. The Lord will take care of us."

Would he? Or had he decided they weren't important anymore either?

"Monique, many people are suffering much worse right now. We can make the best of this. We have to."

Monique nodded. Maman was right. They would manage.

"Who told you we had to move, Maman? Was it someone we know?"

A look of regret passed over Maman's face. "Yes, Captain Lefevre."

"Captain Lefevre was a friend of Papá's! How could he do this?"

"I don't think he had a choice, Monique. He was following orders. But I think he regretted it. He apologized and told me he had selected a fine apartment for us. In fact, he said it would be on the top floor of the building."

A million thoughts ran through Monique's mind. How was she going to ride her bike on the same route she had before so she could visit Sarah? Now, more people would see her coming and going. How would Mr. Alexis be able to help them?

"Will Madam Bouton still be our cook?"

"I do not think so. They do not think the two of us need a cook, but the official taking over the house does need one. After all, we are women and should know how to prepare food for ourselves." Maman's tone bordered on sarcasm. "Besides, we won't be throwing any parties."

How could Maman make light of the situation? But Maman was strong, and Monique needed to be strong as well.

"And Matazan? Will he still work for us?"

Maman slowly shook her head. "Not officially." She placed her hand on Monique's arm. "But he will always help us however he can, officially or not. He is devoted to us, especially to you. He's practically raised you!" Maman smiled. "Or at least, he's been your guardian your entire life. He can't let you out of his sight for long, you know."

Monique's heart was so heavy watching her whole world turn upside down. Remembering the message she'd received earlier that night, Matazan was working for the resistance, and he would be her contact. Somehow, he would advise her on what to do. And now, she was more determined than ever to do whatever she could to undermine this awful government that was controlling their country. If she could only protect Matazan. He was risking his life for her and for the Jews, and he was neither French nor Jewish.

If she could only talk to Audrey. Where was she now? Monique had received a cryptic telegram a month ago that her friend had joined the nurses traveling with an old friend of Monique's father, one she'd seen at the funeral. It was obvious Audrey could not say where she was going or who the friend was, but she'd guessed it was de Gaulle. The government-controlled radio station had reported some of de Gaulle's actions but condemned him as a traitor. Knowing how much Audrey admired the man, Monique would not be surprised to know Audrey had joined the Free French, as his anti-Nazi army was called. Monique's heart swelled at the realization that now she and Audrey were joined in their effort to resist the Nazi regime.

Chapter 24

Audrey

North Africa, 1941

Landing at a port on the Red Sea, Audrey was relieved to find that nobody in the harbor gave them a hard time for having women on board. They disembarked, then took a train to a town to set up camp. The camp was on a plateau above a typical Arab village with a Greek restaurant. Audrey was bored with the lack of activity. No one was sick, so there was no work to do. They lived a primitive lifestyle in tents with no amenities and had to wash their things in the nearby sea.

Audrey discovered the British disliked the Legionnaires, based on their reputation for being mercenaries instead of patriotic soldiers. Many of the Legionnaires were from countries besides France, like Hungarians, Russians, and Turks. Despite their reputations, Audrey found the men very interesting and fun to be around. Since she looked like one of them with her short hair and uniform, she was treated disdainfully like they were, especially since she spoke in French most of the time, not revealing her British origin. She chuckled under her breath when she thought of how differently she'd be treated if she were at a party in her grandmother's mansion.

Unfortunately, one of the side effects of the British treatment was that they had assumed command of the area and gave the Legionnaires very little to do. Audrey was relieved when the British left and moved on, replaced by some men from a native tribe who arrived with their witch doctors in tow. Thankfully, the French chief medical officer, Dr. Andre Venet came with them.

Dr. Venet was bald, short, and chubby, but friendly. Audrey's role changed when she discovered he needed a chauffeur. The doctor couldn't drive, nor could his orderly, and all the other drivers were tied up with other vehicles. She was appointed the position of chauffeur out of sheer need, despite the fact that she was female. Finally, she had a real job, in her opinion. Sadly, the 1938 Humber she was given to drive was the only vehicle available, so she had to learn how to work on it to keep it running. Some of the accompanying troops made fun of her and insinuated that she and the doctor were involved romantically, but she scoffed and ignored them. She couldn't have been in a less romantic situation with a less romantic man.

When it was time to roll out so they could join the troops that had gone on ahead, her car was put in front of the convoy. Being in the front was a great advantage, as they didn't have to breathe the other cars' dust as they moved. The Humber stalled twice, but she got it restarted for the eight-hour trip. The next day, they were up before dawn to hurry and catch up, since their pay may be cut if they were late.

The road grew worse, stony and bumpy with huge dips

as she wrestled with gears. As if that weren't enough, the next part of the journey was through sand. Audrey got stuck in the sand a couple of times and had to be towed out. But Venet was gracious and did not blame her. Once they finally reached the soldiers, they were sent to their new "Home," a small hut in the middle of nowhere. Dropping off the doctor first, she got out of the car and asked where the nearest well was while brushing tons of dirt from her clothes. Finding the well five more miles, she was thankful she could drive there, where she added water to the radiator and filled her canteen.

The next morning, after six long hours, they traveled up to the high plateaus on some dangerous mountain roads, driving among noisy baboons in the trees, and they arrived at the battlefield. Gunfire sounded in the distance while the doctor and the nurses set up a field hospital. Wounded men were brought to them from various battlefronts where the Free French had joined the British, Sikhs, and Senegalese to fight the Italians. Audrey stayed by the car, nervous about the gunfire and hand grenades going off near her. She witnessed the first air drops of food and ammo as two aged Allied planes roared overhead.

Several days after arriving, she and her troop were invited to lunch at brigade headquarters. When she stepped out of her vehicle, brushing the dust off her uniform, she was greeted by a familiar smiling face, Colonel Phillippe Fontaine. "My dear Miss Reynolds. It appears that you could use a bath."

"I can think of nothing I'd enjoy more," she said.

He reached for her hand, but she drew back.

"Let me clean up before you touch me. I don't want to contaminate you."

Phillippe laughed. "Fine. I'll arrange for you to use my canvas bath. We'll hang a rug for privacy. Feel free to lie down and rest afterwards. I'm sure you are very tired."

"Thank you." How kind of him to realize how she felt. Audrey followed his orderly to the tent where the mobile bath was set up. After a glorious cleansing, she lay down on his cot and fell asleep. She had no idea how long she slept, but when she awoke, she scrambled out to find her assigned place. She didn't see Phillippe again and learned that he and his men had been sent to another part of the country. She wished he had seen her cleaned up, but duty separated them again.

Audrey was quite the spectacle in the area. Being one of the few women for miles around, her fair, freckled skin and light-colored hair attracted attention not only from her comrades, but also from the natives. They looked at her curiously and pointed. However, their opinion of her was the least of her concerns. The old car she drove was barely holding together, and she spent most of her time trying to find spare parts from the mobile machine shop. The tires were bald, and the worn seats were terribly uncomfortable.

With her job to drive the doctor to various military camps, she had to keep the car working. She drove through harrowing mountain passes, up rocky trails and across the flatlands. Occasionally, she'd run into the two nurses who were spending most of their time treating men with dysentery. She thanked her lucky stars she was no longer a nurse.

Not that her job was easy. She ran into those who didn't want her in their company because she was a woman, considered inferior by certain people, like the Chadians who fought alongside the Allies. When the doctor visited the Chad camp, she had to eat alone in a corner and was not allowed to speak because the Chad leader didn't like women and would not allow women to eat with men.

Her hands developed calluses from gripping the steering wheel of the car while traveling through the rough terrain. Driving though sand was even worse, and avoiding wheel ruts other vehicles had made was difficult. In addition, the roads were pocked with shell holes from air raids and could rip off part of the undercarriage. Plus, the ever-present danger of mines required her to drive very carefully. Too often, she had to climb out of the car and pile rocks and brush under the tires for traction.

But that car was her responsibility. Not only did she have to keep it running, but she also had to protect it from the constant risk of air raids, covering it with camouflage material or hiding it under trees. However, since the doctor was so important, she had become important too as his driver.

The car became her home as well. She often slept in it at night or rested in it during the day. The doctor knew nothing about cars and expected her to do everything related to it. Thankfully, her curiosity about how things work and her understanding of mechanical things came in handy. If she didn't know how to repair something, she'd ask another driver who would show her. As a result, she knew how to change tires, repair a radiator or a fuel tank, and replace a fan belt. Unmechanical-minded Dr. Venet never even offered to help. What could he do anyway?

Despite the doctor's lack of help, they got along well together. She and the doctor drove into the bush to look for small villages where they could set up camp ahead of the battalion to prepare for casualties. Each night, they stopped at a new encampment where Audrey would find a hole in the ground and erect her tent. The heat was insufferable during the day, but the nights were very cold, so she wore all her clothes to try to stay warm. She tried not to think of the comforts she'd given up, because she couldn't have them now, and yearning for them only made her more miserable. Maybe someday she'd enjoy those comforts again, but she wasn't the only person here who had to deal with the inhospitable situation.

The good news was that they were defeating the Italians. The bad news was that Audrey's camp was always under fire. One time, she was sitting in the Humber under a tree when one of the cooks yelled at her to move because that area was often bombarded. The whistling of an incoming shell made her jump from the car and run as fast as she could before diving into the ground and covering her head with her hands. When the dust settled, all around her were craters and destruction. A warm trickle ran down her leg, and she realized she was bleeding. She applied first aid, but the next day, the leg was infected, and she developed a fever. She mustered the energy to go to the hospital, where one of the doctors pulled a large piece of shrapnel from her leg.

When the Italians finally surrendered and were taken prisoner, Audrey and the Free French army took some time to relax. They moved their camp beside the Mediterranean, where they swam and enjoyed the atmosphere, the sea life, the pelicans, and the dolphins. When it was time for everyone to leave, Audrey looked forward to being on the ship with all the officers again. Unfortunately, Phillippe was not on that ship, which was a slight disappointment, and she didn't know where he was. If he had been injured or killed, surely she would have heard about it.

She and the doctor, the old Humber, two ambulances, and the nurses were loaded onto another ship for their next assignment. Audrey was happy to get a large private room and begged the cook for an omelet. As she lay down in the bed that night, relishing the comfort of a real bed, she recalled the last few months and how isolated she'd been as the only woman assigned to military duty. Her role distanced her from the men as well as the few other women who were nurses. But she'd gotten used to being alone. In fact, there were a few people she wanted to spend a lot of time with.

Monique came to mind. What was she doing now? Audrey envisioned her at the house on the hill in Algiers, and she missed her and wished they could talk. But they were worlds apart. While she hadn't developed any deep relationships, and the nurses she'd worked with had only been acquaintances, there was one person who intrigued her, whom she believed that if they had more time together, something more could develop, even though they'd only talked on two occasions. Phillippe Fontaine. Would she ever see him again or should she hope to? Was she risking heartache? War was cruel and made commitments tenuous and complicated. She'd better not count on any future involvement with him or anyone else. Besides, she was here for the adventure, not romance.

Three weeks later, the ship landed at their next assignment and the next, dangerous adventure.

Chapter 25

Nicole

Algeria, 2019

Nicole was thankful to have Aisha as her tentmate and glad to have company. She couldn't explain her situation to Aisha and make her worry too much, though. Sami was just a few feet away in his tent, giving her some comfort and less fear about anyone harming her at night.

She lay on her cot wide awake, trying to identify all the sounds outside. Aisha spoke softly from the other cot as if reading Nicole's mind. "It takes getting used to, sleeping out here. I used to have a problem with it too, but now I fall asleep because I'm tired."

"Every noise makes me jump," Nicole said. "I want to know what's making the noises."

"I know. I did that too. But it doesn't matter. You're safe in here. There aren't any wild animals that bother our tents. They stay up in the mountains." Aisha yawned. "Good night."

"Good night." Nicole closed her eyes and listened to the sound of Aisha sleeping. Then she heard footsteps outside and sat up. She listened intently. What would she do if someone came into the tent and grabbed her? She didn't even have a weapon to defend herself with, much less, call 911 out here without cell service, if they even had such a thing in this country.

A male voice came through the front flap of the tent. "Nicole, everything is okay," Sami said. "You can go to sleep now."

How did he know she was still awake? She smiled to herself, thankful she had someone looking out for her. She remembered he had a gun, and hopefully, any intruder wouldn't have one.

Somehow, she fell asleep but woke at the first sounds of voices outside the next morning. She glanced at Aisha, who was waking up and stretching.

"Did you sleep all right?" Aisha said.

Nicole shrugged her shoulders. "I slept, but I don't know how long. I'll be okay."

They got ready and went outside. Nicole pulled the drawstrings of her hoodie tight to stay warm in the chilly mountain air as they joined the others around a low grill with some small pieces of meat on it. "Have a seat and make yourself a pita sandwich," Sami said. Nicole took a paper plate and grabbed a piece of pita bread from a container near the fire while Sami speared a piece of meat and put it on her plate. "We have some oranges too." He motioned to another container.

"I need coffee," she said, shivering while holding out the camping mug she brought with her.

Sami laughed. "Of course you do. Or you can have some tea. We have both." On another grill sat two stainless steel coffee pots. He pointed to one of them. "The one on the right is coffee."

She poured the hot coffee into the cup, cradling it for warmth and inhaling the aroma before she took a sip of the strong brew. Then she followed Aisha as they found a place to sit. Nicole listened as the other students discussed what they'd found the previous day—a few pieces of mosaic tiles, mainly, so they surmised they were part of a larger floor mosaic.

When she finished, Sami motioned her over. She stood and walked to where he was sitting. He pointed to the place beside him, and when she sat, spoke in a low voice. "I don't know if you realized it or not, but when I had the ring under the microscope, I took pictures of it with a digital camera attached to the microscope. I sent those images to an App on my phone. I've tracked down an expert in ancient languages and have sent the pictures to his email. He'll get back to me when he figures out the symbols."

"Why didn't you tell me before?"

"I wasn't sure where I would send them right away. Actually, I was thinking of asking Nadir about them before he walked in and surprised us. When he did, I got the distinct impression that showing him the ring would not be a good idea."

Alarm raced through her. "Are those pictures still on the microscope at the lab?"

"No, I deleted them. At least I got that done before Nadir arrived." He paused, then, glancing each way, he said, "I have an idea that might work, if you're willing to go along with me."

Nicole lifted an eyebrow. "What is that? And why

wouldn't I want to go along with you?"

"What if we gave them a decoy? We could find a ring in a market somewhere that's similar, and you can wear that around your neck. Then we set them up with a camera and let them steal it."

"So we'd know who was after it, right? But that wouldn't tell us why."

"Maybe, maybe not. It might depend on who is trying to get it."

"When and where are we going to do this?"

"Soon. There's a souk not far from here on the road to Constantine. Why don't we go there around lunch time?"

"I'm not getting much work done here. But I'll do what I need to do to solve this puzzle."

"Good. And don't worry about the dig. Once we get this settled, you'll have plenty of time to work." He looked at the other students. "All right, gang. Time to clean up and get started."

The students sprang into action as some took dishes to wash and others collected the trash. Everything was cleaned up quickly. Nicole and Aisha took their insulated water bottles to a large cooler that had a tap on it and refilled the bottles before returning to the spot where they'd left off the day before. Nicole removed her trowel from her back pocket, squatted down, and began digging.

Aisha whispered to her. "Are you and Sami dating?"

Nicole snapped her head to look at Aisha. "Dating? Oh no, not at all." Her face heated as she stumbled over words to make excuses. "He's just my escort and supervisor while I'm here in Algeria."

Aisha cocked her head. "Hmm. Maybe so, but you two

seem to have a connection."

"Really? Well, he's just easy to be around."

"The way you look at each other says there's more to it than that."

Nicole glanced down. Was it possible that Sami was attracted to her? No, he couldn't be. And her attraction to him was a schoolgirl crush like the other girl students had on him. There was nothing special. She was just a colleague, probably still a student in his mind.

"Well, trust me. We're not a thing. I'm here to learn, just like you are."

Aisha shrugged. "If you say so."

Nicole resumed her digging, thinking about what Aisha said, for the next few hours. When her trowel hit something hard, she smoothed the dirt away with her hand to reveal part of a design. "Hey, I think I've found something."

Aisha moved over and brushed her hand over the area. "Yes, it is a design. Let's get the brushes and see how big it is."

They worked together to smooth away dirt with their hands and brushes as the mosaic design got larger. "This is exciting," Nicole said. "I wonder how big it is?"

"Who knows? This is the fun part, when you really find something," Aisha said.

Sami walked up and watched them. "What have you found?"

"It looks like a large mosaic, maybe part of a floor," Nicole said.

"Great. I think I'll put a couple more people over here and see how far it extends," Sami said.

Nicole hid her disappointment at not being the only one

to find it, but she pushed her thoughts away, knowing this was a joint project. It wasn't like she'd be famous for discovering a mosaic floor in a centuries-old palace.

"Are you getting hungry?" Sami asked whoever was listening.

Nicole's stomach had been growling for some time, but she hadn't wanted to quit working on the mosaic. She glanced up and nodded while some of the others answered, "Yes!"

"Then let's take a lunch break. Asher, would you be in charge of the meal today?"

A skinny, black-haired boy with his scarf wrapped around his head turban-style stood and brushed off his hands. "Sure. Schwarma?"

"That's right. Everything you need is in the coolers in the kitchen tent." The students stood and brushed dirt off themselves, then headed to the area where water was used for washing.

Looking at Nicole, he said, "Let's go run our errand."

She thought for a minute before she remembered what they were going to do. "Oh, right. Let me wash some of this dirt off first." Aisha gave her a knowing look as Nicole turned to walk back to Sami. Nicole shook her head when Aisha winked.

When Nicole and Sami walked to his car, he said, "The site manager said something showed up on the camera and showed it to me."

"Really? What?" Maybe they would see who took the backpack.

"The video shows a black car driving past and stopping by my car. A man got out of the car, and the car drove away.

Then he ran to my car and used the button release on the back of the car to open the trunk. He grabbed the backpack and closed the trunk. He put the backpack on his own back, then trotted off in a different direction before ducking behind a wall. A few minutes later, he stood up and waved, then he jumped over the wall and sprinted toward the black car, which was parked a few alleys away. He gets in, and they drive away."

"Could they see what the man looked like?"

"The same description the boy gave us. No distinguishing characteristics."

Her gut tensed anyway, assured the car belonged to the people who had been following them. "But I bet it was the car that passed us on the way here."

"From what I saw, you're probably right."

Nicole knew she should've trusted her gut instincts.

As they were driving away from the site, Nicole thought about what Aisha said. Much as she wanted to deny it, there was electricity between her and Sami, just sitting in the car with him. Or at least she felt it. But did he? She turned and looked out as they passed the large archaeological site, forcing herself to focus on the reason she was there. How long had it taken to excavate this whole area? But soon, her thoughts returned to the people trying to get her ring.

"Sami, you must have some ideas about why the ring is so important."

He glanced at her, then nodded. "I've given it a lot of thought. I have a couple of theories. One is that there could be a ring of black-market antiquities thieves, and the ring is much more valuable than we realize."

"That makes sense." But why didn't she know this

before? "And the other theory?"

"There are a few religious cults here. I wonder if it has some religious value to one of them?"

"Sounds intriguing. What kind of cults?"

Sami shook his head. "I'm not sure. I need to do some more investigation because I don't get into a lot of religious controversy."

"Would any of those groups be dangerous?" Would they kill for a ring? "I mean, a religious cult would be non-violent, right?"

He twisted his lip. "Well…not necessarily. There have certainly been a lot of religious wars in history, unfortunately."

"True. What a shame. Didn't God tell us to love each other?"

"The God you and I worship said that, but other people worship false gods that tell them to kill anyone who doesn't believe as they do."

Nicole's eyes widened. "Do you really think someone would kill for this ring?" Her hand went to her chest and felt the ring under her shirt.

Sami reached out and put a hand on her arm. "Hey. I didn't mean to scare you. Let's pray this whole thing can be resolved peacefully." His gesture was comforting, sending warmth up her arm.

Ahead on the side of the road, Nicole spotted some tents and canopies.

"Here it is." Sami pulled the car over and parked. "These marketplaces usually have jewelry. Let's see what we can find."

Nicole put her scarf over her head as they got out, aware

that the more remote areas had stricter customs regarding a woman's attire. They strolled among the booths while the vendors called out to them. The aroma of cooked food drew Nicole to one of the booths. "What is this? It smells wonderful," she said to Sami.

"Couscous." He leaned over to inspect it. "Looks like it has vegetables in it."

"I've had couscous before. It didn't look quite the same, but it looks good."

"Are you hungry? Would you like some of this?" Sami asked, motioning to the food.

"Is it safe?" Nicole had read about food-borne diseases while traveling. This would be a bad time for her stomach to get upset.

"Yes, I believe so. We'll share. Are you okay with that?"

She nodded, and Sami spoke to the woman behind the table, who scooped some of the food into a cardboard container and handed it to him. He took it and paid her. "I'm afraid there are no forks. But there is some pita bread you can scoop with."

Nicole had become familiar with the practice while observing diners at other places. It took a little effort to eat this way because it was messier, but she needed to adapt. Where were French fries when you needed them?

"Sure." They each carried their water bottle on their belts with carabiners, so they had something to wash down their food with. They walked slowly through the market as they shared the food, stopping frequently to study items for sale.

"Look," Sami said, nodding toward a booth across the

way. "I see jewelry. Maybe we'll get lucky."

The vendor had quite a few rings, so Nicole and Sami scrutinized them carefully. They needed the right color and size of her ring, especially if the thief knew what hers looked like. It had to be orange, in the shape of a large octagon in a plain gold setting. They looked at each one, but didn't see one that was similar. "Do you have more?" Sami asked the man.

He nodded and looked under the table, withdrawing a box. He put it on the table and opened the lid, extending his palm, inviting them to look. They fingered through the rings in the box, then Sami lifted one. "How about this one? It looks pretty similar to me."

Other than the modern setting and the etching, the ring closely resembled hers, the same rectangular shape and color. "Yes. That one is perfect," she said.

"How much?" Sami held it up.

The vendor responded by lifting two fingers.

"$200 dollars?" Nicole asked. Was Sami going to pay that much for it?

"No, he means $20. I think that's fair, even if it is worthless. I don't mind spending $20." Sami pulled out some money and gave it to the man.

"Thank you," Nicole said. "I want to compare them side by side, but I'm afraid to take mine out."

"You don't need to. I'm sure this is a close enough match." He snapped his fingers. "But we need another chain." He purchased one from the vendor, then turned to her as they stepped away. "I'm going to have to ask you to put the new ring on your chain. You can use this chain to put your ring on. It's not as nice as yours, but they might notice the difference. If they take it, I'll replace your chain when we get back to the city."

What did he mean "if they take it?" How would they do that?

"All right, but I don't see how this is going to work. I'll have to take your word for it, though."

"You'll see."

So he was setting her up to be mugged?

Nicole glanced at another booth and was intrigued by what she saw. "Look at these unusual shapes. Some even look like flowers. What are they made of? Some kind of crystals?"

"They're made of sand and are a natural phenomenon. Many are found in the Sahara, and they're very popular souvenirs with tourists." He stopped and stared. "Nicole. I should've thought of these. They're called desert roses."

Her mouth fell open. "Desert roses? Sami, this must be what Mimi was talking about! It wasn't a real flower. Now I get it. So she wants me to buy one and bring it to her. Great! Help me pick out one that looks the most like a rose. Will they travel well?"

"They're pretty sturdy, and if you pack it right, it should stay intact. I'm so glad we found these here."

"Me too." Nicole took a couple of pictures with her phone. "I'll send these pictures to Mom."

"Good luck finding cell service. It's difficult out here in this remote area."

Nicole could finally rest in knowing she'd found the right desert rose. But she wasn't ready to celebrate yet, knowing she was about to be set up to be mugged.

Chapter 26

Monique

Algiers, 1941

Monique stepped out on the balcony of their new apartment. The view of the Mediterranean Sea was amazing. Here on the top floor of the building, she had a vast panorama of the sea as far as she could see in any direction. She missed the lush greenery of their home and the trees she looked through from their patio, but this view wasn't too bad.

Inwardly, she seethed because they were forced to move, but she would get back at them another way. From here, she could see almost everything, and the good thing about it was that other people couldn't see her. Even the duplicate seven-story white stucco building next to theirs was set at an angle so that its balconies didn't look at hers.

A cackle next to her made her laugh. Mademoiselle Poulet had settled into her cage on the balcony without too much fuss, still producing eggs, even though she had missed a few days after the move. "She has to get used to her new home," Maman had said. "Just like we do." The hen got plenty of fresh air and enough food. Monique made sure the hen didn't get too much sun or wind by pushing her cage back against the wall.

Actually, the chicken had adjusted better than Minette, who had spent most of her time hiding under the bed since the move. She and Maman had to coax her out just to feed her.

Turning with her back to the sea, Monique stared into her new home, still difficult to comprehend. At least half of their furniture had been hidden by Mr. Alexis, so the apartment seemed sparse. It was comfortable enough, but it didn't feel like home and never would. She vowed to get their home back someday.

Her classes were over for the time being, so she had no excuse to ride through the Casbah to deliver food to Sarah's family. But ever since her encounter with the mysterious man, Matazan had taken the food and somehow delivered it. She wasn't sure it went directly to Sarah anymore, since Sarah's house was likely being watched because her brother had been arrested. The authorities might suspect her father, too, so it was best not to call attention to them. At least Monique and Matazan were helping the Jews.

Maman had taken to doing more sewing for the troops, joining the other women at church who also wanted to help the soldiers. She never mentioned the fact that she was not supporting the Vichy government, but hoped someone was helping Rene, wherever he was. While there, she had begun the habit of praying for him at the altar, getting some peace from turning her son over to God's care.

She did not ask Monique about anything, turning a blind eye to Monique's attempts to help the Jews.

One day Matazan came to the apartment with her new

assignment.

"Mr. Robert Murphy, the United States consul to the Vichy government in France, has been assigned to Algeria as the personal representative of President Roosevelt. He is setting up office in the government building and needs a secretary. You will go apply for the job."

"But I've never been a secretary. I can type, but I'm sure someone that important will hire a more experienced secretary," Monique protested.

Matazan shook his head. "You will go and apply, and you will be hired."

The conviction in his voice left no doubt as to the truth of his words. She studied him. How had someone who had always seemed so submissive become a leader in the resistance? No one ever needs to question his quiet strength, though.

"When?"

"Today, at 10:00. His office is on the fifth floor of the government building. Tell the guards you have an appointment with Mr. Murphy."

Monique glanced at the clock which showed 9:00. "I will be there. Thank you, Matazan."

He nodded and was out the door before she had time to ask him any more questions. She quickly dressed in a white blouse and a gray suit, combed her hair, then put on lipstick. Glancing in the mirror, she caught the reflection of a professional woman instead of a schoolgirl. She was on the verge of something important. She could tell by the excitement pulsing through her body. Papá would be proud. Her thoughts flashed to Audrey.

A few days before, she had found the journal in its

hiding place in the fountain and penned a note to Audrey, telling her they had to move and where. It was foolish, she was sure, to think Audrey would ever see the journal again, but it made Monique feel better just to know she had communicated with her friend. She hoped she would hear from Audrey, too.

Monique put on her black beret, picked up her purse and gloves, and marched out the door. At the government house, the guards stepped aside when she told them where she was going. She tried not to act surprised, but she had gotten more opposition when she was riding her bike. Could it be because she looked more mature now? Or was there another reason?

She took the elevator to the fifth floor and followed the sound of voices down the hall. The sign outside said, "American Consul," but the door stood open, and she heard men talking inside. She knocked on the door but got no answer. She waited a few minutes, then knocked again. Still no answer. Sucking in a breath, she stepped into the room, which had an unoccupied desk in front of the windows. Another door to the right was open, directing her to the voices she heard. She stepped to the doorway and observed three men standing together, each trying to talk over the other. Two of the men spoke rapid French while the man nearest the desk replied in French with an American accent. She assumed the latter, wearing a navy-blue suit, was Robert Murphy. She stood for an undetermined period of time, wondering when they would notice her. Should she say something? Cough? Clear her throat?

The phone rang, and Mr. Murphy looked around while the other men continued talking.

"Would someone please get that?" he shouted.

"Yes, tres' bien," she said, and grabbed the phone on his desk. "American Consul office." The caller asked for Mr. Murphy. "Un moment, s'il vous plait." She looked at Mr. Murphy, who stared at her with a stunned look on his face, along with the other two men.

"The caller would like to speak to you. Mr. Murphy?"

He blinked, then said, "I'll take it." Looking at the other men, he said, "Please excuse me. We will continue this conversation later."

The two men glanced at each other, then left the room. Mr. Murphy motioned for her to close the door after them, so she left the office and closed the door behind her. Then she also closed the door to the hallway. She walked around behind the desk in the room and took stock of what was on it—a phone, a steno pad, pencils, and a typewriter. Sitting down in the chair, she glanced around the room, which had boxes waiting to be unpacked. Should she do that?

A few minutes later, the door opened, and Mr. Murphy stepped out. He extended his hand to her. "Robert Murphy, and you are…"

"Monique Clermont." She took his hand and shook it, smiling.

"And you are my new secretary?"

"So it seems."

He smiled at her. "You speak English, I see."

"I do, and French."

"Good. My French is not so good, and some of those men talk so dang fast, I can't understand them, so you can translate for me."

"It will be my pleasure."

"Fine." He looked around him. "Please forgive the

mess. I guess you can see we haven't quite gotten settled yet."

"Would you like me to unpack the rest of the boxes?"

"That would be splendid."

She removed her gloves, stood, and walked to the nearest box. Marked "Files," she looked at Mr. Murphy. "Would you like these in your office or in here?"

He eyed the box. "I believe that one should go in my office. You do understand that what we discuss in my office is confidential?"

"Yes, sir. You can trust me."

"Very well."

She carried the box to his office and began placing files in the file cabinet while he began unpacking another box. Why she was here, working for the American consul, she had no idea, but the resistance must want her there for a reason, and she was eager to help in any way she could.

"May I ask you a question, Mr. Murphy?"

"Of course."

"The United States is not in the war, from what I understand."

"That is correct."

"But is it true that the US unfroze French money so they could buy American goods for North Africa?"

"That is true. But they can only buy limited quantities and non-strategic goods. In other words, basic necessities and not weapons."

"Oh. Thank you for explaining that to me."

"Now, Miss Clermont, may I ask you a question?"

"Yes, of course."

"When you asked that question, you referred to the

French as "they" instead of "we." I find that odd."

"Oh, did I?"

"Miss Clermont, I heard that you have recently been forced out of your home."

She paused. "That is true."

"How did your parents take that?" He cupped his chin with one elbow, resting in his other hand.

"My Papá, a hero from the last war, passed away a few years ago. My maman and I have lived, along with our servants, in the house I grew up in on the ridge above the city. Now, it is just Maman and I."

"Do you know why you had to move?"

"We were told a Vichy officer wanted the house."

"I see. I assume that was quite the shock."

"Yes, sir. But we have a new view of the sea, plus we are well, not like some of our other people."

"I understand. A good positive attitude will serve you well."

"We do what we can to survive, Mr. Murphy. And we will."

He nodded slowly. "Yes, we will, Miss Clermont. Yes, we will."

"Did you say you have a nice view of the sea?"

"Yes, our apartment is on the top floor of the building, so we can see for miles."

"That's nice to know. Your position may come in handy someday."

She raised her eyebrow. What did he mean by that? She thought of Matazan and how she ended up with this job. It was no accident or coincidence. She had been placed here for a purpose, and now it seemed her new apartment might not be a coincidence either. Change was in the air, and she would be part of it.

Chapter 27

Audrey

North Africa, 1941

By the time they arrived in the next camp, Audrey was weak and tired. Although the camp was full of tents, there was no place for her. She shuttled Dr. Venet to the hospital, and when she stepped inside, she spotted Louise, a familiar nurse, trying to set up an operating table.

"Good to see you, Audrey," Louise said. "Can you help me with this contraption?"

Audrey and the nurse worked with the awkward equipment until they got it ready.

"You look terrible," Louise said. "You should get some rest before we have incoming."

Audrey nodded, but she had no tent of her own at that camp. When Louise left, Audrey just lay down on the operating table, so tired that she dropped right off to sleep with no concern for the discomfort of her unusual bed. The next day, she was somewhat rested when she got up at dawn as usual to take Dr. Venet closer to the battlefield at the front of a convoy to provide on-site medical attention. The road was uphill and full of boulders, and Audrey questioned whether the old Humber would make it. They reached the top of the hill with steam coming out from under the hood, but the car was still running.

At the sound of airplane engines approaching, everyone shouted "Seek cover!" She and the doctor scrambled out and sought refuge beside the mountain, balled up with their hands over their heads. The ground shook as bombs fell around them. As if that wasn't enough, the planes' machine gunners fired bullets repeatedly. One bullet came so close to her ear, she thought the next one would kill her. Men yelled as they were hit, while the incessant drone of the planes and pinging of bullets created a hellish situation. Finally, the planes flew away, and Audrey opened her eyes.

She helped the doctor up and was happy to see he had not been hit. Others had not been so lucky. She and the doctor ran to help those who were wounded. An ambulance and a motorcycle had been destroyed, and the driver as well. But unbelievably, her old vehicle had not been hit. The convoy began again, this time carrying injured, and she deposited the doctor at a tent near the battlefield. Then she turned around and returned to the other encampment with two injured soldiers who needed surgery in the hospital.

When she reached the hospital, she was parched with thirst and exhausted.

The operating room nurse took one look at her and said, "You're sick. We need to get you hydrated and some food in you."

Audrey was hungry but couldn't eat. She trembled with a fever and stomachache and assumed it was dysentery, common among the troops. But the doctor diagnosed her with a jungle fever and ordered her to leave the camp and get help away from the battlefield at the next civilized town. After several days of rest and a boring, bland diet, her energy was renewed, and she was ready to go back to the battlefield.

The camp was in a flurry when she returned due to a new camp commander who had stirred things up by adding new drivers. Dr. Venet hurried to greet her and told Audrey the commander had tried to replace her with another driver while she was away. However, the doctor stood up for her, saying she was the only driver he could work with, so he won the argument, and she kept her job. She was so happy to hear how the doctor had been her advocate. In the months they'd worked together, they'd become friends and fellow soldiers. He was a dear man and one of the nicest men she'd encountered on the field.

She resumed her old job with the same old vehicle. Would her replacement have gotten a new vehicle? By now, she could fix almost anything on it, but when it got stuck in the sand, she welcomed the assistance of villagers in the area. Seemingly out of nowhere, a handful of men and boys would appear and help push, then cheer when the Humber got free. In return, at times when she had taken the doctor somewhere and returned alone, she'd often pick up the villagers walking down the road.

She was always more frightened to be alone in the vehicle instead of being in a convoy with others. Keeping her vehicle on the road was challenging as she tried to navigate boulders in the road. Planes flew over daily, dropping bombs and strafing the ground with machine gun fire. Sometimes it was hard to hear the bombers coming with the road noise of other vehicles drowning out the warning roar of the engines. But watching the road and the sky at the same time was almost impossible.

If one could call it an advantage, she had learned how to tell planes apart by the sounds of their engines. A deep roaring noise meant a heavy Vichy bomber or German Junker was on its way, but a high-pitched whine was evidence that Stukas and Messerschmitts were approaching. Sometimes, though, she was caught off guard. She had not realized planes were flying over until a bomb landed in front of her, narrowly missing the truck and blasting sand all over the place. One afternoon in August, a bomb knocked a troop truck off the road. The entire convoy abandoned their vehicles to scramble for safety. The Humber was too low to crawl under, so she sought cover under another truck that had gone off the road into some dunes.

She wriggled underneath, finding herself in the company of a young British soldier, also seeking safety. They glanced at each other, then turned face down in the dirt, hands over their heads as bombs began to rain down on them, followed by the sound of machine guns. The noise subsided, and the drone of the plane engines faded. Crawling out from under the truck, she surveyed the damage.

As if resistant to attack, the Humber had not been hit. But all around, chaos ensued. Several trucks were on fire, and many men were dead or injured on the road. Audrey glanced around. Who should she help first? To her right, another person crawled out from under a truck and straightened. Her heart leaped as she recognized the man. Phillippe. She hadn't known they were even near each other. She offered a smile and gave a short wave. Recognition crossed his face, and he nodded. Much as she wanted to run toward him, Audrey needed to provide aid to those who needed her most. She ran to the nearest soldier, moaning from his injuries. She assessed his injuries and gave him some water from her canteen. "I will be back to take you to the medical tent."

She went from one person to the other, administering what aid she could. Phillippe appeared by her side. Her heart pounded in her chest being so near to him. "Where is Dr. Venet?"

"I dropped him off at another camp where he'll be for a few days. I was returning to our base camp."

Phillippe nodded. "I see. Can you take these men to the hospital?"

"I can carry five," she said. That would be pushing the Humber capacity to the limits, but the men needed help as quickly as possible.

"Good. We'll get five into your vehicle, and I'll commandeer another truck to help."

Once her vehicle was loaded, she climbed into the driver's seat. Phillippe leaned over, his hands on her door. "I will meet you at the hospital."

Audrey nodded, then shifted her attention to the injured men who needed her driving skills to reach the hospital. Keeping her eyes on the sky, the road, and the injured men, she made her way back to the camp hospital. After helping to get them unloaded, she helped the nurses as much as she could. When they'd finished, she remembered what Phillippe had said about meeting her at the hospital. Her heart raced with excitement as if she were waiting for a date, but in these times, promises were often broken only because situations meant they couldn't be kept.

She went to her tent and rinsed dust and blood off her face and arms with the allotment of water that was provided for such things. How she would love to have a real bath again. Phillippe must think she looked dreadful, compared to their first meeting on the ship. Would he ever see her clean again? She poured water over her head in an attempt to wash her hair, now cut shorter than she'd ever worn it. If he did show up, she wanted to look more decent. She grabbed one of her two clean shirts and put it on, noticing how tanned her arms had gotten. Her reflection in a small handheld mirror reminded her she was much blonder now as well. Her mother wouldn't even recognize her. Nor approve. But would Father? She shook the thoughts from her head as she toweled her hair dry. Putting on a tad of lipstick, she strode toward the hospital, hoping to run into Phillippe.

Dusk approached as she spotted his tall, lean figure walking toward her. He smiled his endearing smile, and her insides melted. He, too, looked like he had washed up and was even more handsome than she remembered.

"Ah, there you are! Would you care to join me in the canteen for supper?"

"That would be lovely," she said, catching the irony in her statement as the mess tent had never been lovely. But being in the company of this nice man would make up for it.

He laughed as he fell into step with her. "I'm sorry it doesn't qualify as fine dining, but we can pretend, can't we?" He finished his sentence with a wink, and she was undone.

"I'm pretty good at pretending, but that may stretch the limits."

When they entered the mess tent and got their food, he led her to a table as far away from the other people in there as possible. "I'm glad we ran into each other again," he said.

"I am too. I didn't have a chance to thank you last time for the use of your shower."

"I knew you appreciated it." He swept his hand through the air. "Out here, you learn to appreciate small conveniences."

She nodded in agreement. "True. Simple things like clean water to drink."

"You know, you've acquired quite the reputation," he said.

Her mind raced through incidents, wondering if the reputation was good or bad. "I have? I'm afraid to find out what that means."

He sat back and laughed. "Oh, it's good. Quite good, in fact. The men respect you for your courage and ability to handle whatever happens. And your expertise with a vehicle is notable as well. I like your nickname. It suits you well."

"A nickname? What on earth could it be?"

"You didn't know? It's the 'desert rose.' I feel it is most appropriate. You are like a lovely rose that is a welcome refreshment here in the desert."

Her face flushed, and she laughed. "Are you sure you don't mean one of those things the sand forms into a rose-like shape? It's rather stiff and gritty, not quite the same as your typical soft and velvety garden rose."

"Actually, I'd say you're both. Although you're a woman, you are gritty in a way that endures in the desert, a combination that is quite attractive."

She lowered her gaze, unable to meet his. Was that really the way the men saw her? The way he saw her? She mustn't read too much into what he said, despite her feeling that there had been a mutual attraction. Looking up, she forced a casual smile. "Well, if I must have a nickname, that's a great one to have."

"So now you're Sergeant Rose. That's what I'll call you from now on." He glanced at his watch. "Well, I hate to end this enjoyable evening, but I'm leaving very early tomorrow." He stood, and she did as well. "I hope we meet again before too long."

"Me too," she said, trying not to show her disappointment that their time was over.

"Until then, au revoir, Sergeant Rose."

Reality sank in once again, knowing the chances of another meeting like today's might never happen again, despite her wishes. War was no place for romance.

Her life returned to its new normal the next day, ferrying the doctor back and forth. One day, the doctor needed to go to a high-risk area filled with mines, and he wouldn't let Audrey take him. "It is too dangerous for you," Dr. Venet said. "Stay here and be safe."

She protested, but he was firm and selected another soldier to drive him. His concerns proved valid when the vehicle he was in struck a mine, the driver was killed, and the doctor was seriously injured. Word of the attack raced through the camp, and she rushed to meet him at the hospital. When he was carried in on a stretcher, Audrey was shocked to see how much blood he'd lost. He just couldn't die. But seeing his injuries, she knew that if he lived, he'd never return to the battlefield. She held his hand as they tended his wounds, then loaded him into an ambulance to be taken back to a real military hospital, where he would stay a long time, if he recovered. Her eyes filled with tears as he looked at her in so much pain.

"You are the best driver I could ever have," he struggled to say. "You make a fine soldier."

Protocol or no, she kissed him on the cheek. "You take care, doctor. I have enjoyed serving with you."

As she watched the ambulance drive away, she realized her desire to be in the war for the excitement and adventure was naïve. The truth hit her hard. Not only could she be killed, but those she'd come to care about could be too. There in the desert, Audrey learned the value of life and also the brevity of it.

.

Chapter 28

Nicole

Algeria, 2019

When they climbed back into the car, Sami pulled the new ring out. "May I see yours, please?

Nicole removed her ring and chain from around her neck, reluctantly giving them to him. Sami took her ring off the chain and put the new ring on it. Then he took the new chain and put her ring on it. Handing them both back to her, he said, "Can you wear both of them for a little while?"

"I guess so." She slipped each one over her head. "My neck is getting heavy."

Sami smiled. "It'll be okay for a short time, I'm sure."

"So what's your plan?" Nicole asked.

Sami started the car and turned around to head back to the archaeological site.

"When we get back today, I'll announce a marshmallow roast tonight, so we'll stay out later. Then I'll go into your tent and set up a camera in the corner of the tent facing the flap opening so we can get a picture of anyone who enters. Tonight, I want you to go into your tent before supper and put on your hoodie, then *accidentally*— he gestured with quotation marks in the air—drop the chain with the new ring on the ground by your cot. Then come out to eat. I expect that anyone who's watching for an opportunity will search your tent while we're out tonight."

Nicole sucked in her bottom lip. "I don't know. Sounds dangerous to me."

"It'll be okay. You won't be in there, and I'll be with you when you return. And Yanis will be here too."

"Are you going to tell Yanis about the plan?"

"Yes, I think he needs to know what's going on. He might even have some ideas. He at least needs to be ready in case of trouble."

Trouble. That didn't sound good. "All right. I'll try it," she said, sending up a prayer for protection. Thieves and kidnappers? She hadn't expected to have to deal with those when she applied for this study.

Everything went according to Sami's plan as far as keeping the students out of their tents longer. When they began to yawn and get up to go back to their tents, Nicole wondered if anyone had gone into her tent. What if they did and were still there, waiting for her to return, when they discovered the ring she left was not the real ring?

Yanis stood and walked toward the tents. A gunshot rang out, and he started running.

"Stay here!" Sami said. "And stay together!" He pulled out his gun and took off running toward the noise, too.

Two of the girls screamed and huddled with the other students, who all started guessing at what had happened. Nicole kept quiet, but prayed Sami and Yanis would not be hurt. Shouting was heard, then more shots, then the sound of a motorcycle, then silence. What had happened?

Time crawled as the students waited nervously for their leaders to return. Finally, at the sight of Sami and Yanis returning, they relaxed. Nicole looked for a sign of injury as they approached, but didn't see any.

"It's all right, guys," Yanis said. "We had some intruders, but we scared them away. You can return to your tents now."

Nicole hurried to Sami. "What happened?" she whispered.

"Someone took the bait," he said.

"Did you see anyone?"

"No, it was dark, but there was more than one."

"Oh my. You could have been outnumbered."

"Maybe so, if they were working together," Sami said.

Her mouth dropped open. "Do you mean to say there's more than one person after the ring?"

"It appears that way. We heard people scuffling and yelling at each other when we got there. Yanis shot his gun into the air, and the two parted company and went their separate ways."

"So you're saying there might be two different groups trying to get it?"

"I think so. Let's get the camera and see what's on it."

"I'll stall Aisha so you can go in before she does." Was it fair for her roommate to be at risk and not know about it? Nicole didn't like that idea. Maybe they could tell her now. She called out to Aisha, and Sami hurried back to the tents. Nicole walked slowly, trying to keep Aisha away from the tent until Sami retrieved the camera.

When Sami returned, he gave her a nod. "Aisha, go on

ahead. I need to ask Sami about something."

After her tentmate was out of earshot, she looked at Sami for answers. "When can you look at the camera?"

He glanced around, then pulled the camera from his pocket. "Now." Nicole stood close to him so she could see the picture. The video showed a man wearing black with a black scarf covering his face peeking into the tent, then slipping inside, bending down to pick something up, then leave the tent. Seconds later, the tent moved as if something pushed against it.

"I think that when he got outside, another person encountered him and they fought," Sami said.

"But we don't know who won the fight, who ended up with the ring, do we?"

Sami shook his head. "No, we don't. Does anything stand out about this person?"

"Just that he looks like the same person who took my backpack."

"I agree. So let's assume these thieves know the ring is valuable and want to sell it on the black market. That, I understand. But who would fight over it? Another antiquities thief?"

"Could be, I guess," Nicole said, trying to comprehend the situation. "Who else?"

Sami shook his head. "Something just doesn't make sense. And I'd like to know why it's so valuable. Maybe that would explain who's after it."

"I wonder how long it'll take until the person who took it realizes it's not the right ring?"

He blew out a breath. "I don't know, but I need to get to the internet tomorrow and reach my contact, see if he came up with anything. And the sooner, the better."

"Sami, I'd like to go with you, since I don't have cell reception out here either, and I'd like to send a picture of the desert rose to my mom. I want Mimi to know I've been successful in the search." Did that seem like an unimportant issue to Sami, considering what had just happened? Maybe so, but it was something she could do, whereas she felt helpless to solve the other situation.

"All right. Let me talk to Yanis and see who can take my place here. We have a graduate student who was here before we arrived, and he might be coming back. When he gets here tomorrow, I'll feel better about leaving."

"I haven't spent much time on the dig," Nicole said. "I sure didn't expect to have such a distraction."

"I know. I didn't either, so that's another reason to get this problem solved, and right now, it takes priority."

The next day, the graduate student returned, and Sami decided it was safe to leave. Nicole told Aisha goodbye and apologized for not being a better helper. Aisha smiled and said she enjoyed working with her for the short time they had. Nicole and Sami left for the return trip to Algiers. On their way back, they went over possible suspects.

Nadir was at the top of their list because of his unusual timing and the suspicious way he acted. "But it wasn't Nadir in the video," Nicole said.

"True, but he could've been in the car, and the guy who took the items might have been working for him," Sami suggested.

"Yes, that's possible. But what about the man with the camel that I saw watching us back at the Royal Mausoleum?" Nicole could not get the image of that man out of her memory.

"Well, we haven't seen any camels around here," Sami said. "Not that they couldn't get here. If encouraged, they can average 25 miles per hour, so it would take one about a day to get here from Algiers."

"Someone at the hotel? Or maybe someone working in cahoots with the bad guys at the hotel."

Sami chuckled. "You sound like you're talking about a movie – bad guys."

"What else would you call them?" she said.

"Let's think about this some more. I don't think anyone else has seen the ring besides me," Sami said. "And I hope you know I'm a good guy."

Nicole rolled her eyes. "Of course you are." A tiny doubt niggled her mind, but she wouldn't allow it to take root. Sami was the only person she could trust here. "Okay, is there anyone else who has seen it?"

All at once, they looked at each other and said in unison, "Amid."

"Wouldn't he be working for the government?" Nicole said.

"He's supposed to be. But if he's working on the black market, he may be using his position in the government as a front."

"And he could have us followed?" Nicole remembered the black cars they kept encountering.

Sami nodded. "He could. But someone could figure out where we are without being followed."

"How?"

"I have to file my itinerary to the department every week, so even if we make some side trips, my plans would still be on record. However, the whole world wouldn't have access to them."

"Let me guess. Nadir could get access to them."

"Yes. That's true. Which means he might be working with the black market," Sami said.

Nicole drew the next conclusion. "Or working with Amid."

Sami gritted his teeth. "Or even working against each other."

"Good grief. Is everyone my enemy?" Nicole sighed. "Who knew?"

Sami patted her shoulder. "Remember, I'm a good guy. I'm not your enemy."

Thank God for that. But what could they do about the others? As Algiers' gleaming white buildings came into view with the blue of the Mediterranean as their background, Nicole checked her phone for coverage. "Hey, I've got a signal," she said before sending the pictures of the desert rose back home. "I really wish Mimi could tell me more about the ring. I'm going to ask Mom if she knows anything about it."

Sami's phone buzzed, and he pushed the answer call button on the car. "Hello. This is Sami…

A man's voice with a British accent spoke. "Sami, it's Matt. I'm calling about the pictures of the ring you sent me."

Sami glanced at Nicole. "Yes, did you find out anything about it?"

"I did. Tell your friend she needs to take out an insurance policy on it." He chuckled.

"What do you mean, Matt? What did you find out? Don't keep us in suspense."

"Us? Oh, is the ring owner with you?"

"She is."

"Hello, Matt. I'm Nicole," she said to the dashboard.

"Nice to meet you, Nicole. That's quite a nice ring you have there."

"Come on, Matt. Tell us what you found out." Sami pulled into a parking space on the street.

"That ring dates to the first century or a little later. The face on it is the face of Cleopatra Selene II, who was the queen of Mauritania who lived from 40 BC to somewhere between 6 and 17 AD. There are coins from that period with her name and picture on one side and her husband, Juba II's picture and name on the other. What's different about this ring, though, is that in the background, there are symbols that probably mean mountains, and there's also a cross, which is kind of strange because she dies a few years before Jesus's ministry."

Sami and Nicole exchanged glances. The Royal Mausoleum was called "the tomb of the Christian Woman." But the years didn't jive.

"Wow, Matt. That's amazing. Do you know if any more of these rings exist?" Sami asked.

"Well, if there are, they haven't been found, which makes your ring, Nicole, *extra* special, I mean one of a kind special. Which makes it *very* valuable."

"How valuable?" Sami asked.

"Hard to pinpoint, since there isn't another to compare. Most of Cleopatra's jewelry has disappeared, been lost or stolen, or is in some private collection somewhere. Let's just say, it would bring at least seven figures, maybe even eight."

Sami whistled. "Well, that explains a lot."

"As I said, get insurance, Nicole, that is, if you can afford it."

Nicole shook her head. The ring she wore around her neck at this moment was worth millions of dollars. She knew it came from Mimi's father, given to him by a friend, but where did the friend get it? The news terrified her. People would kill for that kind of money.

"All right, Matt. Thanks a lot. And keep this to yourself, right?"

"Of course. That goes without saying. But Sami, if I were you or Nicole, I'd find some very safe place to keep it. If Nicole wants to sell it, she can contact one of the major museums, although the native country probably thinks it belongs to them. You know, there were some artifacts turned over to the museum just a few years ago. Local natives had given them to a Peace Corps volunteer who worked in the area in the 1980's."

"Thanks, Matt. Bye." Sami signed off, then looked at Nicole. "Well. Now we know."

"Sami, now I know why the letters looked familiar! They are the same ones on the door to Cleopatra Selene's tomb." Her heart raced, trying to wrap her head around the facts. "If I hadn't been chased, I'd never have known about the ring. But Sami, where is a place that would be safe? I'm sure we're being followed, so they would see wherever we put it, like a bank or something."

"I know. I'll try to figure something out. But I don't want you to keep it because I think your life may be in danger."

His concern for her warmed her heart, but where could she be safe? Even if they could hide the ring, would she still be targeted? After all, how would the people who wanted the ring know if she didn't have it?

"I wish I could ship it back to the States."

"That would be risky."

Nicole's phone buzzed. She glanced at it. "It's Mom," she said to Sami.

"Hi, Mom. How are you and Mimi?"

"We're fine, darling. How are you? For some reason, I've sensed some stress in your messages."

"Really? I'm fine. No worries." Nicole was not a good liar, so she needed to change the subject. "Was Mimi happy to see the right desert rose?"

"I'm sorry, Nicole. She said no."

Nicole's heart sank. "You're kidding! That wasn't it? I thought I had finally found the right thing! Well, I'm out of options now. I'm so sorry to disappoint her."

"Honey, maybe she doesn't really know what she wants. I know she seems pretty lucid, but maybe she's just confused. When I showed her the picture, she shook her head, said no, then she said "person." It makes no sense. I'm so sorry."

"Mom, I don't think her mind was damaged by the stroke, just her body. But I need to ask you about something. The ring Mimi gave me, you know, the one I wear around my neck, I need to find out how Mimi's father got it. She told me a friend gave it to him."

"Yes, that's right."

"Do you know who the friend was?"

"Why no. She never mentioned a name. She said it was a tribal chief, but I don't remember any name. Why?"

"Oh, nothing. I've been trying to research rings like it,

and the more I know, like what year it was made, the better I can research it."

"Well, that's all I really know about it."

"Okay, Mum. Thanks. Gotta go now. Love you. Bye." Nicole had thought she'd solved at least one mystery today, but instead, she was no further along in figuring out what Mimi's desert rose was nor who was after her ring. Was this all about money, or was it something else more important?

Chapter 29

Monique

Algiers, 1942

With her job at the consulate, Monique was no longer the delivery girl to the Jews, but she provided for them with most of her income. She also continued to coordinate activities between Mr. Alexis and Matazan, who used his contacts to help the Jews. If only she could get Mr. Murphy to help them and free the prisoners at the work camp outside the city. Matazan told her there were people trying to get food to the prisoners, but it was very dangerous to do so.

The Americans were officially in the war against Hitler, providing much-needed encouragement to those under Nazi control. Monique enjoyed working for Mr. Murphy. Besides the fact that he was a nice man, she liked being the first contact any officials had when they came to meet with him. She came to know who all the Vichy officials were in Algeria and was particularly pleased at the reaction some of them who had known her father had when they saw her working for the American consul.

American "Vice Consuls," who were actually Mr. Murphy's assistants, were also assigned to North Africa to keep an eye on the American shipments and make sure they were not diverted to Axis powers in the country. She soon learned they had other duties as well, serving as undercover intelligence agents. One day, she was called into Mr. Murphy's office with the Vice Consuls present. She expected to take notes of the meeting, so she was surprised when she was addressed directly.

"Miss Clermont, I understand you have a top-floor apartment with a balcony facing the Mediterranean," Mr. Murphy said, the others looking at her.

"Yes, sir. That is correct. We live on the ninth floor." Monique's shoulders tensed. Why did they care about where she lived?

"Good. We'd like you to help us out if you don't mind." The other men watched her response.

"Of course." So now she'd know her role. She straightened her spine, eager to find out her assignment. "What can I do?"

Mr. Murphy leaned forward on his elbows, clasping his hands in front to him. "We'd like you to monitor activity in the harbor. Do you have a good pair of binoculars?"

"Yes, sir, I do. I have my father's army binoculars that he used when surveying the land."

"Perfect. What we'd like you to do is keep a record of ships going in and out, what you see unloaded, and if you see anything being transferred from one ship to another. Can you do that?"

She relaxed, glad she'd been given such an easy yet important assignment. She smiled but felt like she should salute. "Yes, sir."

"I have no doubt you can and will handle the assignment well."

"When should I start?"

"Right away."

Right now? What about her secretarial job?

"Don't come into the office before ten so you can monitor morning movements. Then go home at four o'clock to watch the afternoon and evening movements. I will increase your pay for this extra work."

She started to refuse the extra pay, but then realized the more she had, the more she could share. "Thank you, sir," she said. She paused, wondering if this was the right time to mention the prisoner work camps. But why wait?

Monique broached the subject with her boss. "Mr. Murphy, I know the United States sympathizes with the Jews."

He nodded. "That's true, but unfortunately, the Axis powers are not."

"But what about here in Algeria?" Her heart raced, but she needed to calm down. She took a breath. "Can you help them here? I have Jewish friends who are suffering from loss of food and jobs, and some of their families have been arrested and put in the work camp."

He shook his head and spread his hands out on the desk. "I'm so sorry. I'd like to help them, but I do not have that power here. The Vichy government is in control, and they have to be the ones to make those changes. Unfortunately, that is one area they aren't interested in changing."

"Mr. Murphy, if the allies ever come to Algeria, won't they liberate the prisoners?"

"I hope so, Miss Clermont. I hope so."

Despite the familiarity she had with the Vichy officials, she harbored a strong dislike for them. How could they treat people like they did the Jews? Keeping her eyes and ears open, she learned about a Jewish resistance group in the city. Many Jewish citizens were being harassed by the pro-Vichy French, who had bought into the Nazi propaganda against the Jews. In order to protect their own people, the group formed, meeting and training in a gym named for the French military boxing champion, Geo Gras.

At the center, the members of the group engaged in sports and physical training right under the noses of many Vichy sympathizers who knew nothing about their existence. As a result, the group members were physically able to respond to any violence they saw in the city and go to the aid of people who were being attacked.

She met the leader, Jose' Aboulker, when he came to see Mr. Murphy, and they were introduced to each other.

"Nice to meet you, Mademoiselle Clermont," he said, giving her a knowing look as he bowed slightly.

She had heard of him and wanted badly to ask questions about her friends, but knew she had to remain silent and play dumb.

She smiled. "Nice to meet you as well."

He went into Mr. Murphy's office, and they closed the door behind them. After some time, he came out. As he was leaving, he glanced over his shoulder and said, "Your friends are doing fine." Then he put his hat back on and left. It was only when he was out of the office that she recognized his voice. He was the one who had approached her from behind in the Casbah and told her to work through Matazan. How nice it was to hear about Sarah's family, even though there would be no details.

She kept a daily record of ship activity and passed the information on to Mr. Murphy. There was a sense of expectation in the air, as if the scene she saw was an illusion of what was really going on.

When General Charles Mast was announced as the Vichy leader of the army in Algiers, he came to visit Mr. Murphy. They met two days a week for several months, and when she built up her courage, she asked Mr. Murphy about the man.

"He may be a great ally one day," Mr. Murphy said.

"An ally?"

"For one thing, the Vichy French need us, so they're trying to stay on our good side. Germany has not been able to send them any aid as we have. Besides, you know what they say, "Keep your friends close.""

"And your enemies closer," she finished, her arms crossed in front of her waist as she stood in the doorway to the office. "That's what my father used to say."

"Smart man, your father."

"Yes, he was. But Mr. Murphy, do you really trust these Vichy officials?" She frowned, uncomfortable with the Vichy friendship.

"Not entirely. That's why you and our other colleagues are watching them."

"I'm happy to do it."

"Miss Clermont, you should know we're working on a plan, and I think it will include you too."

"I'll be happy to help."

He motioned her into his office and closed the door. "I

will tell you this much. The Allies are going to invade North Africa. I do not have the date yet. One of the things I've been working on is convincing the Vichy officials to switch sides and fight with us against the Axis powers in North Africa."

Monique trembled with excitement. Finally, they could get rid of the Vichy. "I'm so glad to hear that. How long before it'll happen?"

"Later in the year, I believe. But it'll have to be coordinated very well, and I'm enlisting the help of Mr. Aboulker and his friends."

"Sir, can you tell me where the Free French are fighting? I have friends that I'm concerned about."

"They're over in Tunisia fighting alongside British forces. We hope to meet up with them and provide reinforcements once we land." He paused. "A relative?" he asked with concern etched on his face.

She didn't think her brother Rene was in Africa, but she knew Audrey was. "Yes." Audrey was her sister, wasn't she? Was she safe?

The meetings between General Mast and Mr. Murphy were almost daily now as tension filled the air. Other officials visited when Mast wasn't there.

"I'll be out of the office for the next two days," Mr. Murphy said.

Monique raised her eyebrow, wanting to ask where he was going. One of the messages that had come across her desk mentioned a submarine and a General Clark whom she had not met. From what she knew, the Allied subs came from Gibraltar. Is that where he was going and meeting Clark?

"I can't tell you where, but I'm going to an important meeting. You can take the time off, too. That way, you won't have to answer the phone and explain why I'm not in the office."

"Yes, sir." What would she do with her time? She could visit Sarah's family, since she hadn't seen her in several months.

Going back into the Casbah was like reliving a bad dream. Where once she had run and played hide and seek from Matazan, now the streets were dark and almost empty. Several stores previously owned by Jews were closed, and some had been damaged, a sign of the antisemitism in the city. Remembering her last time there, she kept looking over her shoulder. Hearing shouts coming from the alley, she turned the corner and toward the noise. What she saw made her blood run cold. A group of young Muslim men were yelling at a Jewish woman and getting closer to her as she tried to shrink into the wall behind her. They were surrounding her, and her face was filled with fear. What would they do to her? Jolted by recognition, Monique's gut wrenched to see Sarah the object of the attackers. Someone had to help her. "Someday, you'll be brave," Audrey's words echoed in her head.

She glanced around and found some empty bottles beside the wall. She might not be a good tennis player, but she could throw a ball. Stepping closer to the group, she threw one of the bottles with all her might and hit one of the attackers on the back of the head. "Ow!" The man turned to see what hit him. She picked up another bottle and threw it, but it hit the wall and broke into pieces. By now, the whole group had turned around and saw her. She yelled, "Run, Sarah!"

The men were now coming towards her, and she had no time to throw another bottle. She turned and ran as fast as she could, hearing their footsteps and shouts behind her. *Lord, help me.* Her heart was in her throat as she rounded a corner and didn't know where she was. Had she run down a blind alley? Suddenly, a door opened behind her, and she was pulled inside as the door was bolted shut. She spun around and saw a young Jewish woman who put her finger to her lips.

Feet pounded outside, then the angry shouts of her pursuers turned into shouts of fear and pain as they were attacked from behind. Monique peeked through the side of the window and saw a group of men fighting the men who had been chasing her.

"Geo Gras," said the woman.

Monique recognized the name of the Jewish gang she had heard about, the ones who met at the gym. Their workouts proved advantageous as they overpowered the attackers, forcing them to scatter.

She turned to the woman. "Thank you."

"No, thank you. We've heard what you've done for us."

Surprised, Monique offered a smile, thankful for the woman's intervention.

They opened the door, and Monique stepped out. No one was in sight. Before the woman closed the door, she said, "May God bless you."

Monique found her way out of the Casbah and hurried home. As she stood on her balcony that evening, she thanked

God for letting her know her efforts to help others were a blessing to them and to her, too.

Chapter 30

Audrey

North Africa, 1942

Audrey's new boss was the opposite of kind Dr. Venet. Dr. Gaudet was tall, thin, and indignant to have a woman as his driver. Since no other driver was available, he insisted on driving the Humber himself with her sitting next to him in the passenger seat. His driving terrified her as he drove too fast and did not try to protect the old tires. He crunched through the gears and hit every rock in the road. Audrey doubted the old vehicle would survive or would she.

She endured his driving for two days until he crashed into a wall, almost killing them both and badly damaging the steering. She snapped, having her fill of his boorish behavior. "You're a horrible driver," she said, as they waited for mechanics from the tank regiment's workshop to come to their aid. "This car is my responsibility. Kindly remember that fact."

While they waited, the doctor jumped up every five minutes, cursing the mechanics who were coming for being so slow. She kept quiet, knowing the futility of his actions.

There were few left in camp now, since most had gone on to the next assignment.

When the mechanic finally arrived, his face was pale from trauma, and his car was full of wounded men. "The road's been bombed, and I couldn't get through," he said. "There are many more injured back there." He unloaded the men, then, without a word, Dr. Gaudet jumped in the mechanic's car and ordered the man to drive him back to the scene of the air raid, leaving her with the wounded men.

She tried to make them comfortable and get them under some shade. Fortunately, most of the men were only slightly hurt, with flesh wounds from shrapnel, concussions or shock. However, one of them had suffered severe abdominal injuries, and Audrey doubted he would survive. She removed her jacket and laid it over the shivering young man.

Several hours later, the mechanic returned, his shaking hands covered with blood as he worked on the Humber. The doctor had returned with him and began to work on the wounded men who had been left there before. When the poor mechanic announced the Humber was repaired, the doctor barked at her and said, "Let's go. I need to get to the advanced dressing station before dark."

Audrey slipped into the driver's seat before he had a chance to and stared up at him. "I'm driving from now on or this car won't make it."

He started to protest, but realized she meant business, so he begrudgingly took his place in the passenger seat.

She learned that over four thousand men had been killed that day, some of whom she had known. Visions of maimed and dying men paraded through her mind, and the next few days were some of the toughest she'd ever experienced. Dr.

Gaudet was the most infuriating man she had ever known. He was still angry because she wouldn't let him drive, so he worked her extra hard. In addition to ferrying him everywhere, he would make unreasonable demands and impossible deadlines, never giving her a moment's rest.

Audrey was terribly tired trying to keep up, yet she could not give in to exhaustion and give him an excuse to proclaim her incompetent. He expected her to get up early and drive all day until dark, knowing she'd have to drive slowly and without lights while avoiding craters and abandoned vehicles. But even though she was tired beyond her limit, she was more stubborn than he was and never complained, hoping her attitude would anger him even more. Their relationship was stretched about as tight as it could be as they barely tolerated each other.

One day, he commandeered the Humber and ordered her into the passenger seat. Then he drove in silence to the main encampment ten miles from where they were based. She was too tired to argue or question where they were going, so she allowed herself the rest until he jerked to a stop outside the main command tent thirty minutes later.

He climbed out and ordered her to wait, so she complied. He returned minutes later and angrily said, "You have a new assignment. Take your things and report to headquarters."

She jumped to her feet. "What does that mean?" she asked.

"It means, get your things out of this car. Now! From now on, I will be driving myself."

He climbed back into the driver's seat and started the car, barely giving her time to grab her tools, suitcase, guns, and other belongings from the boot before he sped off in a cloud of dust. She didn't worry about herself, frankly glad to see the doctor leave, but it saddened her to say goodbye to her dear old Humber.

Carrying all her worldly possessions, she walked toward the headquarters tent. Like a mirage, a familiar figure appeared coming out of the tent toward her. Smiling, he said, "Sergeant Rose, you will be my new driver," Colonel Phillippe Fontaine said.

Had she died and gone to heaven? Later, he filled her in on what had happened. The doctor had gone to the colonel to complain about her incompetence. Phillippe knew the opposite was true, and since his driver had been killed the day before, he needed a new one, Phillippe told the doctor he could have his wish.

Audrey had never driven a colonel before, and it was a big promotion. Of course, all the other senior officers' chauffeurs (as they were called), were treated with the highest regard because they had the premier jobs. They were at the center of the action and were responsible for the safety of their commanders, ready to move at a moment's notice.

She was surprised to find that not only would she drive the colonel, but she would also drive his staff as well. Her new car was not new at all, and there was a period of adjustment before she and the car got along well.

She saw Phillippe often now but stayed professional. Their brief moment when they seemed to be on equal footing was pushed to the back of her mind, and calling him by his first name was out of the question, so he was Colonel Fontaine. He called her Sergeant in return, not letting her nickname slip again. Even so, the prospect of seeing him each day made her eager to get up in the morning. She looked forward to the times the two of them were alone in the car and could relax their attitudes a little.

Never had she appreciated a boss so much, even in the middle of danger. Phillippe was known for not shying away from battle, so she never lacked for adventure anymore. She admired and respected him as her commanding officer and would serve him with the commitment any soldier would give their leaders.

They had their share of air raids and close calls, which they fortunately survived, and each time she thanked God for protecting them. Not that she knew God very well. But the fact that they survived was reason to be thankful. The more time they spent together, the more relaxed and comfortable they were with each other. She couldn't help herself. She was falling in love with the man. She had to keep her head, though, for it was truly a matter of life or death, and she couldn't be caught off-guard fantasizing about the colonel.

Their position was getting closer to Rommel's army, and they were now getting shelled often by tanks. Since their camp was in the sand, they built tunnels underneath and shored them with whatever they could find. When German planes flew over, they burrowed under the sand like moles. Audrey wanted to climb in next to Phillippe and endure the attacks together, but he was still her commanding officer, and a public display of affection was not protocol.

After one particularly long shelling, their unit suffered many casualties. Men she'd come to care for had been killed. But where was Phillippe? She searched all over for him but didn't find him. Finally, she found him underneath a truck that had flipped over during the attack. She breathed a sigh of relief.

As she felt his forehead under the truck, his eyes opened. "Audrey, I thought I lost you."

"Lose me? I'm not that easy to lose." He'd called her by her first name.

He coughed and spit out sand, as she helped him out. Turning to her, his face grew somber as he brushed her cheek with his hand.

"I truly am glad to see you are not hurt."

His hand, though tough, felt gentle as a silk glove against her face, and the look in his eyes as he gazed into hers spoke volumes. He cared for her, and he was letting her know. Her eyes moistened, so she wiped them with the back of her hand. There was no denying the bond between them now. He straightened and glanced around him. "We should take care of the others."

"Yes, sir." She moved to step away, and he grasped her arm.

"If we have time, I'd like to talk with you later."

She nodded and walked away. But what did he want to talk about? Was he going to tell her they wouldn't be able to work together anymore? Was the attraction between them improper for a commander and his aide? Audrey steadied herself to prepare for the conversation. She would understand his decision, whether she liked it or not.

That night, he came to her tent and asked her to come out.

"Let's go for a walk," he said.

As they strolled away from the tents and listening ears, he stopped and faced her. "Today, I realized how much you mean to me, and I cannot risk you getting hurt."

She fought back tears, knowing he was saying goodbye. She focused on the ground.

"I've suspected you have feelings for me too, but I've tried to pretend they didn't exist."

Too? Was he saying he had feelings for her?

He put his hand under her chin and lifted it so she had to face him. "Am I right?"

She nodded as a tear slid down her cheek.

"So we cannot stay on the battlefield together."

She nodded again while her heart was ripping apart.

"There's only one thing to do."

Here it was. She was being dismissed.

"Marry me."

Her head jerked up, eyes wide. "What did you say?"

"I suppose I should say I love you first, because I know I do. Sorry, I'm used to issuing commands, not questions. So let me ask you a question. Will you marry me?"

How she wanted to jump at the answer and say 'yes.' But then they'd be apart because they could not stay together and be married.

"Rose? I know what you're thinking, that we will not be together anymore."

She nodded. "How can that work? I don't want to leave you."

"I don't want you to leave me, but if we're married, I can come see you where it's safe and we can be husband and wife. Please tell me you want this too."

How could she say no? She loved Phillippe desperately. Perhaps it was time to hang up her chauffeur's cap and be a wife.

They married a week later in a tiny Catholic church because Phillippe was adamant that they should marry in the church "in God's sight." He was the most handsome man she'd ever seen in his crisp khaki uniform. She wore a simple, cream-colored dress she'd bought from a local vendor. Phillippe had never seen her look so feminine, and his face radiated pleasure. Phillippe's staff, the nurses, and several doctors were present, but of course not Dr. Gaudet. Afterwards, they took a three-day honeymoon at a villa on the Mediterranean at a location that had been won by the Free French weeks before.

Audrey had never been happier in her life nor felt more loved. Spending so much uninterrupted, peaceful time in each other's arms was the definition of bliss. So this was what marriage was supposed to be like. She doubted her parents had ever enjoyed such pleasure. But what if they had at one time, and it disappeared? No, this was love that would last forever.

"My Desert Rose," Philippe said, kissing her deeply.

"My colonel," she replied, kissing him back.

"Not anymore," he said.

"I am already jealous of your new driver," Audrey said, somewhat seriously. She had signed her separation papers from the military, so she was now a civilian again.

Phillippe laughed. "You are jealous of the man who will drive me? Do not worry. Whoever he is can never replace you."

Audrey embraced her new role as Phillipe's wife, staying in the villa by the sea. They planned to make it their home because of its lovely view and the relative proximity to each other.

Life couldn't be better.

Chapter 31

Nicole

Algiers, 2019

S o what do we do now?" Nicole glanced at Sami with his hands on the steering wheel. They had been driving around the city since they returned from the dig, making sure they weren't followed.

Sami glanced at her, his brow creased in thought. "We need to find a safe place for the ring."

"I agree. We need a safe hiding place," Nicole said, stating the obvious.

"A bank safe deposit box seems like a good place," Sami said without conviction.

Nicole lifted an eyebrow. "Yes, it should be. But do you trust the banker?" In fact, did they trust anyone?

Nicole paused, a niggling thought in her mind. "You know, talking about a hiding place reminded me of something Mimi told me years ago."

"About a hiding place?"

"Yes. Let me think… Yes, it was at the convent school where she attended, in an old fountain. Do you know if there's a convent school here now? I'd love to see it and maybe find Mimi's hiding place."

"Are you thinking of hiding the ring there?"

"No, not really. I'd just like to look for it."

"Let's go find that convent," Sami said. "Now, where was it supposed to be? "

"It's where Mimi and her friend went to school. She said they walked down the hill from her house to get to it."

"Then it must be below where the house is. Let's drive back up there and see what we can find."

Sami drove back to the neighborhood at the top of the hill, where Mimi's house stood, and pulled into the driveway. "I wonder if the man who lives here knows anything about it."

Nicole shrugged. "I hate to bother him again, though."

"Maybe he won't mind. Come on." They climbed out of the car and went to the door. The man met them, his brows raised in question.

Sami asked the man about the convent. He nodded his head, then motioned for them to follow him. At the edge of his patio, he pointed down below to a cluster of trees. Barely visible were some stucco walls.

"That's it," Sami said to Nicole. "He said it has been vacant for years."

"How can we get to it?"

After some discussion and pointing, the man gave him directions.

They turned to go back to the car when the man stepped in front of them, blocking their way. The back door to the house opened, and a young man Nicole recognized stepped out, arms crossed.

"What's going on?" Nicole said.

Nicole and Sami returned to Mimi's former home as uncertain guests. Why did the man want to speak with them? Were they in danger? The man motioned them to sit down in the colorfully decorated living room, replete with traditional Berber-style woven rugs and pillows.

He took his place opposite them with the younger man by his side.

Alarm raced through Nicole as she realized the younger man was the man she'd seen at the Royal Mausoleum in Mauritania. But today he was not wearing the clothes he'd worn that day. Today he was dressed in Western-style clothes like Sami was.

The man began speaking in his native Tamazight tongue and the young man, whom she learned was his son, translated into English.

"My name is Yuba Amastan. You need to know the story of the ring you possess," he said.

Nicole and Sami exchanged glances. He knew about the ring?

"Yes, the ring your great-grandmother gave you. It was given to her father by Chief Badis Amastan in 1932. Chief Amastan was my grandfather Matazan's uncle. We are the protectors, the Sacred Society of the Christian Queen Cleopatra Selene of Mauritania. You visited her tomb."

Shock jolted Nicole, knowing this man was aware of every place she had been since she arrived in Algeria.

"Many people wonder how she could have been Christian, even though there is a cross on one of the entrances, because she died around 7 AD, before Christ came to be known. But she knew about him because she entertained many scholars, philosophers, and wise men, being an intellectual woman. One of those wise men was Balthazar, who was our ancestor. Balthazar was one of the wise men who followed the star to find the Christ child. He explained to her the prophecy of the child and that he would be the Savior of the world one day. Like many in the Old Testament, she put her faith in him, not ever seeing him but trusting he was the Messiah. Balthazar was a student of the prophecy of Isaiah, which tells of a suffering Messiah who would be persecuted. At that time, the Romans used crosses for persecution and execution, and being the queen of a Roman colony, she was familiar with the horrible practice they carried out against their enemies in other parts of the Mediterranean world."

He paused as an elderly woman brought in cups of tea on a tray and passed them around. "My wife," he said, nodding to the woman. After taking a sip, he continued.

"The queen had churches built to worship the Messiah and teach others about Him. She looked forward to meeting Him when He began His ministry, since He was still a child. However, she became ill and died before that could happen. She was buried in the Royal Mausoleum that was built for her family, and her husband Juba II, who died a few years later, was also buried there. Her son Ptolemy was supposed to be buried there as well, but he was killed when visiting Rome, and his body was not returned.

"The mausoleum was a sacred place because the queen was so revered by her subjects. It was protected by Balthazar's descendants until 429, when the Vandals entered the country, destroying everything. Knowing they were coming, the protectors of the mausoleum took the queen and king's bodies and the treasures they were buried with out of the mausoleum and carried them to another place to keep them safe."

Sami and Nicole leaned forward. "Where were they taken?" Sami asked.

Yuba gave a slight smile. "It is a secret kept for centuries. The protectors were the only ones who knew, and they wore special rings that told of the place. Your ring is one of those."

Nicole's hand moved to cover the ring underneath her shirt.

"The front of the ring shows a likeness of Queen Selene. It also shows a cross and some mountains. The mountains are where she was buried again. On the back of the ring are some ancient words that say, "Her soul rests with Him.""

"The protectors knew where she was buried, but they took an oath to never tell anyone else. Our people knew where our ring was and that it had been given away. However, the man who received it did not know the history."

"The man who was Mimi's father?" Nicole asked, receiving a nod in return.

"But why would the chief give it away?" Sami asked.

"When his son died, he had no one to pass it on to, but he was aware there were those who wanted to find the burial site and loot it for its treasure. Giving it away was his way to keep the knowledge safe. Matazan knew about the ring and that your great-grandmother had it, so when she moved to the States, he was confident it would never be found in our country again, so the site would remain safe.

"But now that you are back and have the ring, there are thieves who want to get it and find the burial site and the treasures and get rich from them. We have been following you to make sure you are safe, and they do not get the ring."

"So you're telling us that we are being followed by the guys who want it for that purpose?"

He nodded. "And the ring itself is very valuable now as well."

"Where can we put it to keep it safe? I'm not returning to America yet, or I'd take it back with me," Nicole said.

"I doubt they'll let it leave the country again."

"These men, they know you are a protector?" Sami looked from one man to the other.

"Yes, so they might expect you to give it to me."

"So now, you're in danger since we've come to your house," Sami said.

"Yes. So we must hide the ring."

"But where?" Nicole said. She withdrew the ring and studied it. Did Mimi have any idea about the history of the ring?

"We can pretend we're mailing it to the States," Sami said. "The people who are trying to get the ring will follow us to the post office, and maybe then they'll leave us alone."

"Good idea," Yuba's son said.

"But we will hide the ring for you," Yuba said. "Then it will remain here in Algeria where it belongs."

Sami glanced at Nicole. "Would you be willing to give these people the ring?" Sami asked.

She sucked in a deep breath. Could she trust them? "I want to believe you. You know for sure you can keep it away from them?"

Yuba and his son nodded.

"But you must go through the motions of acting like you're mailing it to get them off track," Sami said.

Nicole glanced from one man to the other. Sighing, then removed the chain from her neck and the ring from the chain. Clasping the ring, she let her gaze drift towards the high ceiling where an ancient wrought iron light fixture hung. The beveled glass panels were covered by iron filigree, detailed with metal stars. "Is that light from Morocco?"

They all looked up at it. "It is Amazigh made, but we do not know where it came from. It was here when we moved in," Yuba said.

They looked at each other as if communicating the same thought.

"Balthazar followed the star, a great light, to find the Christ Child," Yuba said.

Nicole smiled, then handed the ring to Yuba. "I trust you to be its protector," she said. "I can't wait to tell Mimi the story. I believe she will agree that the ring should be returned to you."

"Thank you," Juba said, giving a slight bow. "You have made the right decision."

Chapter 32

Monique

Algiers, November 1942

The air in Mr. Murphy's office was electrified by tension when Monique arrived for work the morning of Saturday, November 7, normally her day off. She had been briefed on the series of events that were supposed to take place and eagerly awaited the process to aid the Allied invasion of Algiers.

Casablanca and Oran would be captured first, then her city. Mr. Murphy had continued negotiations with the Vichy officials, hoping to convince them to fight with the Allies. But many were afraid to commit to the Allies for fear of retaliation by Germany. News from the Tunisian and Egyptian battles vacillated between good and bad as one army, then another, won and lost battles.

The Allies had to win. So many, like Monique, counted on their victory. The anti-Vichy French wanted their country back from Germany, while the natives wanted their country back from both of them. Monique watched the clock anxiously, knowing the order of planned events. If the plan to overthrow the Vichy government didn't work, she and her co-resistance leaders would be in big trouble.

From his office, Mr. Murphy called out. "Miss Clermont, do we have any fresh coffee?"

"I'll make a new pot straightaway, sir." How long had he been there? He must be tired, but the next twenty-four hours were going to be crucial, and they both needed to stay alert. She made the coffee, then carried a cup to the man, who stood looking out his window at the city. "I brought some croissants from home." She offered a tray of the pastries to the man.

"Ah, thank you, Clermont. Your mother makes the best croissants." He took one and bit off a huge piece, then swigged a drink from the cup of coffee. Using the pastry as a pointer, he motioned to her. "Have one yourself. We have a long day and night ahead of us."

She complied, savoring each bite and inhaling the coffee's aroma before taking a sip. The phone rang, and Mr. Murphy answered it himself. "Uh huh, Yes. Set the Torch." He hung up and said, "All's a go. Now we wait."

Monique recalled the proposed schedule of events. Everything must go smoothly. Members of the resistance would seize control of the police station, the power stations, Radio Algiers, telephone switchboards, and army headquarters. The plan was to ensure a peaceful takeover without harm to anyone, unless in self-defense, telling the captives that the American forces were landing and to surrender, and convince the Vichy leaders to join the Allies. In the meantime, the American and British ships had to back up the threat by landing on time. After taking control of Algiers, the Allies would head toward Tunis to aid the fight against German forces there.

The hours moved slowly, as one by one, throughout the day, calls came in verifying the success of each area of operation. When all was secure, Mr. Murphy would go to the Villa des Oliviers, an Arab palace where the French commanding officer of all Vichy ground troops in North Africa, General Alphonse Pierre Juin, resided. There, Mr. Murphy would inform Juin that the invasion had begun and ask for him to command the surrender of the Vichy forces. Monique would go along with Mr. Murphy to interpret and make sure the two men understood each other.

Later that day, one of the resistance officers came to the office with food for Monique and Mr. Murphy as they continued to wait. Mr. Murphy paced the floor and drank coffee while Monique embroidered, listening to music from the office radio. Around nine o'clock, the radio went silent. She and Mr. Murphy exchanged glances. Did that mean the station had been taken over by the Resistance? Shortly afterwards, the phone rang, and when Mr. Murphy answered and listened to a brief message, he said, "Bien," and hung up the receiver.

More time passed in silence, and Monique's eyelids grew heavy. She must have dozed until the next call came in, waking her with a start. She glanced at the clock. Midnight. She sat up straight, glancing at Mr. Murphy who returned her gaze. "Rested up?" he said.

"Yes, sir. Sorry, I dozed off."

"It's fine, but now it's time to move. The invasion is underway." She stood and grabbed her hat, purse, and steno pad. Mr. Murphy plucked his hat from the hat stand and stuck it on his head. They left the office and hurried downstairs to his car. They drove to Juin's villa, arriving at

12:45 a.m. After getting out of the car, Nicole followed Mr. Murphy as he brushed past two fierce-looking Senegalese sentries. Mr. Murphy rapped on the door until a short, swarthy mustachioed man dressed in pajamas opened the door.

The man's brows furrowed at the intrusion as he waited for Mr. Murphy to speak first.

"I am happy to say that I have been instructed by my government to inform you that American and British armies of liberation are about to land."

"What?" the man exclaimed. "Do you mean the convoy we've seen in the Mediterranean is going to land here?"

Mr. Murphy nodded with a cautious grin.

"But you told me the United States would not attack us."

"We are not attacking. We are coming by invitation."

"Whose invitation?"

"General Giraud."

Monique tried to keep her face expressionless since she knew Mr. Murphy was bluffing. At this point, Giraud had not yet arrived, to their knowledge.

"Is he here?" blustered Juin.

"He will be here soon," Mr. Murphy said, then described the invasion forces waiting offshore, exaggerating the size. "Our talks over the years have convinced me that you desire to see the liberation of France, which can come only through cooperation with the United States."

"I'd like to comply with you, but Giraud outranks me, so I must wait for his order first."

A phone call was made, and twenty minutes later, Admiral Darlan, commander of the Vichy French fleet, arrived. Darlan was one of the most detested figures of the

Vichy regime, and he was not usually in Algiers, but was there to visit his sick son. Monique tried to close her ears as Juin and Darlan spoke with vulgarity to each other. The Allies needed Darlan to comply and order his fleet not to fire on the Allies, and had heard he might be persuaded. But when he was told about the invasion, he was angered and responded with insults.

For fifteen minutes, he paced the room and sucked on his pipe. Mr. Murphy pressured him to comply, saying, "The moment has arrived!"

But Darlan refused to act before he called the Vichy president in France for guidance. However, when he set foot outside, he was surprised by the presence of forty rebels with white armbands and rifles. "Does this mean we are prisoners?" he asked.

Mr. Murphy nodded. "It does. Until you send orders to your men to step down."

Darlan finally conceded at dawn on Sunday morning, giving Monique and Mr. Murphy freedom to leave. Mr. Murphy drove her home to her apartment. "Thank you, Clermont. We did it."

When Monique stepped out on her balcony, she saw the American ships in the harbor. Church bells pealed throughout the city, calling Christian worshippers to church. Now she could rest, couldn't she?

For the next several days, Algiers was turned into an Allied headquarters. The Hotel St. George at the top of the hill became the new temporary offices of American General Eisenhower, as he set up a command center for the rest of the North Africa campaign. Americans were all over the city, elation about their success visible on their faces.

When Mr. Murphy went to visit the American general, he took Monique with him.

"You need to meet this man," he said. "He will make sure the Germans are sent running out of Africa."

"He is your boss?" she said.

"Not officially, but he's calling the shots here."

"Calling the shots?"

Mr. Murphy laughed. "That means what he says, goes, and we will do what he says."

As her boss drove up the hill, they entered her former neighborhood. She sighed as they passed her old residence, her loss weighing heavily on her heart. Murphy glanced at her in the passenger seat. "Are you all right?"

She nodded. "That used to be my house."

"It did? Now I remember. Didn't a Vichy officer take it over?"

"Yes."

"Well, guess what? He's out now, and an American official lives there."

The announcement came as a surprise, but she didn't know whether to be happy or sad because someone besides her family still lived in the house. However, she did prefer an American to the Vichy.

Mr. Murphy looked at her with sympathy. "Monique, when we get out of here, I'm sure you can have your house back."

She would like that, but worried about what the other

inhabitants would have done to the house by then.

They pulled into the parking lot of the hotel, and two American guards opened the car doors for them. "Ma'am," said the one by her, smiling as she stepped out. What nice-looking men they were in their crisp uniforms.

She and Mr. Murphy climbed the stairs to the second floor, where other guards stood outside some of the hotel rooms. Mr. Murphy identified himself to the guard, who then opened a door for them to enter. Mr. Murphy motioned for Monique to go in front of him, then he followed. "Good morning, sir," he said.

A bald man with a pleasant smile stood behind the desk across the room. "Murphy! Good to see you, man." He extended his hand, and Mr. Murphy shook it. "Who is this lovely lady?

Mr. Murphy looked at Monique. "This is Monique Clermont, my secretary and translator. Monique, this is General Eisenhower."

The general's eyes twinkled as he smiled at her. "Very nice to meet you, Monique. I understand you have been a great asset to Mr. Murphy here and instrumental in the success of Operation Torch."

Heat flushed to her face. Surely, she was not worthy of such praise.

"This is my aide-de-camp, Lieutenant Paul Davis."

Murphy shook the lieutenant's hand, and Monique acknowledged him with a nod.

"Sit down, sit down," Eisenhower motioned to two chairs across from his desk. They complied, and Mr. Murphy and the general began discussing the progress of the campaign. Her gaze returned to the tall blond lieutenant standing at attention to the side of the general, and their eyes met. He gave a small nod and a slight smile. Her insides flipped. This man was incredibly handsome and appeared friendly. What was he like? Would they ever have a chance to talk without the others around? She hoped so.

When she and Mr. Murphy left, the Lieutenant requested permission from Eisenhower to escort them. The general responded with a wink and a "Of course, go ahead."

Lt. Davis walked them back downstairs and to their car, where he opened her door.

"I look forward to seeing you again soon," he said.

Monique shared that desire.

For the next six months, as General Eisenhower remained in Algiers to command the American military engagement eastward across North Africa, Monique and Paul saw each other on a daily basis. Her attraction for the tall, gentle American grew into love, and she dreaded the day he would leave. Paul began talking about a future together, but Monique feared making a commitment based on their uncertain future. Paul would be going with Eisenhower whenever and wherever he went next, but he assured her of his love. As a result, she accepted his proposal when he knelt before her the following May.

Despite their happiness, Algiers was now subject to German air raids. Monique's apartment was in a dangerous place, being at the top of a tall building, so Paul tried to convince her to move. But she and her mother had no other place to go since their home was still occupied. So when the sirens wailed, they'd hurry to take shelter on lower floors. Once, the building next to them was hit, leaving half an apartment missing, which was quite a surprise to the unsuspecting tenant when he opened the door.

Maman loved Paul and was happy to see his interest in Monique. But she worried that he might take her away from Algiers. "I'm not going anywhere, Maman. I am staying with you. Paul is the one who will be leaving."

However, the prospect of his leaving made her and Paul want to be together even more.

"We need to get married, Monique. I love you and want you to be my wife," Paul said. "I do not want to wait any longer."

"I don't either," she said.

"I believe we will be leaving here in September. Let's get married soon, so we have time together as husband and wife before I leave."

She agreed to have the wedding in two weeks. Maman altered her own wedding dress to fit Monique, stitching some of her own pearls into the headpiece. Paul was Protestant, so they married at the Anglican Church. Her brother Rene was unable to get to Algiers, so Mr. Murphy stood as her witness.

Two months later, Paul was shipped out, and Monique was left in Algiers expecting their child. She wanted badly to share her news with Audrey, wherever she was. Monique remembered the journal. Was it still there?

One day, when she knew the sisters would be in mass, she went to the convent school and sneaked in. She went straight to the fountain and found the loose stone. When she pulled it out, she reached into the space and was thankful to find the journal was still there. Quickly opening it, her heart leaped when she discovered a separate sheet of paper stuffed into the journal. On it was a message from Audrey. When had Audrey left her a message? Had she been in the area?

Married my true love, the dashing General Phillippe Fontaine of the Legion. I am now living in a coastal villa in a peace zone. I am no longer in the army, as I am a wife and soon-to-be mother! Hope to see you and introduce you to my baby someday. P.S. M, a mutual friend of ours, entered this message for me, as I am not able to.

What an amazing coincidence that they were both married now and both expecting. Wouldn't it be wonderful if one day their babies could meet, even become friends like her and Audrey?

Monique quickly added her news to the journal and slid it back into its hiding place.

Chapter 33

Audrey

North Africa, 1943

The baby kicked in Audrey's stomach, and she rubbed the area.

"Little one, are you anxious to meet your daddy?" Audrey said. "I don't blame you. He is quite handsome."

Phillippe had been to visit twice since their marriage, but the time dragged by in between. At least she had the baby to prepare for. Who would have thought she'd be a mother?

Patting her stomach, she said, "I promise you will be loved and will know you are loved." Audrey would never let her child live with two unloving people. She wouldn't worry about being accepted or disappointing her parents. This child would know the kind of love Audrey and Phillippe had for each other.

"If you're a girl, you can be my little rose, since I'm the desert rose."

Audrey was amazed at how much she'd changed. At one time in her life, she'd had servants. Another time, she was an almost-sister living with Monique's family. Then she'd been a soldier living with bare essentials in ever-present danger. And now she was a wife and mother-to-be.

Because Phillippe had suggested she hire someone to help her, one of the local women came in to do housework and wash clothes. She didn't need the help. After surviving in the desert, taking care of herself, she was capable of doing her own chores. Plus, how much work was there to do with only herself to clean up after?

But she was glad to have someone else around, even if that someone wasn't conversant in the same language. Even though Audrey had spent most of her life as a loner, she didn't like being alone. She liked company sometimes, if not all the time. She especially liked Phillippe's company, relishing every moment they had together, and she couldn't wait to spend her life with him when the war was over.

Audrey had gained weight and filled out since retiring from the military, as well as from the pregnancy. As she grew larger and larger with the baby, she hoped she didn't look ugly to Phillippe. He came home a month before the baby was due. Did he still find her attractive? His next campaign was going to be farther away and expected to be intense. Phillippe was unsure if he would be back in time for the birth, but promised to return as soon as he could. She now lumbered around like an elephant, but consoled herself that soon the baby would be here, and everything would be wonderful.

As he feared, Phillippe was not there when their baby girl was born. Only the midwife and the housekeeper were with Audrey. But once Audrey saw her baby, all else was unimportant. Her beautiful little girl was perfect, except that she had inherited Audrey's fair skin tone and light hair color instead of Phillippe's. "What will we name you, little one? It is almost Christmas, so you should be Noel and not Rose, especially not a desert rose. I will send word to Phillippe that his little Noel is here and ready to meet him."

She didn't hear from Phillippe right away. Word got back to her that the fighting was heavy, and it was difficult to get messages through. Audrey tried not to worry, though, because she and Phillippe had been through many dangerous situations and survived. She knew how unpredictable war was, too. For now, she'd focus on taking care of her baby.

Audrey loved to watch Noel, reveling in every movement she made. The way she stretched and yawned, the way her bright blue eyes looked around. Audrey loved the velvety touch of Noel's skin, her fine, silky hair, and her special baby aroma. Her heart swelled with love for her child, the result of her and Phillippe's love. She never thought she could love a baby as much as she loved her husband, but she did, and she would do anything to protect her.

Noel was three months old when Audrey got the letter. Her hand trembled when she saw it, knowing what it was before it was opened, but refusing to open it and make its contents real. Phillippe had been killed in battle. Her heart broke into a million pieces as she fell to her knees, sobbing.

"No!" It's not supposed to be this way!" For days, she could not eat or stop crying, and the housekeeper told her the baby cried because she was hungry, that Audrey's milk would dry up without nursing her. Pulling her out of a trance, the housekeeper placed Noel in her arms and said, "Feed child."

As Audrey fed her precious child, she saw the future fall

apart. Noel would never know her father or his love. He'd never hold her in his arms. Audrey would not be able to give her the perfect family she'd wanted to. Why had she thought she could be a wife and a mother? She would fail. She was not cut out for domestic life, and it was not fair for her to subject Noel to such failure. Noel needed a better life, one Audrey could not provide. Audrey made a decision, one that would be the best for her daughter.

Chapter 34

Nicole

Algiers, 2019

S ami drove to the main post office and parked along the curb. They went inside the cavernous colonial building and found the display of padded envelopes. Selecting one large enough for an international label, they took it to a counter on the side of the room.

"Are we going to put anything in it?" Nicole asked.

Sami eyed the bandana around her neck. "Would you be willing to part with your kerchief"?

Nicole frowned, then understood.

"Give me your mother's mailing address. While I'm addressing this envelope, why don't you nonchalantly walk around looking at the architecture while removing it from your neck. Then stuff it in your pocket. Act natural and don't look over your shoulder. Next, mosey back over here where you can discreetly put it in the envelope."

Nicole walked away as he suggested, then returned. Sami tried to block anyone from seeing while she put the bandana in the envelope. Then he sealed it, and they carried it to the postal clerk who weighed it.

"Contents?" the clerk asked.

"A scarf," Sami said. "We're sending it to a relative for a birthday gift."

The clerk nodded and stamped the envelope that contained no valuables the government had restrictions on. After quoting the fee, Sami paid him, and the clerk tossed the envelope into a bin behind him. Sami and Nicole walked away. "Let's stay awhile and see what happens to the bin." The two glanced up at the arched windows while Sami pointed, and they discussed the history of the building while keeping an eye on the bin. After a while, the bin was picked up by a postal employee and carried to the back.

"Guess we can leave now."

"Where to next?" Nicole said.

"Let's get some coffee, then we can go find that old convent."

They left the post office and drove past one of the entrances of the Casbah. Nicole thought it was odd that he didn't park closer. She walked with Sami to the coffee shop where he'd brought her the first day she'd met him. Inside, Sami greeted Hassan, ordered the coffee, and paid for it. "áer cups, please," Sami said, then leaned toward Hassan and whispered something.

When the coffee was poured, the half-full cups were handed to them. "Let's stand," Sami said. They sipped the hot brew with their backs to the door while Hassan faced it. A couple of minutes later, Sami asked where the restrooms were. Hassan motioned to a curtain-covered doorway behind him. Sami nodded, putting his cup down, glancing at Nicole to do the same.

"Come," he said, moving toward the curtain. Hassan

tossed the cups in the trash as Nicole followed Sami through the doorway into a private room behind. Taking her hand, Sami led her to a back door that he opened, motioning her to go through. When she stepped outside, they were in a small alley. Walking briskly, they wove through a maze of other alleys before coming out to the street near their car.

They hopped in and drove away.

Nicole eyed him curiously. "That was strange."

"Just one more step to make sure we weren't being followed.'

"Hope it worked," she said.

"Me too. At least, it'll stall them a while," Sami said. "So let's go find that convent now."

They drove back toward Yuba's house, but instead of going all the way up the hill, they began to search in the area they'd seen below Yuba's patio.

"He said the road is overgrown and hard to spot," Nicole said.

"There!" Nicole pointed. The entrance to a road through the forest was barely visible.

Sami turned onto it, then eased along, pushing through dense undergrowth, the brush making a scraping noise against the car.

"I'm sorry your car is getting scratched," Nicole said.

Sami shrugged. "Maybe it won't be so bad. It's pretty obvious no one has been down this road for a long time."

As the walls of an old building came into view, the road ended with a gate across it. A padlocked chain kept it closed. Sami stopped, then he and Nicole exchanged glances. "Should we try to open it?" Nicole asked.

Sami pointed to a sign on the fence in Arabic. "It's a no-trespassing sign."

"But who's going to know? You can tell nobody has been around here for a while."

They got out of the car and walked up to the gate. Sami grabbed the gate and shook it. He then lifted the rusty padlock. "I wonder who has the key?"

"Or if they're still alive?"

Sami jerked on the padlock, then stopped, raising a finger in the air. "I think I have a tool that might work." He went to his car and opened the trunk. He reached into the backpack that he took with him to the dig and pulled out a slender metal tool, holding it aloft. "Let's try this." He closed the trunk, then returned to the lock and inserted the tool. Holding his ear near the lock, he moved the tool around inside it until it clicked. Then he jerked on the lock, and it opened.

"Wow. Now I know what else that tool is for," Nicole said.

Sami smiled, then unwrapped the chain from one side of the gate and pushed it open. Leaving the car behind, they walked into what was once a yard surrounding the yellowed stucco walls. Sami pointed to the top of the building where parts of the wall were missing. "I believe that damage is from World War II when the Nazis dropped bombs on the city. I think I remember reading about a bomb hitting a convent back then. Yes, that's right, and several nuns were killed."

"That's terrible," Nicole said, staring at the damage.

They walked slowly through the overgrown yard before reaching a concrete plaza in front of the vine-covered building. Etched in the masonry arch above the door were the words, Soeurs de Saint Cyprien. "Sisters of Saint

Cyprien," said Nicole.

"He was the patron saint of Africa," Sami said.

They pushed through the unlocked double wood doors into a courtyard. The sky opened above them, evidence of the bombing. In the middle of the courtyard was a fountain surrounded by rubble, with only half the statue in the center still remaining. "The fountain—I think that's where Mimi said the hiding place was." She strode over to the fountain, stepping over rubble, then walked around it as well as she could.

"I doubt if anything hidden in that would have survived the attack," Sami said as he studied the fountain.

Nicole began feeling each of the stones that made up the base of the fountain. "Mimi said one of these was loose."

"They're probably all loose now," Sami said, looking on.

Nicole continued checking each stone until one moved. She jiggled it and pulled it out. Glancing at Sami, she said, "I'm not sure about this, but I've got to try." Then she reached her hand into the space behind where the stone had been, and her fingers felt something. She grabbed it and withdrew a small, leather binder, the leather frayed and peeling. She carefully opened the binder to reveal yellowed sheets of paper. She stared at it. "Sami, this was Mimi's journal."

"Grab it and let's get out of here," Sami said, batting mosquitoes.

A noise came from part of the building above them, and they froze, glancing up.

"Do you think we were followed?" Nicole said. The noise grew louder as they stood watching. Then they spotted the source as a monkey swooped down on a vine that hung across the building. "Monkeys!" Nicole said.

"Hurry. They bite," Sami said.

One of the monkeys ran across the courtyard and up onto the fountain, reaching for the book in Nicole's hand. "No, you don't!" she said, clutching it tightly against her chest.

The two of them ran out of the building and back to the car, closing the gate behind them. Sami relocked the padlock.

Strangely, the monkeys didn't follow, preferring to stay and protect their reclaimed domain.

"I thought there weren't any monkeys around here anymore," Nicole said.

"I didn't think there were. But it looks like the jungle is reclaiming the area, so I guess the monkeys come with it."

"Or maybe they escaped from the zoo?" Nicole suggested.

That's a possibility." Sami motioned to the book she still clutched. "I'm sure you'd like to read that. Do you want to go back to your room?"

She shook her head. "No. I don't feel safe there anymore, knowing someone broke into it."

"Tell you what. Why don't you come to my house? My mother would love to meet you, and you'd feel safe there."

Sami's house was a modest two-story stucco home in a neighborhood outside the busy city. The house had a walled garden around it where colorful flowers abounded. Sami's smiling mother met them at the door and ushered them in. Nicole towered over the little woman who spoke in French, so Nicole was able to understand her. Sami explained about the journal and where they found it. His mother nodded, telling him the convent was indeed the one where several nuns were killed during a Nazi bombing. She said they never rebuilt it because the surviving nuns left Algeria after the war and went back to France.

Offering them tea, Mrs. Kateb went to the kitchen to prepare it, motioning for them to sit. Nicole opened the journal underneath the nearest light and began to read. She smiled at the words of young girls written so long ago. Most of the book's entries were written during a short amount of time, then the entries were few and years apart. Nicole read the words of Mimi, who was Monique, and her friend Audrey, as they left messages for each other. Some were silly, others more serious. She scanned the messages, faded with time. The last message was left in 1943 by Audrey. Nicole looked up. "I wonder what happened to Audrey?"

"Do you know her last name?"

"No. But she left to join the Free French early in the war." Nicole looked up at Sami. "I can't see these very well. I'll have to have stronger light and a magnifying glass."

"Did you say she joined the French Foreign Legion, the Free French, under de Gaulle? I wonder what she did with them?"

"I'm not sure. Maybe the journal will tell us."

Nicole studied the journal more closely, holding it closer to the light. "Look, Sami. Each entry is signed by the person who wrote it, either Monique or Audrey. But these last two entries were signed, The Desert Rose." She glanced up. "Sami, do you think Audrey was The Desert Rose? Mimi said it was a person, so it must be her. But find her? I don't even know if she's still alive or where she would be if she is.

She would be about the same age as Mimi, so chances are, she's not around anymore."

"At least you have some idea about what or who you're looking for. We can go from there. There must be some records with names of the Foreign Legion. And there can't have been that many women. Do you know her last name?"

"The front of the journal says, "This is the private journal of Monique Clermont and Audrey Reynolds. Keep out."

Sami chuckled. "I'll look on the internet and see what I can find."

"Thank you, Sami. But what about the other problem?"

Sami glanced at his mother, bringing in the tea and setting the tray on the ottoman. She poured a cup and handed it to Nicole. "I will speak to her." Sami explained to his mother about the ring without all the details, just that it was an heirloom and Nicole's room had been broken into. Mrs. Kateb responded in rapid French and a forceful tone, pointing to Nicole. Nicole drew back, wondering what she said, since Nicole's French wasn't that good.

Nicole sipped the tea, glancing at Sami. "What did she say?"

"She wants you to stay here and not at the hotel. Would you mind?"

"Thank you," Nicole said, looking at Mrs. Kateb. "I don't want to put her out, though."

"It is not a problem for her, and she practically insists."

"Well, in that case, yes, I accept."

Chapter 35

Monique

Algiers, 1943

Paul had been gone eight months now. At first, Monique had sent him letters telling him how she felt and how she had started knitting and preparing a nursery for their child. But he couldn't tell her where he was or when he'd be back. And when she lost the baby at nine weeks, she didn't tell him about it. He didn't need to hear sad news and be disappointed while he was away.

Maman had consoled her, telling her she'd get pregnant again, and that she should tell Paul. But Monique couldn't bring herself to tell him in a letter. He'd know soon enough. When the Americans moved out of the city, her house on the hill became available again, and she and Maman moved back in. The house had different furniture, but Mr. Alexis recovered their old furniture so they could restore the home to a semblance of its former self.

The home was so different now, so empty. She had not seen Matazar since the invasion in which he'd played an important role in the resistance. One night, Monique stood in what was supposed to be the nursery as tears ran down her face when she heard a knock at the door.

Maman had gone to bed, so Monique slipped down the stairs, harboring hope that perhaps Paul had come home to surprise her. But when she opened the door, Audrey was standing there cradling a blanket in her arms. "Audrey!" Monique threw her arms around her friend. "I have missed you so. Come in." Monique peeked at the tiny face in the blanket. "Let me see your baby."

Audrey pulled the blanket away from the sleeping baby's face. "This is Noel." Tears streamed from Audrey's face. "Phillippe is dead. He was killed in battle."

"Oh, Audrey. I am so sorry." Monique hugged Audrey. "There is so much sadness. I lost my baby." The two women leaned into each other and sobbed.

"Where is your husband?" Audrey asked. "Is he…?"

"He is on a ship somewhere in the Mediterranean, I think. He could not tell me where. But I think he is still alive. I hope so."

"Monique. I have to ask you a favor," Audrey said.

"Anything," Monique said. "What can I do for you?"

Audrey handed the baby to Monique. "You can take my child and raise her for me. Raise her as your own. I am not a mother. I am a soldier, and I'm returning to the Legion."

"Audrey, I can't. She is yours. She needs you."

Audrey shook her head. "No, she does not need me. She needs someone who will raise her in a loving family. I know she will be loved by you and hopefully, your husband. Tell him it is his baby."

Monique held the beautiful baby and studied her little face. Her empty heart filled with love for the child. She looked up at Audrey. "Are you sure you want to do this?"

Audrey nodded. "It is what's best for her. She's yours now. Don't ever tell her you aren't her real mother. From now on, you are."

"I'll have to tell Maman, but she will keep the secret. Plus, I'm sure she'll love the baby. She was, after all, expecting a grandchild." Tears pooled in Monique's eyes.

Audrey gazed at her daughter. "Her name is Noel. That means "good news." She was supposed to be Phillippe's good news. Now she is yours … and Paul's… and your mother's."

Monique hugged Audrey again, and they cried together. The baby stirred, and they separated and regained their composure. Neither of them wanted to upset the child, sharing the need to protect this child from their own heartaches.

Carrying the baby close to her, Monique walked Audrey to the door.

"May God bless you and protect you, Audrey. We will take care of your precious child."

Audrey leaned down and kissed the sleeping baby on her forehead. "Au revoir, mi amor."

And then she walked briskly away, leaving Monique with the most precious thing she had ever had.

Chapter 36

Nicole

Algiers, 2019

L et's go to the library and do some internet searching," Sami said.

At the library, he searched for a list of people who had been in the French Foreign Legion during World War II. "The war started in Europe years before the United States got involved, so I'm going to check from 1939 to 1945."

"Her name was Audrey Reynolds when she and Mimi were friends, but she could have gotten married."

Sami opened the list of names, scrolling down the page. "I don't see an Audrey."

Nicole pointed to the screen. "Look for A Reynolds. Since most of the legionnaires were French, I doubt there were many named Reynolds."

"Good thinking." He scrolled slowly down the list. "There. There's an A Reynolds. It says this person was a chauffeur. And received an award for bravery in the desert of North Africa. Hey, look. The name changed to A Fontaine. Looks like this person was born in 1923."

"That's the same year Mimi was born," Nicole said. "Does it give a date of death?"

He studied the information. "No."

"She's still alive?"

"If this is up to date, then yes."

"But where is she now?"

"Last known address, Paris, France."

He searched for the address listed. "Looks like a retirement home."

"Let's call and see if she's still there," Monique said.

"I'll do that," Sami said.

While he was looking for the number of the place, Monique pulled out her phone and texted Mom. "Ask Mimi if she knows Audrey Reynolds or Audrey Fontaine. Also, ask her if Audrey was the desert rose."

"Audrey Fontaine is a resident of the retirement home," Sami said, disconnecting his call. "And she's lucid, though in a wheelchair."

Nicole's phone dinged. "Mimi said 'yes." She looked up at Sami. "We found her."

"Ready for a trip to Paris?" Sami grinned. "I hear there's a lot of history there."

Nicole beamed. "Absolutely. I can't wait to meet this person, and we can set up a Facetime call with her and Mimi."

"But first, we have to find a box and mail something."

"Oh yes. We'd better do that right away."

In the Uber ride to the retirement home, Sami's phone pinged, displaying a message.

He laughed. "Well, how about that!"

Nicole glanced at him, her eyebrows lifted. "What?"

Sami looked at the phone and read out loud. "It's from Matt. He says a big ring of antiquities thieves has been arrested in Algeria. And you'll never guess who was part of it!"

"Well, tell me!"

"Amad Hamid and Nadir!"

Nicole's mouth gaped, and she put her hand over it. "Sami, do you think they were the ones after us and the ring?"

"Apparently so."

"I wonder how they got caught?"

"I bet a not so little bird told on them."

"Yuba?"

"Apparently. Some thieves were caught breaking into his house, and when they were arrested, they implicated Nadir. When Nadir was arrested, he implicated Amad."

"Wow. Thank God they got caught."

Sami nodded. "Indeed."

When they arrived at the retirement home, an attendant led Nicole and Sami down a sunny corridor. Sitting in a wheelchair, a woman looked out of the window at a colorful garden with a fountain in the center.

"Madam Fontaine, you have visitors." Turning to Nicole and Sami, she said, "You may sit here," pointing to chairs on either side of the wheelchair.

Classical music played softly on the intercom as they sat beside Audrey. She slowly turned her head to look at them. Her eyes registered confusion as she asked in French, her voice shaky, who they were.

"My name is Nicole Bennett, and this is my friend Sami Kateb."

"Do I know you?" The elderly woman's pinched expression showed confusion.

"No, but I believe you know my great-grandmother, Monique Clermont."

Her eyes widened, and she reached for Nicole's hand. "Monique?"

Nicole's heart leaped. She remembered! "Yes."

Madam Fontaine's eyes filled with tears. "Is she alive?"

"Yes. In fact, she asked me to find you, that is, if you're the desert rose."

Her light blue eyes crinkled at the corners as a smile worked its way across her face. "I haven't been called that in a very long time."

Nicole explained to her where Mimi lived and that she asked Nicole to find the desert rose when she went to Algeria for her archaeological study. "You've been hard to find," Nicole said.

"I didn't want to be found," Audrey said. "But I'm glad you found me now."

"Me too. Mimi will be so happy." Audrey squeezed Audrey's hand.

"Mimi?"

"That's what we call Monique."

Audrey's eyes had a faraway look. Was she remembering the past?

"You said you are her great-granddaughter? Did she have many children?" Audrey asked.

"No, just my grandmother, Noel."

Audrey's face pinched. "And how is she?"

Nicole shook her head. "I'm sad to say Grandma Noel passed away several years ago from cancer."

Audrey's face fell, her eyes filling with tears. "I am so sorry."

"We miss her. She was so much fun, and quite the adventurous woman. She loved going on trips and took me and my mom with her many times." Nicole paused, looking at Audrey. "Did you know her?"

Audrey's voice softened. "Only when she was a baby."

"Mimi says I look like her, or like she did when she was my age."

Audrey's gaze roamed over Nicole, and she nodded.

"I'm going to call home and get you and Mimi together on a Facetime call so you can see each other. Unfortunately, Mimi can't speak well anymore since her stroke. She understands, though."

Nicole opened her I-Pad and dialed home. When Mom answered, Nicole said, "Mom, we're here with Audrey, aka, the desert rose. Can you put Mimi on the screen?"

A few minutes later, the screen showed Mimi. "Hi Mimi. Here's Audrey, the desert rose."

Mimi's eyes grew wide as she looked into the camera.

Audrey spoke. "Bon Jour, Monique!"

Mimi reacted with the happiest smile she could muster. She stuttered as she tried hard to repeat the greeting.

"Monique, my dear old friend. I am so happy to see you again. And I am so happy to meet your great-granddaughter. She is Noel's granddaughter, yes?"

Mimi nodded, but her eyes grew sad.

"Nicole told me about her. I am sorry to hear of her passing."

Mimi nodded again, lip trembling.

"She had a good life?"

Another nod.

"And a beautiful granddaughter, Nicole."

Mimi smiled and nodded.

"Nicole says she looks like Noel did when she was younger."

"S.s.s.h.h.e. e. d.d.does."

Mimi held up a picture that usually sat in their dining room. It was a photo of three women and a young girl, each standing on a paddleboard in shallow water. She pointed to it.

Audrey squinted at the picture.

Mom's face showed on the screen. "Hi, Audrey. I'm Noel's daughter, Natalie, and Nicole's mother. Nice to meet you! We had a hard time trying to figure out what Mimi meant when she asked Nicole to find the desert rose." Mom pointed to the picture Mimi held. "That's the four of us." Pointing to each one, she said, "That's Mimi, my mother, Noel, me, and Nicole. It was taken about ten years ago. My mother was always adventurous and enjoyed having all her 'girls, ' as she said, with her. This is a picture of the time she made us all go paddleboarding together, even Mimi!"

Audrey laughed. "What fun. I'm so thankful Nicole found me. Monique and I had many happy times together when we were young. She was like a sister to me."

"She's spoken of you before and said the same. She said you were the adventurous one, like my mother, Noel."

Audrey smiled. "I was. And Monique was the sensible

one." She looked at Mimi.

"Thank you, Monique. Thank you for taking care of Noel."

Nicole frowned. What a strange thing for her to say.

"S..s..e.e.c.c.ret."

"Yes, you kept our secret. You did a good thing. I prayed for her, and God answered my prayers."

Mimi nodded again as a tear fell down her face.

Nicole spoke up. "I visited Mimi's old house in Algiers recently and saw where the swing was."

"Ah, the swing. What fun we had on it," Audrey said, with a twinkle in her eyes.

Natalie spoke again. "Mimi's birthday is tomorrow. She will be 100. I wish you could come to her party."

"I do too. My 100th is next month."

Mimi smiled, and she tried to say "Happy birthday."

Audrey clapped her hands together, smiling broadly. "Happy Birthday to you, my friend! Seeing you again is the best present I could ever have."

Mimi nodded, her eyes bright with joy. "T.. t. than k y… you. "

The End

Acknowledgments

Thank you to Karena and Travis Miller, who shared his grandmother's journal about growing up in French Algiers. Thank you also to Michelle Clarke, an underwater archaeologist in the Mediterranean who taught me about historical gemstones of North Africa. I must also thank my patient husband Chuck for putting up with me during the writing and researching of this book. And to my publisher, Cynthia Hickey, who makes sure my books see the light of day. Thank you for supporting my writing. And finally, I thank God for the stories He's given me and the ability to share them with you, the reader.

Marilyn Turk's roots are in the coastal South, born and raised in Louisiana, now a Florida resident. An award-winning author, she calls herself a "literary archaeologist" because she loves to discover stories in history that her fictional characters can experience. A fascination for lighthouses spawned her popular weekly lighthouse blog and inspired her to write Lighthouse Devotions. She has published 20 award-winning books and novellas. They include several World War II era books and a series set in Florida during and after the Civil War. Marilyn loves hearing from her readers. Sign up for her newsletter at https://pathwayheart.com/subscribe/.

WANT TO HELP MARILYN?

If you enjoyed reading this book, the best thing you can do to help Marilyn is easy – tell others about it. Word-of-mouth is the most powerfu form of marking there is.

Leaving good reviews is the best way to ensure Marilyn can keep writing. She'd greatly appreciate it if you'd consider leaving a rating for this book on Amazon and writing a brief review (a sentence or two will help).

Here's the Amazon link for *Secrets of the Desert Rose.* https://www.amazon.com/Secrets-Desert-Rose-Marilyn-Turk/dp/1968792759/. Scroll down on the left side to the area that says "Consumer Reviews, below the graphic that shows the number of stars. You'll see the words: "Review this product, and below that is a box that says, "Write a Customer Review."

Marilyn thanks you very much for reading her books!

SIGN UP TO RECEIVE MARILYN'S NEWSLETTER

If you'd like to get an email alert whenever Marilyn has a new book coming out or when special deal is being offered on any or Marilyn's books, go to her website and sign up for her newsletter here, https://pathwayheart.com/subscribe/ .

You can also follow Marilyn on Facebook. Facebook.

Discussion Questions for Secrets of the Desert Rose

1. Of the three female characters – Audrey, Monique and Nicole – which personality do you most identify with and why?
2. Do you think there were Christians before Christ was born? How is that possible? What were the Magi looking for?
3. Which of the three women showed the most bravery? How?
4. In times of war and also times of peace, we struggle with whom to trust. Under Vichy rule in France, trusting the wrong person could be dangerous. Do you have a hard time trusting others?
5. When Monique and her mother were forced out of their family home and moved to an apartment in the city, it worked to her advantage, even though she wasn't initially happy about the change. Have you ever been forced to change your situation, only to discover Got had a better plan for you?
6. Audrey had a hard time getting approval from her parents. But Monique's parents were very loving, and Audrey thought Monique had a perfect home and wished hers was like it. Have you ever sought approval from others – parents, friends? Whose approval really matters?
7. Nicole had no idea that her family keepsake was valuable, but it was valuable to her because it came from her great grandmother. Do you have anything that is more valuable to you than it is to anyone else?

8. Audrey's faith is weak but seeing how Monique and her family demonstrate their faith makes her more open to it. How has someone else affected your own faith?

9. Monique was appalled by the ways her Jewish friends were treated and went out of her way to help them, putting herself at risk. Would you have done the same?

10. Audrey made a supreme sacrifice, believing it would be in the best interest of someone else. Do you think she made the right decision?

11. Matazan has looked out for Monique since she was a child, risking his own safety to help her. Did you have a Matazan in your life? How does his devotion to her remind you of Jesus?

12. Audrey's life motto was "adventure," motivating her to keep taking risks, almost like a game. But once she became part of the army, she became attached to her fellow soldiers and realized life was more important than the adventure. Have you ever had a moment when you realized what was most important in your life, and it wasn't what you thought it was?

13. What was your favorite part of the story?

14. Did you learn anything surprising about North Africa, particularly Algeria, that you didn't know before? What?

15. Monique's and Audrey's characters were based on real people. The woman Monique is based on kept a journal which I was privileged to read. The woman based on Audrey was based on an autobiography of

the first woman to join the French Foreign Legion. I am very thankful they wrote their stories. Without their records, we would not know all the details of the story. Have you ever wished you could ask an ancestor questions? What do you think about keeping a journal for your own descendants to know what your life was like?

WANT TO READ MORE?

We hope you enjoyed this book. If you'd like to read more of Marilyn's books, here's a list of what she's written so far.

Other Books by Marilyn Turk

Historical Novels

Coastal Lights Legacy
Rebel Light
Revealing Light
Redeeming Light
Rekindled Light

Suspicious Shores
The Gilded Curse
Shadowed by a Spy
Seaside Strangers (coming soon)

Standalone Novels
Abigail's Secret
The Escape Game

Novellas
The Wrong Survivor
Love's Cookin' at the Cowboy Café
Between Two Worlds
The Christmas Gift in *The Christmas Gazebo*
Kaetlyn's Cup of Christmas Cheer
Not My Party
The Old Beach House
Book Lady of the Bayou (The Librarian's Journey)

The Gilding of Minnie Tucker
The Missing Chapter (Secrets Between the Shelves
collection)

Short Story
A Stranger's Visit to the Lighthouse (Guideposts Books)

Nonfiction
Lighthouse Devotions
*Walking in Grace (*compilation*)*